Silent
Trauma

Judith Barrow

ACKNOWLEDGMENTS

I would like express my gratitude to Tony Riches for his advice, patience and, above all, his skill and expertise in formatting and enabling me to publish this Work.

I am indebted to Pat Cody who, in great faith that I could write this novel, generously sent me her book: DES Voice: *From Anger to Action*, signed, and with the words to use any part of it that would send out the message for DES Action.

I would also like to thank; Fran Howell – Executive Director DES Action USA for all her help and advice, Jill Vanselous Murphy – President, DES Action USA and Joyce Bichler (all DES Daughters) for allowing me to quote them. Jane Kevan and Heather Justice (DES Daughters), from DES Action UK for their contributions over the years towards the facts within this novel. And many thanks to Marion Vickers: DES Action Australia for her contribution.

I would also like to convey my appreciation to The Sunday Independent, Jaymi McCann and Sarah Morrison, Domino (DES Daughter) and Heather, for their permission to reprint the article, first published, 22 January 2012, on Diethylstilbestrol (DES) which included the interviews with Heather and Domino.

Thank you also to the Senior Rights Assistant, Yale University Press, 47 Bedford Square, London, WC1B

3DP for permission to quote *from the* publication To *Do No Harm: DES and the Dilemmas of Modern Medicine*.

To Abacus: A Division of Little, Brown &Co (UK) , Brettenham House, Lancaster Place, London, WC2E 7EN for permission to quote from the publication *Our Stolen Future*.

And to Dick Clapp for allowing me to quote from his article in *The Pump Handle*: Public Health Classic: DES Daughters.

Special thanks to my dear friend and fellow author, Sharon Tregenza, for her diligent and unstinting encouragement and support during the writing of Silent Trauma.

Lastly to David, my thanks for his love – and for taking on the grocery shopping and coffee making so I could finally finish this book.

In remembrance of Pat Cody:

"Today and always, Pat is the DES Mother who is the Mother of DES Action."

— Kari Christianson, DES Daughter and DES Action USA: Program Director

The whole gamut of experiences associated with trauma has been seen in the aftermath of DES. The insults inflicted by DES are social, personal, external and internal, public and private, sudden and enduring.*

*Roberta J Apfel, MD.,M.P.H. Susan M Fisher, M.D. To Do No Harm: DES and the Dilemmas of Modern Medicine Chapter 4 p60

Judith Barrow

Foreword

The Sunday Independent: Sunday 22 January 2012

Thousands of women could be at risk from 'silent Thalidomide'
A drug intended to prevent miscarriage is blamed for causing cancer in the daughters – and possibly even granddaughters – of women who took it decades ago.

By Sarah Morrison and Jaymi McCann

Diethylstilboestrol (DES), a drug given to women for 30 years up to 1973, has been found to cause a rare form of vaginal and cervical cancer in some of the daughters of the women who took it, as well as fertility problems …. There is even a suspicion that DES – known as the "silent Thalidomide" – can affect the grandchildren of those who took it….

The saga surrounding DES, developed in England in 1938, began when it was prescribed to millions of women in the US, Australia and Europe, despite the fact that research published in the American Journal of Obstetrics & Gynaecology in 1953 revealed that women receiving it suffered a higher rate of miscarriage. In 1971, the US Food and Drug Administration told doctors to stop prescribing DES when it was discovered that one in 1,000 daughters of women who had taken it developed a rare form of vaginal and cervical cancer, known as clear cell adenocarcinoma (CCAC)....

The Royal College of Obstetrics and Gynaecology estimates that 7,500 women in the UK were given the drug and 3,500 exposed girls were born between 1940 and 1971, but this is believed by many to be a gross underestimate. Other reports estimate that up to 300,000 people in Britain were exposed, but no source can confirm this figure. Some children will be unaware if their mother took DES during her pregnancy, especially as some of those who took it have since died.

The "children" that do know, most aged between 35 and 65, are not only concerned about their own health, but also that of their children. Research into the effects of DES exposure on the third generation is in early stages, but studies done on rodents suggest the drug can cause DNA changes in women that can be passed from generation to generation. It was not until 1973 that UK doctors were advised against prescribing the drug....

Dr Julie Palmer, professor of epidemiology at Boston University's school of public health, who is leading a study on the effects of DES exposure in second and third generations, said she does not think we have uncovered all the side effects of this drug. "Women who took it were given very big doses. They often took one pill every day, all the way through their pregnancy – sometimes a week before their due date," she said.

All DES daughters carry a lifelong risk of CCAC and

are 40 times more likely to develop it than unexposed women. Most cases have occurred in women in their late teens and early twenties, and it is estimated that at least 25 per cent of those diagnosed died from the illness. But this is only one of a rapidly increasing list of side effects. According to a recent study, led by Dr Robert Hoover at America's National Cancer Institute, breast cancer risk is nearly doubled in DES daughters over the age of 40, with women recording a one-in-25 chance of developing the disease by 55….

Several studies have found increased risks of premature birth, miscarriage and ectopic pregnancy associated with drug exposure, while "DES sons" run a higher risk of genital problems, such as undescended testicles, cysts on the back of the testes and lowered sperm count…

The first recorded "DES daughter" in Britain, **Heather Justice**, 59, from Jarrow, was 25 when she found out she had vaginal cancer and would have to undergo a hysterectomy and partial vaginectomy. Although she found records showing her mother had been given DES in the 1950s, she was unable to bring a case to court - (in the UK, because she could not identify which manufacturer had produced the drug. However, a US lawyer did help her get some compensation there. Also, she says –"it is impossible for anyone to find the manufacturer of the drug in this country, not just me, as it was never patented. It was the surgeon who performed my hysterectomy who asked my mother if she knew what she had taken. He knew it must have been DES because of the rare type of cancer I had. He was also the one who found her medical records with the generic name of the drug":- *added after this interview*)

After years of fighting the legal system, she says she feels disillusioned.

"One of the problems is that unlike Thalidomide, where you see the problem the minute the baby was born, women who took DES had healthy babies," she says. "Problems were hidden until the teens and twenties, by which point we were forgotten about. When I asked my mum what she had taken, she didn't even remember the name of the stuff. It is a complete and utter minefield."...

Dominique, 40, lives with her husband and her three daughters, aged between three and eight. She discovered that she was exposed to DES when she was 13 years old and found out she had a T-shaped uterus when she miscarried 11 years ago. After being refused surgery by the NHS, she returned to France for surgery.

"It is really tiring to have to educate GPs when they should be the ones telling you they will take care of you. When you have to convince them, it makes you feel paranoid. There needs to be more awareness. It has been a battle for me; DES daughters are at risk of [breast] cancer over 40, yet my GP said I can't have regular breast examinations because I am not 50. It means I'll have to pay for it.

"There are definitely women who don't know their mum even took the drug. That's the main issue in the UK, because they may be infertile or have breast cancer without knowing it is because of DES. My mum really blamed herself, but it will be worse for me. My mum didn't know what it could do when she took it, but when I had my children, I knew there were some concerns for the third generation. I'm sure many women will make that decision. If my daughters get ill, I'll definitely feel guilty, but I don't want to be a victim of it. It can't rule my life."

Silent Trauma

Prologue – Lisa - 1989

It was the first time they'd made love: the first time for both of them. It would be the last. Lisa hadn't told him. He'd find out soon enough. But it had been perfect. Daniel had said so, 'perfect', he'd said, circling her nipple with his fingertips and kissing her throat, 'you're perfect.'

The rush of warmth spreads slowly from her stomach down between her thighs. Taking a deep breath she closes her eyes, leans back on the wrought iron garden seat and savours the memory; the weight of him, the feel of him inside her.

The breeze ruffles her hair, presses the long cotton skirt to her legs and her skin puckers against the rapidly cooling September evening. Winding her mother's scarf closer to her neck she breathes in the familiar perfume of the pale blue material and lies along the bench, pulling up her knees and wrapping her clothes around her. She twirls a length of hair between her fingers and chews the end of it, a habit from childhood. Through the branches of the apple tree the sky is a blend of gold and red streaks against a backdrop of deepening blue. This is her favourite place.

The tree, planted the day after she was born, had grown with her. 'In celebration of their first child,' her father used to say but she hadn't heard that phrase for years. It had stopped after her mother had the last miscarriage. So the tree had just become 'a celebration of Lisa'. There was no further talk about having more children: there'd been no brothers or sisters. It hadn't bothered her; she'd always felt special.

Until lately: lately she wished she had a sister, someone to confide in, someone to talk to about what was going to happen to her; about the threat, coiled patiently waiting since the moment she was born: since before then.

She reaches over the arm of the seat and strokes the trunk of the tree. It used to be smooth, slippery, under her fingertips but now there are sharp raised bumps and tiny cracks in the bark. And as far as Lisa remembers there's never been any fruit.

The sun slides slowly downwards. Turning her head she watches it, the bright radiance hurting her eyes. She blinks, clearing the tears that blur the rapidly changing patterns: strands of yellowing cloud that dissolve, transform and race across the sky: lines of fiery colours merge and flow.

A musty smell of burning wood fills her nostrils: a spiral of smoke twists and turns, rising from a garden somewhere down the lane.

The leaves on the apple tree rise and fall in the breeze. One comes to rest in the folds of her skirt. She picks it up, strokes it. Not yet brittle and dry, the surface is still a dull green but is pitted with small holes, each flaw edged with rusted orange. Rubbing it between her palms she holds it to her face and inhales but the fragrance of summer has vanished. She brushes the remnants of the leaf off her hands and sits up, swinging her feet to the ground and looking across the lawn. The grass is long; her father will have to do another cut before winter sets in and everything slows into a long sleep.

It's almost dark. Lisa stands, pulls at the hem of her cardigan, smoothes down her skirt.

The hedge at the far end of the garden is now a line of blackness, above it the last streaks of red fan upwards. Anxious to catch a final glimpse of the sun as it dips out of sight she kicks off her sandals, climbs onto the bench and raises up on her toes. Now there is only a blood-gash in the blackness.

She pulls her long hair over one shoulder. It lies, dark and silky across her breast. She hears Daniel's words again when he stroked her hair, kissed her, licked the flatness of her stomach, the inside of her thighs. 'Perfect, you're so perfect.' She waits for the heat to rise within her again but it's not there; the cold is deep inside her now.

Barely able to see the tree she works the scarf around the branch above her, the material, traced with her mother's perfume, smooth between her fingers.

Jerking the knot tight she yanks on it, tests it. The branch bends, creaks loudly, holds.

For a moment she stares into the darkness. Her heart is beating so fiercely it fills her whole being with a loud insistent throb. Drawing in a long breath she waits, smells the smoke still in the air, feels the sharpness of the cold night in her lungs. She pulls the loop over her head, letting the scarf slide taut around her neck.

Then Lisa steps off the bench.

Chapter One – Meg - November 2001

My intention is to present a book to fill (the) silence, a book for DES mothers, daughters, and sons that shows how positive change can be made by working, often against indifference, to bring people together affected by a dangerous drug.[1]

Good morning and welcome to Radio Carvoen's Woman's World. In today's programme we're talking to Meg Matthews. She's in the studio to tell us about her daughter, Lisa, who sadly committed suicide twelve years ago. I'll let Meg tell you herself about the circumstances that surrounded this tragic event and why she feels let down by past and present Governments.

Let down? Meg felt the familiar surge of impotent anger. The emotion swept away the terror that had overcome her outside the local radio station when she'd realised what she was about to do. She willed herself to stay calm, hanging on to deep breaths, blowing them slowly out through parted lips. The air in the recording studio was odd, a mixture of warm electronic machinery, stale sweat and lingering food smells.

Sandy Carney, the interviewer, was smiling at her.

---

[1] *DES Voices From Anger to Action. 2008* © Pat Cody, *Introduction* Page 6

There was a whispering stillness in the headphones. Meg adjusted them; they felt strange, unwieldy over her ears. She needed a pee but it was too late. She opened her notebook.

'I just want the facts to be told.' She heard the huskiness in her voice, felt the plastic chair hot and tacky under her thighs.

'In your own words, Meg, tell us first about Lisa.'

Meg cleared her throat. 'Lisa died when she was nineteen. She killed herself after she was diagnosed with a rare form of vaginal cancer. This was because, while she was in my womb, while I was carrying the most precious thing in my life, she was exposed to an artificial oestrogen called Diethylstilboestrol.' She faltered.

'Could you explain to our listeners how that happened Meg?'

'Diethylstilboestrol, it's usually called Stilboestrol in this country,'[i] Meg added, 'was a drug given to approximately seven thousand pregnant women in the UK between nineteen forty-seven and nineteen seventy-one; over five million worldwide: ostensibly to prevent miscarriages, and it was prescribed to me by my GP when I was pregnant with Lisa. I'd lost a baby three months into a pregnancy before and I was told Stilboestrol would stop that happening again.' She swallowed and fell silent: she wasn't angry now, only filled with the familiar grief.

Sandy opened her mouth as though to speak. 'I'm okay,' Meg mouthed.

The interviewer nodded, encouraging her to continue.

'By taking that drug, any future my husband Richard and I could have had with our daughter, was taken away.'

Tears burned at the back of her eyes. She waited, reminding herself of the conversation she'd had with Richard's when she'd told him she'd contacting the radio station.

'You've lobbied the Government for over ten years,' he'd said, 'you promised you'd give up at ten years if we'd got nowhere.'

'Just this one last thing,' she'd pleaded, 'this is the one thing I haven't tried.'

'Well, please make it the last, sweetheart; you're worn out.'

And so she'd given her word. She'd try this one last thing, after this she'd stop.

'But you did carry Lisa to full term.'

'Yes but that wasn't because of the drug,' Meg stressed. 'Over the years it was proved it didn't stop miscarriages. But what Stilboestrol did do was to plant this time bomb in my daughter.' She leaned forward, feeling her body relax under the benevolent gaze of the interviewer. 'I know all this happened years ago,' she said, feeling more confident: it was almost as if they were having a conversation just between the two of them. 'But just because the drug stopped being prescribed so long ago doesn't mean that it's a problem that's gone away.'

'In what way?'

'There are women living every day with the consequence of Stilboestrol.' Meg looked down at her notes 'And it's believed by some that the grandchildren of the women originally prescribed with the drug could also be affected.' She paused, adding, 'though that isn't proved. But this chemical hormone has been described as a 'hand me down poison' for the human race. And I've even heard it called 'the silent Thalidomide.'

'Has it been proved that Stilboestrol is as damaging as Thalidomide?'

'Oh yes.' Sometimes, over the years, it had seemed to Meg that the massing of the facts. The meticulous, painful research, had been the only reason to carry on living. 'Oh yes,' she emphasized, 'that's been proved, it's been proved by many people; women, men; people who've suffered because of it: scientists who specialize in these things. I've seen the evidence.'

She became aware of the heat in the small studio: or was it just her?

Sweat was trickling down between her shoulder blades and when she lifted her knees there was a faint un-sticking noise from the seat. 'I always thought that prescription drugs were safe,' she said, 'and if something was suddenly found to be harmful we would be told. After all they do with everything else; toys, food, cars.' Meg clenched her hands on top of the table, her knuckles white. 'But nothing was made public in the UK until nineteen seventy-nine, almost ten years after the health authorities discovered the damage Stilboestrol caused to the reproductive system in the daughters of the women who'd taken it.'

'What about the doctors? Didn't they say anything?'

Meg shook her head. 'The doctors only knew what they were told was best for their patients. They followed advice from the pharmaceutical companies, from the Government.'

'You told our researchers you'd contacted the Government Health Department.'

'Yes, many times. I've written to every Health Secretary over the last twelve years. Eventually I presume they saw me as a nuisance because I received a letter saying that in future my correspondence to them would be logged but not answered.' Meg smiled; a stretching of her lips.

'The papers?'

'It's seen as old news by the media.'

There was a pause and the strange whispering stillness filled Meg's ear again.

She answered a few more questions almost automatically; repeating the phrases she'd used so many times in the letters written over the years and was surprised when Sandy pointed to the clock on the studio wall and signaled 'four minutes'.

Meg glanced up and nodded to show she

understood. 'The cancer Lisa had is called a clear-cell adenocarcinoma of the cervix; usually found only in post-menopausal women, 'she said. 'The week before her birthday she was given a choice, a total hysterectomy or face dying. In the end she made her own choice.'

'Have you managed to come to terms with the choice Lisa made?'

Meg's voice cracked: always the guilt clenched in her chest. 'No.' She gazed for a long moment at Sandy. 'No, I don't think my husband and I will ever come to terms with losing Lisa; especially because of the way she died. She paused, took a sip of the water. 'Sorry.' She placed the glass carefully on the table. 'There have been many nights I've lain awake over the years and thought about how desperate, how alone, she must have felt, and I think … I know I let her down as a parent.'

'I'm sure you didn't, Meg.' The interviewer made a sympathetic face.

Meg felt like shouting how the hell would you know?

'What do you hope to achieve from this interview, Meg'

'Probably nothing; I just wanted to tell Lisa's story one last time; I've promised my husband I'll stop trying to get the Government to help us after this. He thinks we both need to move on.' She shrugged. 'There's not enough public information out there in this country. The official line seems to be that it would cause unnecessary alarm.' Meg twisted her mouth in an ironic gesture. 'Who knows why the Government really ...?'

Sandy Carney hastily interrupted. *'Just so the listeners know, we did ask our local MP, Stewart Jones, to contact the Government Health Department to ask if someone could come into the studio today to answer these question, and we also asked for a statement from them but we were told there was no one available for either.'*

Meg wasn't surprised but she kept quiet.

'But anyway.' Sandy held out her hands spreading her fingers*,' surely, these days the scientists, the pharmaceutical companies are more aware of the dangers of using these drugs. There must be greater, more stringent rules ... laws, on their usage.'*

Meg lifted her shoulders and let them fall, looking steadily at her. 'The frightening thing is that scientists are still conducting various prescription trials on women who have a history of miscarriages, some good and some bad; ultimately who knows? And it's being allowed by our Government: pharmaceutical companies are given permission to manufacture all kinds of synthetic chemicals each year. I realize that the argument is that there are stringent checks and regulations before they are produced. But the public are expected to believe, to accept, that the scientists know the consequences of their use. They don't, not the long-term use anyway. No one does. Not them, not you, not me ... nobody.'

Sandy tilted her head to one side and glanced towards the tinted glass partition behind Meg, giving a slight nod as if in answer to a question. She frowned at Meg's last words. *'Careful,'* she warned silently.

Meg glanced at her notes; she'd underlined the next paragraph. The researcher who'd been given the task of vetting the interview had decided against it. 'Too controversial,' she'd said.

Meg hesitated for a second and then made the decision. 'What I do know, what I've found out through my research, is that there have been hundreds of synthetic chemicals introduced into our environment over the last fifty years.' She looked over her shoulder where she knew the producer and her team were. 'People have a right to know what's happening all around us, to be warned.[ii] Even though, like Stilboestrol, it will probably be too late.'

Sandy made a gesture, a sideways cutting motion. She made no mention of Meg's final words. *'I'd like to thank you, Meg, for coming here to talk to us today.'*

Meg's fingers trembled as she pulled off the headphones. The glass in the windowed partition distorted her image but she could see how stiffly she sat at the table and how the overhead lights highlighted the greyness of her hair that was stuck up, as always, from her double crown. She flattened it down.

'If you or someone you know has been affected by

Meg's story or you need any information on Stilboestrol, please don't hesitate to contact our helpline.'

It was drizzling: a dark, grey November afternoon. The tarmac in front of the building shone black with splodges of orange from the outside lights.

'We'll let you know if we get any calls at the station.' The presenter pulled a packet of cigarettes out of the pocket of her over-large cardigan and lit one, jigging from one foot to the other, shivering.

'You probably won't. Thanks for seeing me out; you can go in now,' Meg said, buttoning her raincoat and pulling the hood over her head.

Holding on to it she walked to her car, noticing for the first time the lacework of rust over the front wheel arch of her old Ford. Conscious of the young woman still watching, she slid into the driver's seat and, without straightening her coat or fastening the seat belt, fumbled with the key until the engine croaked into life. Her eyes were burning. 'Please go,' she muttered, not looking in the woman's direction and struggling with the stiff gear stick. 'Just go in, why don't you?'

Meg let the clutch out too quickly. She swore under her breath as the car lurched forward.

Once outside the double gates of the entrance she braked, the wheel trims scraping along the raised kerb. Resting her forehead on the steering wheel she gulped against the lump in her throat: then heard the loud wail that escaped as though it came from someone else.

What Meg hadn't said in her interview, what she and Richard had never told anyone, was that Lisa hadn't died quickly; her neck hadn't snapped. The branch of the tree wasn't strong enough; it had bent under her weight and she'd been able to touch the ground with the tip of her toes. By the time the branch broke she'd slowly, it must have been slowly, despite the Coroner's carefully chosen words, strangled to death

Chapter Two

What really worries me is that a lot of doctors have no knowledge of the drug and its effects. They look at me as if I have suddenly started speaking in a foreign language[2]

Alice, Meg's neighbour from across the road, was washing soapsuds off the car in her drive. The drizzle had turned into a steady rain and Alice was enveloped in a large yellow cagoule. Sponge in hand she looked up and down the avenue of neat semi-detached houses and bungalows before struggling to cross the road on legs swollen with phlebitis.

'Why are you cleaning your car in the rain?' Meg locked the Ford and pushed her way between it and the privet hedge that lined their drive, to the gate. 'You're wet through.'

'Waiting for you,' the big woman grinned. 'It wasn't raining when I started.'

'Liar,' Meg smiled. 'You know I'd have come over later.'

'Couldn't wait.' Alice enveloped Meg in a soft squashy hug. 'You were wonderful.' She smelt of

---

[2] Excerpt from letter written to the Royal College of General Practitioners on the 4th August 2008 by Barbara Killick, Mother of DES Daughter Sarah..

detergent and TCP.

'Oh, Alice, it was as bad as I expected. I'll never do anything like that again.'

'Don't talk rubbish, woman, you were great. If that doesn't make somebody sit up and take notice, I'll eat my bloody hat.'

'Not your red feathered hat?' Meg said in mock horror.

Alice nudged her and laughed. 'Watch it you. Just 'cos that lad said I looked like a cockatoo, the cheeky young beggar.' She blew down her nose as if offended while smiling at the same time.

Meg looked up at her. 'All I want, all we've ever wanted, Richard and I, is for someone to say they made a mistake,' she said. 'We don't care who and we've never wanted compensation … nothing could ever make up for losing Lisa. But someone should have admitted it was their fault a long time ago.'

'I know,' Alice's voice softened. 'Our Wendy thought you sounded great too. Lisa would have been proud of you.'

An instant memory of Lisa and Alice's daughter, as small children playing in the garden, flashed into Meg's mind and tears threatened.

'She still misses her, you know.'

'Does she?' Meg put a hand on Alice's arm, remembering how fiercely her friend had protected her and Richard from all the unwanted publicity in the horrendous time after Lisa's death. 'You've both been so good.'

There was a tapping noise and turning round Meg saw her husband signalling at the window. The room behind him, hued in warm colours, was all at once irresistible.

'Go in now, Alice, you'll catch your death. Go on, I'll pop over later. I must see if Richard is okay first.'

'Course love, I just wanted to say well done. You'll get that lot in the Government to help yet.' Meg got another squeeze, her head pressed into her friend's large bosom, the sponge dripping soapsuds down the collar of her coat.

'Thanks, Alice, one day perhaps. Let's hope so anyway.' She looked up at the woman's large smiling face. 'Give my love to Wendy. She set a date for the wedding yet?'

'You're joking', Alice laughed; a long unselfconscious guffaw, her head tilted back on her shoulders and her small eyes closed tight. 'She's too comfortable at home that one; waited on hand and foot. Unless her John becomes as good a cook as me he hasn't a soddin' chance of getting her down that aisle. Still, mustn't grumble, she's a good girl.'

Richard knocked again on the glass.

'You'd better get in; 'im indoors wants you.' Alice gave Meg a slight shove that sent her tottering backwards. 'Oops, sorry love, don't know my own strength sometimes. See you later.' She turned and waddled back across the road.

'She is a good soul, she must have been waiting for me for ages,' Meg called, hanging her coat on the stand in the hall and kicking her shoes off. She heard Richard switch off the television.

'You did well,' he said, 'you alright?'

'Ok, bit tired,' she said, determined to make light of how traumatic the interview had been. What was the point? He'd only blame himself for persuading her into going. She hung her coat on the stand in the hall. 'You?'

'Yes, fine .Come in here,' he said. 'Guess what?'

Meg dropped her handbag on the hall table. Standing in the doorway to the living room she said, 'What?'

Richard swivelled his wheelchair round, a piece of paper clutched between his fingers and the armrest. 'You've had a 'phone call from the radio station. I'd just put the receiver down as you pulled up in the car.' He grinned at Meg. 'They've passed a message on from a woman called ...' he unscrewed the paper and pulled his spectacles lower down his nose. 'Rachel Conway. They said she'd asked if you'd ring her back ... she's a DES Daughter.'

Chapter Three

"DES taught us ... important lessons that can guide our investigations of other chemicals ... The risk of health impacts from exposure to hormone disruptors is especially high during prenatal development ... Girls who were exposed to DES prenatally appeared to develop normally. Only in adulthood did health impacts like uterine malformations, infertility ... become apparent.[3]

To: Megmath222@aol.com
From: info@theconways
Subject: DES

Dear Mrs Matthews,
It was so good of you to return my call. I have been desperate to talk to someone other than doctors.

Rachel Conway chewed the inside of her cheek. Did desperate sound too... well, desperate? But wasn't she? She pushed her cheek further in with her thumb to give her teeth more leverage on the skin of her mouth. She didn't want to sound needy: yet the relief of knowing there was someone who'd been in

---

[3] Review by Kari Christianson. Voice Spring 2009

a similar situation, who, from what was said in the interview, knew how she felt. She stopped gnawing when she tasted blood and gazed hopelessly at the word. She'd leave it in for now.

She reached over and stroked the head of the dog sitting by her side. 'Ok boy?' she said. The end of the long tail of the Golden Retriever flicked and he gave a low whine.

When I heard your name on the radio I realised I knew who you were. My mother, Megan Lewis, was in Beddgaron Hospice - she thought the world of you and the other Friends. And it wasn't just about the money you raised; it was the way you always chatted to her about ordinary things. She said you treated her as an 'ordinary woman' not like a lot of her visitors with their hushed voices and wearing what she nick-named 'the deadly look'. We used to laugh about that.

Rachel felt the ache inside her turn into bleak misery. Over the last year, the wretchedness of all the miscarriages had somehow merged with the sadness of her mother's death. Although she'd trained herself to turn away from the traps set by everyday situations: a young mother pushing a pram, a middle-aged woman carefully linking the arm of an older one, heads close together as they laughed and chatted in the shopping mall, sometimes it was impossible. And yet here she was deliberately bringing both out into the open for her to confront.

Rachel patted her sleeves of her blouse for a handkerchief. She was a mess; forever on the verge of bloody tears. No wonder Stephen was fed up with her.

And was she making things worse by getting in touch with this woman, Meg Matthews? She'd acted on impulse; reaching out for yet another answer as to why the miscarriages kept happening, even though she knew the physical reasons. Hoping it would help to push the situation with Stephen to the back of her mind? She didn't know; had she even been thinking? Now, it seemed she'd replaced one set of awful feelings with another.

Rachel gave a loud sigh that made the dog get to his feet and shove his nose against her arm. She rested her cheek on the top of his head. Okay, enough self-pity. She wiped her eyes and blew her nose loudly. 'Right!'

Well, it was the only thing we could do. She said she knew she was dying from breast cancer; she just didn't want it written all over everyone's face as well. She said you weren't like that and I'm grateful. You may remember Mum passed away just before last Christmas.

The tears spilled over. Furious with herself, Rachel fumbled in the box of tissues; a whole bunch of them followed the one she tugged at and fell onto the floor. She ignored them, scrubbing at her face until her skin stung. The dog pushed at her arm again.

'Okay Jake,' she said, 'it's okay.' His coat was silky under her fingers.

Just before I lost the baby.

Their fourth baby.

She'd seen Stephen's expressions each time she'd miscarried. Grief and pity had changed over time to anger and frustration. Frustration with her. Until the last twenty-four hours that hadn't occurred to her. Now it was so obvious. After all, she despised herself, why shouldn't he? Stephen didn't like failure.

She'd watched him in action with clients and with his family. He would always try to drag situations round to what he wanted, not accept what was. When it didn't work he'd grow tight-lipped and silent.

And it had been the same with her and she hadn't even seen it, let alone acknowledged it. She'd been so tied up with herself she'd completely misread the situation.

When had he last touched her voluntarily except for the almost dutiful coupling, to try again for a baby? She remembered her humiliating pleading two nights before when he'd finally made love to her. But, even then, she knew it was only to shut her up; he had an important meeting the following day, he'd said afterwards, turning from her and pulling the duvet over his head.

She couldn't even remember when he'd last reached for her hand when they walked together, massaged the knot of tension in her shoulders, curved himself naked around her back in bed, so that even if they didn't make love she could feel his warmth against her skin, his hand resting on her hip. She couldn't remember. They didn't even kiss anymore, except for the quick 'hello and goodbye' peck on the cheek, a gesture without regard on both sides.

God, this was all too much, she was exhausted: her head felt so heavy on her neck she let it droop, her chin resting against her chest. She closed her eyes for a long moment.

When she opened them the first thing she saw was the coffee stain on the front of her old green dressing gown and on her pyjama leg, still in the same things from yesterday: she hadn't dressed for two whole days, hadn't even cleaned her teeth. Her mouth felt foul and when she cupped her hand over her lips her breath stank. She raised a hand to her head, her hair hung, unwashed and limp, over her shoulders. She was disgusted with herself; she'd been letting herself go for months. Stephen was justified in leaving her; she was a mess: she deserved to be alone.

Double clicking the mouse she put the email into 'draft' and pushed against the front of the large oak desk. Her chair skimmed back on its wheels across the wooden floor of the office and when it stopped she stood, left it where it was and went into the bedroom, followed closely by Jake.

In the ensuite bathroom she stepped into the shower and turned it on, waiting for the warm water to release the tension in her muscles. It didn't. Now she'd stopped thinking about Meg Matthews and her search for more information on that bloody drug, the fear that Stephen wouldn't come home returned. She hated being alone in the house at night. It was worse since, she made herself say the words in her head, since losing the baby. In the past she'd 'phoned her mother if Stephen was late home or working away; she couldn't do that anymore. And she knew her father, miles away in a different country, was still so lost in his own grief that he could hardly bear to talk to her.

She felt her legs give way under her and slumped down onto the tiled floor of the shower, her sobs lost under the noisy power of the water beating down on her.

Yesterday she'd waited for Stephen to call, now she knew he wouldn't; she'd worked it out, understanding why he'd been so distant over the last few weeks. He'd been psyching himself up to leaving her and when she remembered the cruelty of his words over the last few days they were together she knew he'd deliberately chosen them to hurt, to underline his detachment from her.

'Going out? You were out last night,' Rachel had said, raising her head from the cushion on the settee.

'And, with any luck, I'll be out tomorrow as well.'

'I want to talk.' She swung herself into a sitting position.

'What's to talk about?' Stephen shouted, taking the stairs two at a time.

The dog, fastened in the kitchen, began to bark.

Rachel raised her voice as she followed him. 'I want us to talk,' she said again, holding onto the post at the top of the stairs.

'That's all you ever want to do; you're bloody obsessed,' Stephen went into the bathroom and plugged in his shaver. 'If you weren't such a hysterical cow, we'd have kids by now, like the rest of my family.'

The floor tilted as his words hit her. She sat down with a thump on the landing, the anger gone. 'It's not my fault.'

He switched on the shaver and stretched his chin upwards, rubbing his fingers against the bristles on his neck.

The atmosphere the following morning continued the previous night's row. Sitting opposite Stephen at the breakfast table Rachel watched him. It seemed to her that the tension sparked between them: she sensed it by his refusal to look at her, in the way he snapped the newspaper and folded it onto the table in a perfect rectangle to read the financial page. It showed as he pulled the cuffs of his shirt away from his plate by holding the material between forefinger and thumb and giving it an impatient tug. And then again in the precise slicing off of the top of his boiled egg.

It was when he cracked the shell that she began crying.

Stephen stormed out of the kitchen, leaving behind his half-eaten breakfast. Rachel picked up the coffee he'd left on the table and followed him up the stairs. In the bedroom she held the cup out to him. 'Here.'

He ignored it. 'You're always bloody crying,' he said, his tone cold. He flung open the wardrobe doors and began pulling suits off their hangers.

'My ... the baby ... I need ...'

He pushed past, knocking the cup upwards and coffee splashed over her. 'The baby, the baby! I'm sick to death of hearing about your needs ... your baby. It only ever happens to you, doesn't it?' His voice throbbed with contempt and she knew he was deliberately drowning out her words as he dragged open drawers, threw clothes, shoes, shaver, into a case. She flinched away from his anger. 'You're a mess, Rachel.' Stephen spun around, held his arms out in a wide arc. 'Look at the state of the house. How can I bring clients back here, let alone invite them for a meal. They'd get bloody food poisoning.

Sort yourself out ... because I won't be here to do it for you. I'm gone!'

When the front door slammed she stood by the bed, running her forefinger around the rim of the cup staring into the large wardrobe. She felt numb; worthless. When had that started? That feeling of utter worthlessness?

The doors swung on their hinges: on one side, shirts, half-pulled from hangers, trailed sleeves on the floor making vague lines in the dust there. On the other, the opened drawers were draped with jumpers, underpants, socks. His golf bag was propped up in the corner of the room. He'd forgotten his clubs. He was bound to come back for those. Surely?

But he hadn't come back for his golf clubs and he hadn't called.

Rachel stretched her legs against the wall of the shower cubicle. The warm water turned cold. She stood up, the pain in her stiff legs, the crawling return of circulation, almost welcome. At least concentrating on the sheer effort of making sure she didn't fall over helped. She dressed, refusing to let herself think: ignoring the quivering in her legs that was travelling rapidly upwards through the whole of her body.

Downstairs Jake barked.

In the kitchen, the head-spinning weariness made Rachel hold onto the worktops. She was cold, colder than she'd ever been in her life. She pressed the buttons on the heating panel until the temperature control wouldn't go any higher.

Voices mumbled from the clock- radio on the windowsill. *'Because of Stilboestrol.'* The word hammered itself into Rachel's consciousness, the shock making her skin tingle. She reached over and turned the volume button.

'Because of Stilboestrol there are women who can't conceive or who lose their babies in the first trimester. Many don't even know why. That's the tragedy ...'

Rachel couldn't move. She gripped the edge of the sink. Was it worse not knowing why? No, whoever she was, this woman saying these things, she was wrong. What's worse, Rachel thought, was knowing why and knowing that there was no chance of going to full term: of having that first rush of excitement when you realise you are pregnant and then living with the fear, the knowledge, that it wouldn't last. That was what was worse.

'And there are GPs, doctors, who don't know why these things happen either because they haven't been trained to recognize the consequences of Stilboestrol.'

'So that's yet another consequence of the drug, an inability to conceive?' *'Why is that?'* Another woman's voice.

It was obviously some sort of interview. Rachel couldn't take her eyes off the radio.

'It's either through hormonal imbalances or a small, maybe a deformed, uterus. And, what I find worrying is that some go through infertility treatment in their bid to become pregnant: thus putting even more artificial hormonal drugs in their bodies. It's a vicious circle. It's heart-breaking for the women and it's not fair on them.'

And it's not their fault, Rachel felt sick, seeing the anger in Stephen's face again; whatever the problem it's not their fault. With one part of her brain she was trying to take in what the woman on the radio was saying, with the other half she had the sensation of floating around the room, watching herself disintegrate. This is what it felt like to be completely alone: no longer at the centre of anyone's world. To be nothing.

'... please don't hesitate to contact our helpline 0800123124 or contact us through our website www.radiocarvoen.co.uk ...'

Rachel looked down at her hands; her knuckles had whitened the skin. She pushed herself away from the sink. Before she could think things through, find reasons why she shouldn't, she reached for the telephone.

Opening her email Rachel began to type again.

As I said on the 'phone, Mrs Matthews, I haven't had cancer but I've had an ectopic pregnancy and earlier this year went through my fourth miscarriage. I found out after my first one, that my mother was given Stilboestrol as injections when she and my father were trying for a baby and stopped when she discovered she was three months pregnant with me. After I lost the second baby the gynaecologist told me I have a misshapen fallopian tube and a T-shaped uterus, caused by the drug. I never told Mum, she wouldn't have coped with it.

She sat back in the chair, resting her hand on the dog's head. God knows she'd wanted to tell her mother so much when she grieved with Rachel for the lost babies: weeping for each little soul, but reminding her that she herself had two miscarriages before Rachel was born. 'And all the more precious,' she'd say, holding her daughter closely as though trying to shield her from the despair and anger that welled up so destructively. And Rachel was glad that her mother had died believing that the last baby was safe. That by carrying it past the time when she'd miscarried three times before, this would be the one child Rachel would hold in *her* arms.

I will not be trying for another child.

She nibbled on the inside of her cheek, wincing against the pain of the open sore. Her finger hovered over the keyboard, hesitating over the first word of her last sentence, wondering whether she should change it to 'we'. No, she thought, no, why should I?

She added another couple of sentences, stock phrases to end the email and signed her name. She read the message once more, hesitating again over the 'we' or 'I; left it as it was and then jabbed at the Send button before she could change her mind.

Moonlight lit the front of the house when Rachel returned from a shortened version of the last walk of the day with the dog.

She still hadn't heard from Stephen, his mobile was switched off and earlier, when she'd finally plucked up the courage to ring him at his office, his PA had told her he was in a meeting. She watched Jake dart from shrub to shrub, following a trail of interesting smells. Snotty cow hadn't even offered to take a message, let alone ask if Stephen could ring back. Rachel felt a large tear roll down the side of her nose and brushed it angrily away with her palm. Probably wasn't the woman's fault: she wouldn't be surprised if he'd told her to ward off calls from his wife. It occurred to Rachel that she didn't even know the name of the young woman who organised Stephen's daily life. Unbelievable. Just shows how far apart their worlds were; how little they'd talked.

Jake rushed into the house when Rachel unlocked the door. She'd left the television on and she could hear the canned laughter of a sit-com playing to the empty lounge. Reluctant to go in she studied the sky;

long gauzy clouds, the edges white gold, trailed across the face of the full moon. Twisting her head to one side she found the three bright stars of Orion's belt and followed the lines of the warrior, savouring the beauty of the night sky, feeling tiny and insignificant. T S Elliot was right, she thought; '...*We must leave it all to fate...*' She grinned, hell's bells, pretentious or what and then answered herself, '*pretentious moi*?' She gave a snort of laughter and turned to go into the house.

She loved Stephen. He loved her, she was sure; they'd just forgotten how to show it. For a moment her spirits lifted; despite everything that had happened to them it was still possible they could sort things out.

She followed Jake into the kitchen. His claws scrabbled on the tiles as he ran to drink from his dish, chasing it around until it clattered against the fridge.

Rachel checked the telephone. No messages light blinked. Pulling her mobile out of her pocket she checked it for the umpteenth time. Nothing. The clock showed just past midnight. Reluctantly she turned off the television and felt the silence pulsate throughout the house. Walking from room to room she switched lights on.

In the bedroom she lay on top of the pale blue duvet, still dressed. The occasional clicking of the heating broke into her sleep, disturbing her, and when she woke in the morning, her face stiff with dried tears, the blaze of the overhead light hurt her eyes so much she closed them again. Turning her head in the dent of her pillow she opened them slightly. Stephen's side of the bed was flat, formless.

Curling into a foetal position Rachel waited for sleep to return.

Chapter Four

"But I won't be able to have children." I looked at him squarely.
   "But you'll be okay. And I'll still love you whether or not you have kids."[4]

'Four days? Where the hell is he?'

Rachel stifled an unfamiliar irritation with her friend; if I knew I'd tell you, she thought but instead said in a taut voice, 'I don't know and I don't care.' Immediately she felt guilty; Jackie was the best friend she'd ever had and it wasn't right to take things out on her. 'Sorry.' She poured the boiling water over the tea bags and stirred, breathing in the scent of the camomile. 'I suppose he's at one of his brothers ... or his sister and they'll have closed ranks.' She watched Jake wandering around the garden oblivious to the sparrows scattering as a large pigeon descended onto the bird table.

It was cruel what Stephen had done, to have left her without even letting her know where he was. She felt that in some way it was a punishment: more than the usual 'need for some space', after a quarrel; one of Stephen's mantras: he'd actually walked out

---

[4] Excerpt from - *DES Daughter: A True Story of Tragedy and Triumph: The Joyce Bichler Story 1981* © Joyce Bichler. Ch.4 p54. See Bio

on her to penalize her for losing yet another of his babies. The sob stuck in her throat and knowing Jackie was closely watching her, she covered over it by coughing.

She knew that, over the years since her marriage, her belief in equal rights and women's independence seemed to have diminished, especially in many of the decisions made for the part of her life she shared with Stephen. And now she was lost. Drifting from day to day.

But she had a well-developed radar for Jackie's intolerance for any alleged dependency on the male species. So, resolutely ignoring the image of the flat undisturbed side of the bed upstairs, she said, 'I don't want to talk about it.' She put a beaker in front of Jackie. 'Fraid it's camomile.'

'Yuk!'

'I've nothing else, I haven't been shopping.'

'Have you been out at all this week?' Rachel looked pale and exhausted and Jackie was worried. Damn the man. Even though she'd liked Rachel's husband when she first met him, she'd noticed how impatient he'd become with her over the last year. Jackie thought back to the hissed row in the hospital corridor shortly after Rachel had lost this last baby and had been admitted for a D&C.

'I can only stop a minute.' Stephen had risen up and down on his heels, his fingers tapping on the leather of his briefcase that he clutched to his chest.

'I've a thousand and one things to do.' He glanced towards the ward. The curtains were still around Rachel's bed where the doctor was examining her

'You really are a selfish git, Stephen.' The words were out even as Jackie thought them. He'd been watching the comings and goings on the ward as though any minute he would make a break for freedom and she was sick of him.

'What?' His heels hit the floor with a small thud. 'What did you say?'

'I said you're a selfish git.' Jackie looked him up and down; not a hair out of place, immaculate suit and shoes so polished they reflected the overhead lights. 'Your wife's lying in bed in there, having had the most horrific twenty-four hours … and not for the first time …'

'And don't I know it,' Stephen broke in. He made to put his briefcase down on the floor; thought better of it and, looking around, dumped it on one of the chairs that lined the corridor. Pushing back the cuff of his shirt he checked his watch. 'I've got a meeting with a colleague in half an hour. We've got the firm's books to go through before the AGM.'

'Bastard.' Jackie turned away from him. Some of the student doctors were now clustered together outside the curtains.

'What the hell's taking them so long?' He looked past her.

Jackie faced him. She could feel the hot flush of anger rise, colouring her neck. 'What is it Stephen?'

she said, 'when I first got to know you two you idolized Rachel, couldn't do enough for her. What's happened?'

For a split second he had the decency to look ashamed and then the moment was gone. 'Look, tell her I'll be in tonight to see her.' He picked up his briefcase and walked away.

Jackie's retort hovered; she bit it back, seeing the image of Rachel's face as they'd wheeled her into the operating theatre, tear stained and distressed. She stared at his retreating figure; saw the gracious half-bow of his head as he let a young nurse go first through the door he held open, the flirtatious way the girl looked up at him. 'Creep,' Jackie muttered.

Once, she would have bet her life that Rachel and Stephen were rock-solid. But now this: it was obvious he didn't care. 'What the hell's going to happen to them,' she murmured.

Well, now she knew. The smell of the camomile tea turned her stomach. 'Grief, Rachel, this is gross. I don't know how you drink the stuff.' She pushed the beaker away.

Rachel took a sharp impatient breath. 'Don't drink it then.' There I go again, she thought, flushing. 'Sorry... again.' She smiled apologetically.

'If you're trying to pick a fight it won't work,' Jackie said, 'I've had enough for one day. Besides ...' she folded her arms on the table and rested her chin on them, looking up at Rachel, 'I know it's not me you're mad at.'

'No, you're right.' Rachel's attempts to hang onto anger against Stephen, to blot out the panic, had failed miserably and she lain awake most of the night. 'Lack of sleep.'

'You need to get some fresh air,' Jackie said. 'You can't just give in.' Men, she mused; bloody waste of space.

'I don't know what to do.'

Pack the rest of his stuff up and dump it in the river. Jackie clamped her lips together, determined not to say the words.

'Let's change the subject.' Rachel adopted a false cheerful tone, hoping her friend would follow her example. 'You said you've had enough for today? So, what's happened? Come on; give me all the gossip from work.'

Jackie grimaced. 'Do I have to? I've only just escaped. I came to see how you were, not talk about that bloody place.'

'You came round to mine because you've had another row with Hazel and you don't want to go home.'

'That obvious, am I?'

'That obvious,' confirmed Rachel, sitting opposite Jackie. 'Is it just her? Or work?' Rachel instinctively knew there was something on her friend's mind. And that it concerned the school.

Jackie shifted in her seat to look out of the kitchen

window. The squabbling sparrows had returned to compete for the last of the food before nightfall. 'That lot remind me of the staffroom,' she said.

'Right, what's going on?' Rachel leant back and clasped her hands behind her head. A flicker of nervousness ran through her.

Without thinking, Jackie reached for the tea and sipped it. She screwed up her face at the taste. 'Someone always finding some poor sod to fight with ... or pick on,' she said.

Rachel made a small upward gesture with her chin. She knew it. The silence between them lengthened. 'And I suppose it's my turn at the moment?'

'Mind if I smoke?' Jackie fumbled in the rucksack she carried everywhere.

'Yes,' Rachel said, ' but I don't suppose that'll stop you.'

'Don't nag, woman, my nerves are shot.' Jackie flicked her lighter. 'Useless! Got any matches?'

'No.' Rachel gave her a smile of satisfaction. 'You'll have to do without. Now, school. What's the problem?'

Jackie took the cigarette from her mouth, rolled it between her fingers, hesitating. 'That bloody Carter cow is pushing Thacker to make her permanent Head of Year Eleven.'

'My job?' Rachel made herself shrug; so she was being stabbed in the back by yet another person? Bring it on. 'She's welcome.' Raising her eyebrows, she said, 'so they don't think I'm coming back?' She felt sick.

'Thacker's been making noises for a while,' Jackie said. She tried again with the lighter and was rewarded with a small flame. Sucking greedily on the cigarette she narrowed her eyes against the smoke and tilted her head backwards to exhale noisily. 'After all, kiddo, you've been off since March.'

'I don't feel like facing anybody yet.' Or ever again. It was safer staying within the four walls of the house.

'The staff or the kids?'

'Both I suppose. Each time it's happened ... every time I go back to work I feel like they're all staring at me.'

'They're not, you know,' Jackie said. 'Most of the staff couldn't give a damn about anyone else; they're too busy watching their own backs. As for the kids, the little devils don't think we even exist outside the classroom.' She paused. 'And if that bastard *has* left you, won't you need the job?'

'Yes ... probably.' Rachel unclasped her hands and put them flat on the table. Panic was building into explosive levels. 'It's just that I can't see me going back there.' Just as she thought she was keeping it all together. 'Sorry,' she said, ' I've got to ...' Her voice cracked. She looked up at Jackie. 'Sorry,' she said again. She ran from the kitchen.

Outside Jake was barking.

'Me and my big mouth.' Jackie stood, taking a last

drag on her cigarette. At the sink she squeezed the end until the lit ash fell with a hiss into the pile of crockery. Opening the back door she flicked the remains of the cigarette over Jake's head as he pushed past her into the kitchen. Leaving him in there she went through the dining room to the hall and called out. 'Rachel.' There was no reply. Undecided, Jackie stood for a moment looking around. There was a layer of dust on the wooden flooring. Through the lounge doorway she saw newspapers and magazines strewn across the cream leather sofas and a glass and a plate with something congealed on it on the coffee table. She'd never seen Rachel's house so messy; it was nearly as bad as her own. She lingered; undecided. 'Rachel?'

She climbed the stairs, sliding her hand along the banister and pausing on each soft tread to listen. In all the time she'd known her friend she'd never been upstairs in her home.

Rachel was sprawled sideways on the bed, her face buried into the pillows. Jackie perched on the edge of the mattress and patted her shoulder, looking around at the bedroom; the cream long-pile carpet, queen size bed, overhead light and fan combined and the pale oak Strachan fitted wardrobes all screamed money. Just shows that dosh can't buy everything.

She cast around for something to say before finally deciding on, 'good job Hazel can't see us. She'd think I was trying to seduce you'. Inane, but what the hell.

Rachel twisted round to look at Jackie, her face red and shiny. 'Chance'd be a fine thing,' she grinned weakly, sitting up and blowing her nose on a tissue. 'Fraid you're not my sort at all, sorry.' They laughed softly, but it was an odd sobering sound. Rachel rested her forehead against Jackie's arm, keeping up the pretence. 'You're far too bony for me, madam.'

'Try telling that to Hazel.' Jackie gave a sardonic smile, 'she thinks I'm irresistible to any woman I speak to. She now wants "commitment."' Jackie held up her forefingers, making marks in the air. 'We've quarrelled because she's going to visit her parents and she's finally decided she wants me to go with her and I won't.'

'Why?' Rachel was grateful for the diversion. She sniffed loudly

'A year ago I would've but not now. Things aren't good between us and I don't want the hassle. They don't know about me … about us.' Once, being kept as some sort of secret by Hazel made her angry but now she was more detached from it: now she was relieved she hadn't become part of Hazel's family.

'Would it matter?'

'Too true, they haven't given up hope for grandchildren, even at her age. They don't know it'd be a miracle. Oh sorry, love.' She hugged Rachel.

'It's alright.' It wasn't.

'No it's not, I should stop and think.'

'Well, that'd be a first.' Rachel smiled, giving Jackie

a soft punch on the arm.

'Cheeky mare.' Jackie put on a mock-offended expression, relieved to see Rachel at least half-way cheerful. Or pretend to be. 'No, they think Hazel's too busy being a career police officer to find a man,' she said.

Rachel kept quiet. Jackie made no secret of her sexuality but still she sounded defensive.

She switched on the bedside lamp and studied their reflections in the window. Except for their hair, Rachel's thick mane was sticking out in all directions while Jackie's was spiky-short, their slender silhouettes were almost identical.

Heavy drops of rain hit the window, slowly at first and then with force.

'Bloody rain,' Jackie said.

'Hmm.' Rachel still stared towards the window. 'Can I ask you something?'

'Sure.'

'Stephen's changed these last few months but he says I have.' She spoke quietly. 'He says I'm self-centred and only thinking about how I feel about losing the babies.' She was no stranger to anxiety; sometimes she wished for just one day when she didn't think what Stilboestrol had done to her. But that was unrealistic; the fear had been with her for years. It was worse now than ever before and it was incomprehensible to her that he didn't understand. Or was her own distress blocking out his feelings? Leaving no room to acknowledge that it was as bad for her husband? 'Is that how it seems to you, Jackie? Am I selfish?'

'No, you're not.' Jackie hadn't one maternal bone in her body and didn't understand the desperate need to have children that her friend carried around with her but she'd witnessed the pain of the last miscarriage: seen the growing distance between Rachel and her husband.

'I know he gets as upset as me but he shuts off. I need to talk. He won't listen and he won't talk.' Gradually, over time, they'd lost something in their relationship; she didn't know what, but it somehow made them unable to talk, to communicate properly. 'I don't know what to do,' she said, 'I feel like I should pull myself together; carry on as though nothing's wrong.' She made a face. 'I try to do that, honestly I do but it's impossible.'

'Of course it is.' Jackie drew Rachel to her. 'He should understand.' Insensitive swine, she thought. Her friend was falling apart and he'd just buggered off. When she spoke again she was cautious. 'Rachel,' she searched for the right words, 'will you tell me something?' She tucked a chunk of Rachel's hair behind her ear so she could see her friend's face. 'Tell me to mind my own if you like … but do they know why you lose the babies?' She felt Rachel's body tense. 'I'm sorry, forget it. It's none of my business.'

'No, it's alright,' Rachel said, 'it's just that I've not explained it to anyone before.' She pushed herself off the bed, tugged at the ribbed hem of her jumper and rubbed her hands over her wet cheeks. 'It's because of something that happened before I was born.'

'What?'

'Mum took something when she was pregnant,' Rachel said, adding hastily, 'something the doctor prescribed for her, that he thought would help her. It meant I was born with some problems.'

A jolt went through Jackie. 'What do you mean?' she forced the words out, unwilling to acknowledge the growing comprehension that hovered in the background.

'Come on,' Rachel held out her hand to her best friend, 'it's easier if I show you on the computer.'

Chapter Five

Endometriosis – DES Daughters are at increased risk for this painful chronic disease. They often have anatomical complications ... (or) ... (other) anatomical malformations common to DES Daughters may also increase the risk.[5]

To: Megmath222@aol.com
From: Jacgay@yahoo.com
Subject: DES

Hi,

A friend of mine, Rachel Conway, said you wouldn't mind if I got in touch to talk about Stilboestrol. I've only just found out that, like me ...

There was a sudden shout of 'fight, fight, fight,' from the corridor outside the computer room.

'Damn kids!' Jackie took off her reading glasses, dropped them on the desk and strode to the door. Flinging it open she saw two pupils kneeling on the floor punching another girl. The group crowding over them pushed and shoved, shouting encouragement, some holding mobiles above their heads taking photographs. 'Stop that!' Jackie knew that school

---

[5] www.desaction.org/desdaughters.htm

policy of never touching the students prevented her from dragging them apart so she used the full volume of her voice. 'Stop that right now and get up.' They carried on. 'Now!' The two girls rose slowly to their feet, pushing against one another with bravado. Jackie helped the crying girl to her feet before turning to her tormenters. 'Detention after school all week; report to the staff room at three thirty … shut it,' she yelled again as one opened her mouth in protest. 'Now get to your classrooms, the lot of you.' She looked at the still sobbing girl, surrounded by the friends who'd held back when she was being beaten up. Some mates, Jackie thought. 'Get her to the nurse. I'll be along after the next class.' She spun on her heel and marched back into the room. 'What I'd give to leave this place,' she said aloud to the computer. Putting on her glasses she took a the empty room before sitting in front of deep breath, and began typing again.

… she was exposed in utero. We've been colleagues and friends since I came to Wales from Lancashire a few years ago. It never occurred to me that her losing her babies and my endometriosis had any connection.
My mother was prescribed Stilboestrol when she was expecting me. She denies it (mainly, I think, because I have some other unusual...

She clicked her fingers, wondering how to write

what she wanted to say ... or did she? She settled for

... differences / problems which have not been officially attributed to the drug but were immediately evident when I was born-

Jackie paused; did she really want to tell this woman about her rubbish relationship with her mother? She ruffled her hair, unconsciously leaving the short fringe sticking up. Oh blow it, she thought, why not?

... My consultant says there's no doubt the drug affected me, but he didn't tell me there were other problems (such as Rachel's) caused by DES and I've never talked to anyone outside the medical profession about it. I've had painful periods forever – sometimes I live on Ibuprofen – I've had two operations for lesions and a laparoscopy – but still get dreadful stomach cramps and am now on the waiting list for a hysterectomy.

Jackie glanced towards the door. Through the small window she could see faces peering in at her as the next lot of pupils jostled to be first into the computer room. She hurried to finish.

I find it impossible to talk to my mother about this. It's always been a problem between us and I doubt that will ever change.

Rachel said your interview on the radio was informative and moving. I'm sorry I missed it. I always thought I was a 'one off'. If you could send any details on DES and/or particular websites I could look up I'd be grateful. And I agree with Rachel - we would be more than happy to do anything to try to help you to raise awareness of the drug. Just let me know. My telephone number is below.

Anyway, thanks for your time reading this.

She typed her name. Hesitated. Was she asking for a whole new set of problems? From an early age she had learned to be self-protecting: allowing few to become close to her. But she trusted Rachel and she'd said this woman sounded okay. She drew in a long breath, hit 'send' and waited a moment until the message went from the Outbox to Sent. Then she deleted it and logged out from her password on the computer. 'Little sods would have a field day,' she muttered, and stood up, putting her glasses in their case. She opened the classroom door and, without speaking to any of them, waited until they moved into a line. 'Come on then,' she said, 'and keep it quiet.'

Only one more lesson today and then she was free.

Chapter Six

The friendships I have made with other DES exposed people are incredible. We were brought together because of something horrific and we've moved beyond the atrocities to a much better place in life. One where we embrace the little things and cherish every moment. [6]

To: Jacgay@yahoo.com
From: Megmath222@aol.com
Subject: Re. DES

Dear Jackie,
It's incredible that you, me and Rachel live within ten miles of each other, all linked by this horrible secret. I call it a secret because I've discovered that, for many women it's so personal that they won't ever tell anyone. And, unlike Thalidomide, the damage caused by this drug is hidden. And, for many, isn't understood for years.

Hidden: concealed, secreted, suppressed. Reading the word Jackie unconsciously let others with similar

---

[6] Quote - Jill Vanselous Murphy DES Daughter USA. See Bio.

meanings follow. It was a game she'd started as a child, now it was a habit, an automatic ploy she used to give herself breathing space to think. She pursed her lips. It wasn't just the damage that was hidden, the truth was too, she thought bitterly.

So I am glad that you got in touch and I'm sorry that your exposure to DES has caused problems between you and your mother. It's a shame because it wasn't her fault and I think it most likely she feels guilty.

'Huh!' Jackie snorted.

But it's not your fault either and you mustn't let her make you feel bad.

So there you go, Mother, Jackie thought, clicking the mouse onto the next line.

You hinted you had other problems when you were born? The drug has caused so many side effects who's to know if yours isn't one of them? Anyway, if ever you want to talk about that it's up to you.

Jackie circled her fingertips over her forehead. She couldn't see herself discussing *that* with a stranger; the only person she'd ever wanted to talk about it with was her mother and she refused point blank.

Jackie blinked against the unexpected burning at the
back of her eyes.

*Stilboestrol is just one of many chemicals that
affect the environment and each and every one of
us. Somebody has to stand up and be counted. You
said you wanted to help? As we're so close could
the three of us meet sometime?*
Warm regards
Meg

*PS I've attached an article on DES that I wrote
some years ago.*

Jackie read the email twice, slowly taking in each
word.

Upstairs she could hear Hazel talking to her
mother on the 'phone extension upstairs. How come
someone as confrontational as Hazel could get on
with her parents, she thought bitterly, when she'd
ever only had to be in the same room as her mother
for five minutes for world war three to break out?

It had grown even worse since the Christmas
when she was twenty-one and she'd told her mother
she was gay.

'Gay? Gay? You mean you're a ... lesbian?' Mary
Duffy had spat the word out. Standing in front of the
fireplace her mother lifted her skirts up at the back

to warm her backside. She seemed lost for words, casting her gaze around her tiny kitchen. 'It's not natural; you're not natural.'

'Why do you do that?' Jackie shouted. 'Why do you always try to make me feel bad about myself? Just for once try to listen to me without all this,' she searched around for a way to express how she felt and in the end settled for, 'all this shite.'

'Less of the language, missy.'

'Oh bollocks, Mother.' Jackie flounced across the room and grabbed her duffle coat from the hook by the door. 'I'm going for a walk and when I come back I'm packing and going back to my flat.' She opened the back door, letting in a sweep of hailstones. 'You know why we can't get on,' she kept her eyes on her mother, struggling to fasten the toggles on her coat, 'if you'll only admit it.' She swept her scarf around her neck. 'It's because you feel bad because you took that drug when you were expecting me.' She took a deep breath and made herself calm and still. When she found the words she spoke quietly, watching for a reaction, a softening of her mother's features. 'When will you get it into your head I don't blame you. I never have and I never will. The specialist explained it to me. It wasn't your fault.' She waited.

A cloud of soot and smoke wafted down the chimney.

'Now look what you've done.' Her mother glared at her. 'Either close the door or go.'

Jackie left.

As usual the unwelcome memory upset her. 'Soft cow,' she muttered, don't be such a bloody drama queen.' She rubbed her nose with the back of her hand and scowled; the thought reminded her that her mother was still waiting for her to make a decision about Christmas. If she didn't go, there'd be hell to pay on the next visit.

Yet she didn't want to stay at home either.

Chapter Seven

...don't expect an action program to come out of the first meeting. It is vital that people get to know each other and build trust before they can work together as a team...[7]

'Everything okay, Rachel?' Meg adjusted the telephone to her ear. She spoke in her usual quiet way but, as she listened, her forehead lined with concern. She watched Richard set the table for lunch. He stopped, a placemat in his hand, and looked up at her, an eyebrow raised in question. Meg shook her head in answer. 'I agree; the weather's been awful. I hate being stuck in the house, as well.' She glanced through the window: the shrubs dripped water but there was a pale sheen of sunlight on the leaves. 'Brightening up now, though.' She nodded. 'Right then, we'll see you at three. Jackie's got the address; it's the third bungalow on the right, number seven, off King's Road, The Avenue, first left after the Co-op. See you then.' She put the telephone down.

'Everything alright?'
'Not sure.'

---

[7] *DES Voices From Anger to Action.* 2008 © Pat Cody Ch.6 p.56

'This casserole smells done to me.' Richard expertly backed his chair from the small round table and opened the oven door.

'It should be; it's been in two hours.' Meg smiled. 'Here, let me do it.' She bent down, oven cloth in her hands and lifted the pot out and put it on the metal stand in the middle of the table. 'You get the dishes, love, will you?' She took the lid off.

Scooping out the stew she said. 'I'm not sure,' Meg repeated, passing a bread roll to Richard. 'She sounded upset; she's been through a lot from what I can make out.' Sitting opposite him she said, 'but both of them seem keen. It's quite exciting after all these years, having someone else to take up the reins.'

Richard paused between mouthfuls of his food. 'Do they still want to press for a public enquiry?'

'Yes. Jackie especially. Though I have told her it won't be as easy as she seems to think.' Meg put her spoon down and reached over to hold Richard's hand. 'But, you know what, love? For once … after all this time, I feel we might start getting some answers. This afternoon could be a fresh start.'

Richard lifted her fingers to his lips and kissed them. 'Wait and see. Don't get your hopes up too soon, sweetheart. We've been here before … dozens of times.'

'But this time we're not on our own, Richard. And this time I feel that someone will really have to listen.'

Richard didn't answer. He began eating again.

Meg watched him; she knew from the familiar sadness in his eyes that he was picturing Lisa's room, the shelves crammed with files of research and hundreds of letters appealing for help to raise an awareness of the drug. And when he looked up at her, she knew that he was thinking that nothing had made anyone listen before; why would they now?

Chapter Eight

The DES pill produced trauma in unique ways. DES as a medication is related to sexuality and fertility, to the past and to the future. It touches on issues at the heart of the mother-child relationship. In all grieving, the childlike parts of us return and we seek, literally and spiritually, the care of our mothers ... But one of the most disturbing features of the DES experience is its isolating nature, because the usual sources of help are the very sources of pain.[8]

Rachel hung her coat on the hook and wandered into the lounge, automatically switching on all the lights and turning up the heating. She poured herself half a glass of red wine and downed it in one gulp. Running a finger along the line of books on the shelf she picked out Arundhati Roy's *The God of Small Things*, and took it, the bottle and the glass upstairs.

On the landing she stepped over three rubbish bags. The weight of Stephen's files had tipped one of them over and spilled the papers. Rachel ignored them; packing his belongings had felt good at the time and she tried to convince herself that they

---

[8] *To Do No Harm – DES and the Dilemmas of Modern Medicine.* Roberta J. Apfell,,M.D.,M.P.H.
Susan M Fisher, M.D.Ch..4 p 66 (see Footnote *i*)

represented a life she'd discarded but, miserably frustrated with herself, she knew she hadn't succeeded; she waited every day for a telephone call from him. What she had taken for granted, the sound of his voice, the deepening lilt at the end of his "hi Rach" when she answered the 'phone was a feeling of security, of belonging to someone. And now it was gone. She felt she was at a crossroads with no one to tell her which way to go.

Putting the bottle and book on the floor she crossed the landing and pushed open the door next to their bedroom; the room that Stephen had confidently called the nursery from the first day he'd carried her through the front door and they'd made love in the hall.

The bright sunshiny walls and curtains turned the child-size bedroom units into a creamy white. Rachel opened one of the drawers: the pile of baby clothes, some still in their wrappings was a mockery of her hopes. She picked up a tiny white hand-knitted cardigan and held it to her nose; it smelt of her mother's perfume. Rachel felt the hot pain of tears and, folding up the cardigan, closed the drawer. She looked around: the nursery, like the house, now felt unfamiliar: chilly and empty. Uninhabited. She closed the door firmly behind her.

It had been a good meeting; Meg and her husband seemed to be especially nice people. Their house was what Rachel called homely; matching flowered curtains and three piece suite, warm red carpets and table lamps placed in corners; soft light for maximum cosiness.

She liked to think of herself as a kind, a compassionate person. Yet in that initial moment when she walked into their home she couldn't suppress the stab of resentful envy. It represented everything hers didn't. Love. She was instantly horrified by her feelings but the shame stayed with her, worsened by the fact that both Meg and her husband had made her and Jackie feel at ease right away, even when they'd gone upstairs to what had obviously been their daughter's room. The files and folders, filled over the years of striving for recognition of the damage Stilboestrol had caused, were a sad tribute to their love.

Rachel emptied the glass. God it must have been awful. What was worse? Not having children or a child dying? 'Horrible either way,' she muttered, pouring more wine. 'But definitely worse losing a daughter to suicide.'

She sat on the bed, dropped the book on the floor, and prised off her shoes. Carefully balancing the glass and bottle she shuffled back against the soft, dark blue headboard and mulled over the meeting.

The couple must both be around sixty but they gave the impression of being younger, especially Richard with his thick dark hair, only slightly greying at the temples, and warm brown eyes. Despite the wheelchair he looked strong, reliable. They seemed to be close, even after all the ghastly things that had happened; things that had altered their lives beyond anything they could have imagined in their youth. How was that? How did some people stay loving each other? And others, she rested the glass against her lips, licking the rim with the tip of her tongue, others didn't. The tears ran in two steady lines and dripped unnoticed off her jaw.

Because they didn't lumber themselves with bastards like Stephen, she thought, glancing around. She'd closed his wardrobe and drawers but could see in her mind the jumble of clothes in them: shoving those in a bin bag had seemed a step too final. 'Bastard,' she said aloud.

Dragging the corner of the duvet over her legs she studied the photograph of her mother and father on the dressing table opposite the bed. Meg and Richard reminded her of her parents; it was as if it wasn't only their arms around each other that held them together but their love as well.

In the portrait her parents smiled steadfastly for the camera, even though Rachel had since discovered they'd known then of Mum's illness. Something they'd protected her from in the same way they'd shielded her from problems all her life. She'd been angry when she'd found out; she felt that by not telling her they'd stolen time from her; time she needed to let her mother know how much she was loved by her daughter as well as her husband. To show how she'd stored and treasured memories from her childhood: the smell of baking drifting through the house and the rhythmic push and drag sound of the old-fashioned lawn mower from the garden as her father cut the front lawn on Saturday afternoons. Or, on wet winter days, the way the steam of starched clothes, mixed with the mouth-watering aroma of potato pie, met her when she came in from school and found her mother, red-faced and sweating, hunched over the ironing board. The jingle of her father's keys just before the swift grind of the front door lock, the rattle of the kitchen window from the draught as he stepped into the hall: "I'm home". How safe she'd always felt as a child.

How all that changed when she was older.

Rachel closed her eyes; the image of her mother imprinted behind her eyelids. When she breathed in she thought she could smell Mum's perfume, Youth Dew. Sometimes, when Rachel had hugged her mother she imagined the fragrance was mingled with a hint of Old Spice from when her father had kissed her before he went to work and Rachel could pretend he was there sharing the embrace.

She missed her mother.

But when she slept her dream was of her four lost babies, their cries loud, filling her head, her body, until, growing fainter, they vanished.

Four tiny souls flying away.

Chapter Nine

Some mothers are unwilling to talk to their children for fear of their reaction and the anxiety such knowledge might create[9]

Jackie pulled into the kerbside outside her house, the adrenaline and excitement about forming the group and the pleasure from her time spent with Rachel, Meg and Richard evaporating rapidly. Every window was blazing with light. 'She thinks I've got money to burn,' she muttered.

The key to the front door wouldn't turn. 'Stupid cow!' She left her finger on the bell, listening to the harsh continual chime.

'Okay, okay.' She could hear Hazel slowly walking down the stairs (the last four treads, as always, giving creaking protests) before the door was dragged open.

'Why leave your key in the lock?'

Hazel turned and stamped upstairs without a word.

Jackie watched her, shrugged, dropped the files and papers on the hall table and lifted up her coat to hang on the rack on the wall. Then she saw the rucksack propped up against the living room

---

[9] *DES Voices: From Anger to Action*: © Pat Cody.2008.Ch.4 p41

doorframe. Fantastic. 'You've decided to go then?' she called.

'You don't have to sound so bloody pleased.' Hazel scowled at her from the top of the narrow stairs, shoving her arms into her anorak.

'I'm not ... I'm just saying ...'

'I need a lift to the station,' Hazel interrupted. 'Okay?'

'Okay.' Jackie waited, her arms still raised, her coat between her hands. 'Now?'

'If it's not too much trouble.'

'No it's fine. Your mum will be pleased anyway. How long will you stay?'

'My god, you can't wait to get rid of me, can you?' Hazel zipped her anorak. 'Don't worry; you'll have the house to yourself for a week at the least.'

'I'll wait in the car.' Jackie wasn't chancing another argument. She'd take Hazel all the way to her mother's in London if it meant some peace afterwards.

They drove to the railway station in silence. Jackie neither knew nor cared about Hazel's parents so had no sycophantic message or greeting to send via their daughter. And, in turn, she knew Hazel was refusing to ask how Jackie would pass the time until she returned: although from the martyred sniffs as she determinedly glared through the passenger window and the occasional toss of her head Jackie could tell it was taking all her will power to keep her mouth closed.

In the station car park Jackie lifted the rucksack out of the boot, avoiding Hazel's kiss which landed awkwardly on her cheek. 'Take care,' she said, thrusting the bag at her.

'You could have come with me,' Hazel pouted.

Not an attractive sight, Jackie decided. 'No.' She didn't elaborate.

'What will you do while I'm away?'

Jackie moved her shoulders. 'Not sure.'

'Well, you'll always have the lovely, ever-desperate Rachel to keep you company.' Hazel hitched the rucksack onto her back. 'I'll ring.' She strode towards the entrance to the platform. Before she went through she glanced over her shoulder. 'Miss you.' She waited a moment for a reaction before pushing on the heavy door. It closed with a final swish.

'Oh hell.' Jackie started to follow; Hazel looked so pitiful. She stopped, recollecting the spite in the remark about Rachel, the thousand and one mean and nasty actions that had systematically chipped away at whatever was between them. Was it ever love? Jackie wasn't even sure now. She walked to the car and got in.

Holding onto the wheel, she let the sense of relief wash over her.

To: info@theconways
From: Jacgay@yahoo.com
Subject: Hi

Hi Rachel,
House fantastically quiet - Hazel gone.
Need to make a decision about Christmas - whether / when to go to mother's That sodding cat from next door's shit in our back yard again.
Can I borrow Jake for a week?
Ring if you need to talk - I mean it.

Jackie x

To: Jacgay@yahoo.com
From: info@theconways
Subject: Bloody Christmas

Don't talk about Christmas. First damn card today - to both of us - from his boss. Obviously hasn't the guts to tell them yet!!! Dad's been asking if I'll go to him for Christmas but can't face it.I'll bring Jake round sometime. He loves cats - especially for breakfast – ha-ha .

Rachel
x

To: info@theconways
From: Jacgay@ yahoo.com
Subject: Ref: Bloody Christmas

Ok, made a decision – not going to mother's - you're coming here for Christmas –sorted for both of us - no arguing!

Jackie x

To: Jacgay@yahoo.com
From: info@theconways
Subject: Bloody Christmas

Who's arguing!!
R x

Chapter Ten – Christmas

How does a father of a DES daughter react? ... the unknown fear of what would continually lie ahead for this beautiful child, growing towards womanhood with so many uncertainties and such grave possibilities, would be in my mind daily ... even greater ... was watching the guilt that (my wife) had taken upon herself. The punishment inflicted daily, hourly, on what she perceived she had done to her child. The pain never really left.[10]

Meg snuggled down, her head tucked under Richard's chin. 'Another one nearly over with,' she said, softly patting his chest.

'I know, sweetheart. Don't think about it.'

Her hand stilled. 'But we should, we should think about her.'

'I meant, don't torment yourself, Meg, you'll make yourself ill.'

'She'd be thirty now.' She tipped her head to see his face but couldn't in the darkness. 'Married with children, who knows? We could be grandparents.'

He sighed. 'Let's try to get to sleep, huh?'

She lifted herself up and he moved his arm from

---

[10] Article by Martha Cotiaux (quoting her husband) in DES Action *Voice*, 1989: *DES Voices: From Anger to Action*. ©Pat Cody 2008. Ch13 p169

under her head. Helping him to turn onto his side, she reached down and rearranged the cushion between his knees to stop them rubbing against one another. Resting her mouth on his shoulder she whispered, 'sorry, love.' Still, sometimes she wanted to shout at him, 'talk to me about her. Tell me what you think she would be like now.' But she knew she wasn't being fair; it wasn't Richard's way. And she never doubted his grief was as brutal as hers. 'Sorry,' she said again.

It's okay,' he reached back with his arm and touched her, Night.'

'Night. You had your tablet?'

'Uh huh.' He was soon asleep.

The slant of white moonlight slowly arrowed its way across the artexed ceiling, until the grandfather clock in the hall softly sounded twice. Still she was awake; and thinking of Rachel and Jackie. Because of them she hadn't had the time to dread Christmas as she usually did. She mulled over what they'd done: a friend of Jackie's was building a simple website for them, they'd already set up the email address, deciding on the notice to go into local newspapers throughout the country. Rachel had spent a whole week searching on the Internet for the most useful looking, Jackie had found a website to locate and email MPs and Councillors directly; they were both so clever with all this new technology. Her job had been simpler; she'd drafted letters to their MPs to send out in the New Year

Rolling onto her stomach Meg tucked her hand under the pillow. She couldn't think of anything they'd missed. Everything was ready for them to start their campaign.

She refused to think about all years she'd battled alone to get her voice heard. Who knows, she thought, lifting herself up and pressing her cheek against Richard's back, finding comfort in the warmth of his skin, the movement underneath, with each quiet rumbling snore.

This time it might be different.

When she did sleep, the dream came again. The sound of the wipers splattering the rain across the windscreen in stuttering arcs: the distorted image of the road ahead: the angry words between her and Richard. Her hands holding the steering wheel so tightly she couldn't feel her fingers anymore. Barely noticing the needle on the speedometer curving upwards - sixty, seventy, eighty.

And then, suddenly, the image of shining black ice and a kaleidoscope of senses: the dizzying reeling spin, the squeal of brakes, the protest of the car's engine, her scream, shrill, mingling then lost in his anguished shout.

The wall coming towards them.

Then leaden silence.

Chapter Eleven

According to lead author Robert N. Hoover, M.D., of the National Cancer Institute, researchers can now say conclusively that prenatal DES exposure is linked to a host of health problems for DES Daughters, including infertility, ectopic pregnancy, loss of second-trimester pregnancy, preterm delivery, stillbirth, a rare vaginal/cervical cancer and breast cancer in DES Daughters over age forty, among other health issues[11]

'Thanks, Jackie; it was good of you to invite me.' Rachel raised her voice above the crashing of cutlery being thrown into a drawer, the clattering of crockery in the kitchen.

'Don't be daft; it's been good; better than spending the day on my own with her.' Jackie shoved her hands deep into the pockets of her combat trousers and tipped her head in the direction of the noise. 'Ignore her, it's not you, she hates Christmas.'

That wasn't the reason for the dour silence that Jackie's partner had maintained from the moment

---

[11] DES Action news release quoting the *New England Journal of Medicine*, *"Adverse Health Outcomes in Women Exposed in Utero to Diethylstilbestrol.* October 6, 2011,

she'd arrived but Rachel went along with the comment.

'Well, I'll get off home.' She pulled on her gloves and wrapped Jake's lead around her hand.

'You should have come in the car. I'd run you home but I know I'm half pissed.' Jackie squinted along the narrow street of terraced houses. Under the line of streetlamps the pavement glistened with ice.

'Don't fret, it's only twenty minutes and the walk will be good for Jake.' Rachel kissed her on the cheek. 'See you next week at Meg's, we'll talk about things then.' Adjusting her hat she stepped tentatively outside and tested the ground with the toe of her boot. 'Oh, it's not so bad underfoot. You go in though; it's too cold to be standing on the doorstep.'

At the end of Jackie's street she glanced back. Her friend was still standing at the doorway. Rachel raised her arm before turning the corner. She glanced upwards: in between the bright circles of electric light the sky was blue-black and speckled with stars. Over the roofs of the houses on the opposite side the moon hung large, surrounded by a pale misty ring. It would be a hard frost. Her scarf, held over her mouth, was soon wet with warm condensation.

There were few people about but those who were all seemed to be in twos; everywhere she went these days there were couples. She ran her hand down the dog's lead and touched Jake, padding close to her side. Perhaps she should have gone to her father's for the holidays, she'd heard the loneliness in his voice; it was the first Christmas without her mother. But it wasn't her he wanted. Needed.

So when he'd telephoned, and the crackling line reminded her of the distance from Crete, she'd pushed the sense of obligation to one side and convinced herself to stay at home. To wait and see what happened. She'd been sure Stephen would come home, certain he wouldn't leave her on her own at Christmas, even though she hadn't heard from him in the four weeks since he'd left.

The hot feeling in her chest rose yet again and tears came easily. She pulled up the collar of her coat and ducked her head when a group of mini-skirted girls tottered towards her, their breath swirling in front of them as they catcalled and whistled at two youths slouching on the corner of the road. One girl, her piled-up hair now listing precariously on the side of her head, bumped into Rachel and dropped the bottle she had been waving about. It splintered into small shards of glass and Rachel quickly pulled Jake away, feeling a sudden pain on her leg above her boot.

'Now look what you made me do, you stupid bag.' The girl shouted, staggering into the road as she tried to keep her balance on high wedge-heeled boots.

A low growl rumbled deep inside Jake. Rachel touched his back. She glared at the girl; recognising her as one of the sixth-formers from school. 'I beg your pardon?'

'Should think so too!' The girl sniggered and lurched away.

Rachel bent down and rubbed her leg. She could feel the stickiness of blood between her finger and thumb and no doubt her tights were ruined but there was no glass in the cut.

Straightening she looked around. The road carried faint wet-black tracks of cars away into the distance. The houses here were mostly semi-detached. Unlike the terraced houses, where coloured Christmas lights encircled the blue light of wide-screen televisions in almost every window, these front rooms were lit either by the soft glow of lamps or light that spilled out through half-drawn curtains over the dark flat lengths of lawns and hedges or trees tastefully adorned by large white bulbs. In the stillness of the evening she heard a jumble of sounds; music, laughter, shouted conversations. Despite the warmth of the dog's shoulder against her leg Rachel felt completely alone.

Once Rachel was out of sight Jackie closed the front door and leant against it, trying to balance her anger against the knowledge that she'd had too much to drink. She'd felt the wretchedness in her friend all day, watched her push the food around on her plate until it looked as if she'd eaten something.

Hazel hadn't helped.

Jackie went into the tiny kitchen. 'What the bloody hell was all that about?'

Hazel was emptying the dishwasher. Her voice was nonchalant but Jackie could see the tension in her movements.

'I don't know what you mean.' When she turned around her eyes were narrowed. 'I was civil, wasn't I? I cooked the dinner, poured the drinks ... entertained your ... girlfriend, didn't I?' her top lip curled upwards revealing her two front teeth that protruded slightly (at one time Jackie had thought them endearing ... like Thumper from the Bambi films).

Almost in relief Jackie felt the rage drain away; what was the point, she couldn't, wouldn't, fight anymore. Studying Hazel's scowling face; she saw the lines, deepened by a lifetime of cynicism. Her mouth, pulled in at the corners, emphasised the loose flesh around her jowls. What on earth had she ever seen in her? Jackie resisted the nagging thought that what she'd sought in the older woman was as much a loving mother as a lover. Letting Hazel move in with her had been the biggest mistake she'd ever made. But had it really been her choice? Hazel swept the relationship along from the beginning and, for once, Jackie let it happen in the hope that Hazel was the one to light up all the dark places in her life. She wasn't.

'I bet you wish I'd never come back from

Mother's, don't you?' Hazel challenged, banging serving dishes down onto the glass top of the kitchen table.

Jackie forced herself into stillness. 'And I bet you hoped I'd be on duty all Christmas so you could have little Rachel all to yourself.'

Hazel had her feet apart and her arms folded; she was gearing up for one of her brawls that could spiral into violence. In the beginning these always ended with them in bed, having sex in an equally aggressive way that both sickened and excited Jackie. Now, with sudden clarity she realised she couldn't remember the last time they'd made love.

Hazel started tapping her foot, usually the start to one of her yelling sessions. Once she got going she seemed unable to stop. She took a deep breath.

No more. Jackie held up both hands. 'I'm going to bed, Hazel. I'm sick of everything,' she said. 'We can't … I won't, go on like this. We're finished.'

Chapter Twelve -January 2002

A vaginal clear-cell adenocarcinoma developed in a young woman who had been exposed in utero to maternal Stilboestrol treatment. During 1940-71 in the UK some 7500 women were given Stilboestrol during pregnancy. Thus more cases are likely to appear and clinicians caring for young women should be alert to this possibility. [12]

Avril Breen settled deeper into the bulky old settee and shook her spectacles until they unfolded, then pushed them onto the bridge of her nose. The wind shrilled its way down the chimney causing the fire to burst upwards in wavering yellow licks of flame. There was a thin draft snaking its way around her ankles. God, Satis House had nothing on this place: the old comparison these days brought a wry smile to her face: at least she wasn't sitting in front of a moulding wedding cake and dressed in a tattered dress. She tucked her legs up and covered them with a tasselled throw. Balancing her new state of the art laptop she typed www.avrilbreen.co.uk.

---

[12] Stilboestrol and vaginal clear-cell adenocarcinoma. syndrome.JOHN M MONAGHAN, L A W SIRISENA British Medical_Journal, 1978, 1, 1588-1590 (following discovery of DES exposure in Heather Justice member of DES Action UK - the first recorded "DES daughter" in Britain. See bio)

Waiting for her website to appear she unconsciously untangled small knots in her curly hair with her fingers and hummed along to *Colours of my Life,* playing on the radio in the kitchen.

The Christmas card from her cousin was just in her eye line on the coffee table. By now she knew, word for word, the large scrawl that covered the whole of one side. H*ope you're well. Thought the enclosed might interest you - found it in a local rag. Try to visit us sometime this year. Love Julia.*

Read only once, the square of paper, its folds pressed firmly down, lay next to the card. Heaving a deep sigh Avril picked it up, her lips moving as she read the article.

"*... interesting interview with Meg Matthews, locally known for her charity work and ...*" Avril skipped the following line. "*... talked movingly to Sandy Carney of Radio Carvoen's Woman's World about her daughter, Lisa, who committed suicide in nineteen- eighty-nine, unable to cope with the idea of having a hysterectomy at eighteen ....*' Avril swallowed, it wasn't any easier reading it the second time. "*Lisa had been affected by a drug that her mother, Meg, was prescribed before her daughter was born. At just seventeen she contracted a rare cancer, usually only found in post-menopausal women.*" Avril dropped the paper and slowly took off her glasses. It took a moment for her eyes to adjust and the fire flickered, a hazy yellow in the fireplace. 'Thanks Julia,' she murmured, 'that's all I need.'

She hoped her cousin hadn't been insensitive enough to show the article to her mother. She'd never forgotten the anguish in her eyes the day after the operation or her words as she'd clutched Avril's hands.

'I'm sorry, love. I've done this to you; I've ruined your life and I'm sorry. I wish it was me lying there instead of you. I'd do anything to swop places with you.'

'It's not your fault,' Avril spoke with all the vehemence she could muster. 'It's not. You just wanted to have me. I don't blame you, Mum, and I never will.' She tried to forget the group of students who had stood around her bed only half an hour ago while the specialist explained what he'd done to her; strangers, discussing a part of her that was private; discussing how he'd cut her sexuality out of her. She looked up at her father, saw his confusion and fear but still insisted, 'tell her, Dad.'

For a few moments she watched him. He nodded, licked his lips, attempted to speak. The tears came slowly. 'I have, I've told her every day since we found out about … about all this.'

Avril knew he idolised her mother. She watched him struggle until, in the end, he put his arms around his wife and held her close to him. 'It's not your fault, Enid.'

'See?' Avril gave a small smile even though inside she was screaming against the unfairness of what had happened to her. 'I'll never blame you, Mum.'

And she'd kept her promise.

Now she blinked hard, fighting back the tears. 'Oh, dear lord.'

'Oh dear lord.' A croaky voice echoed Avril's words. Absently she held out her hand. 'Hop up,' she said, looking towards the corner of the room at a large stainless steel cage. 'Hop up,' she encouraged, glad of the diversion. There was a flash of blue and gold as the macaw landed on her wrist and shuffled up her arm to be closer to Avril's face. 'Hello Mr Macawber,' she said. 'Scratch?'

'Scratch,' the bird repeated, ducking its head for her to tickle his neck.

'Clever Mr Macawber,' Avril murmured, 'clever Mr Macawber, I love you.'

'Clever Mr Macawber,' the macaw repeated staring at her with a black beady eye.

'Clever Mr Macawber.' It reached down to chew her jumper.

'No,' Avril said, ripping the Christmas card in two and putting the picture side on the back of the settee, 'chew that.' The bird hopped off and pinned it down with one claw, shredding the thick paper in an instant with its long curved beak. Then he sidled along the back of the settee and began to nibble Avril's hair.

She took no notice; hooking her glasses behind her ears and picking up the newspaper cutting she read the last line. *"Meg is looking for other women affected by DES; she says 'the strength of the group will be in our numbers. I tried for many years to go it alone; it didn't work' ... Meg's contact details are as follows ..."*

Pushing her lower lip out Avril blew a gust of breath upward, lifting her fringe. She dropped her head against the back of the settee.

The Macaw shuffled sideways, picking up pieces of the torn card until it reached the end of the settee. A moment later he flew over to another corner of the room dominated by a collection of branches fastened and decorated with small wooden toys.

Avril turned so she could watch the bird clamber through the play area she'd built for him, but tonight his antics didn't distract her.

'Why send this?' She knew the answer of course. Even though she insisted she worked better in isolation and that she loved the renovated cottage squatting in the middle of the Pennine moors, she knew her family had always thought she was hiding away. None of them, especially Julia, closest to her in age, believed she had come to terms with what happened to her and they were probably right. The memories might be old but they came back in her dreams.

She dropped the article on the small table at the side of the settee and automatically scrolled through the pages of her website. The layout of the new page, showing the cover of her new book with the blurb written within the silhouette of a woman, looked good. She saw, through the link to the Lydfield Players, that her play listed some good reviews. Even the latest photograph of herself at the top of the home page wasn't too bad for once, she thought.

"Meg's contact details are as follows ..." The phrase wouldn't go away. She closed the lid of the laptop and laid it on the seat at her side, studying her reflection in the rust-speckled mirror propped up on the Victorian sideboard. She didn't feel that different but her hair, though still thick, now had grey scattered through the copper and, while her skin was good, there were fine lines around her deep grey-green eyes. Avril felt the blackness of depression hovering; waiting.

And, as usual when this happened, she thought of Bill; wondered where he was, whether he'd married, had kids. As always the last thought hurt and she unfolded her legs and heaved herself to her feet. The leather soles of her Ugg Boots scuffed the gritty stone flags as she went into the kitchen, ignoring the unwashed pots and crammed worktops, and made a coffee. Standing in the doorway to the front room she stared up at the painting in the alcove next to the fireplace. It had been there so long she didn't see it anymore.

'Stay still!' Although the words were sharp Bill had smiled when Avril pouted.

'I'm bored now' how much longer?' She fluttered her eyelashes in comic seduction, trailing her hands from her thighs to her stomach and over her bare breasts.

'Ok, enough.' All at once Bill dropped his paintbrush onto the easel ledge and leapt up onto the platform where she was posing for him.

Avril squealed, pretending to escape as he caught hold of her slender waist and spun her around. She leaned backwards, laughing, her long coppery-red hair glowing in the spotlights of the art room.

'You're trying to sabotage my masterpiece,

woman,' he nuzzled her neck. 'When you're old and fat and ugly, you'll be grateful to me that I captured you in all your beautiful ...wonderful... gorgeous ... glory.'

On the utterance of each word he kissed her hard on the lips.

Then they made love on the old settee the art department's life models used.

It was their first Christmas together in college; she was eighteen. Six months later she was diagnosed with a vaginal clear-cell adenocarcinoma.

Sometimes Avril felt that girl had never existed but now, suddenly she remembered the Dickinson poem she had found in the weeks after he'd left? *'Heart, we will forget him, You and I, tonight! You must forget the warmth he gave / I will forget the light.'*

Well it had taken her a long time: she'd clung to the misery of losing him; in a strange way it had helped to block out what was happening to her physically.

Avril pressed on her eyes with forefinger

and thumb. She couldn't remember the rest of the lines.

She was relieved Christmas and New Year was over; had managed to avoid everyone again despite Julia's cajoling efforts to join in with the festivities. She hated this time of year, the contrived cheerfulness; "high-spirits", her cousin had said; out of a bottle more like, Avril thought. This New Year she'd managed exactly ten minutes of Angus Deayton before switching off.

Gulping the coffee she saw the macaw had hopped into his cage and she walked over to it. 'Night Mr Macawber, sleep tight.' She waited until he settled down on the perch, eyes half-closed, before closing and locking the door. Covering the cage she went around the long room drawing the four sets of curtains over the small deep-set windows. At the last, she stared at her outline, lit from behind by the small lamp on the coffee table. Even though there was only the contour of her from the chest upwards, it was obvious she was carrying too much weight. 'Fat cow.' She raised her beaker to her image, pulled a face and dragged the curtains together.

The fire had settled into smouldering coals. Avril leant over it and threw a couple of logs on, turning her face against the sparks that flew out.

Flopping onto the settee, she slid down into the cushions.

When she woke she'd been snoring; her tongue felt thick and dry as she ran it around the inside of her mouth trying to make some saliva. She stood, rubbing her face and scratching her scalp and crossed to the back door. Standing on the ice-patterned step, her breath came in small puffs of white. She listened to the occasional bleating of sheep from the nearby farm, the swift unseen rush of wings and the high - pitched, far away whine of the wind hustling the thin clouds across the face of the half moon. A scattering of snowflakes shuddered to the ground: she held out her hand, palm upwards, to catch some as they fell, revelling in the sharp instance of cold before the thaw left a wet patch on her skin. *"… for if dreams die … if dreams go, Life is a barren field, Frozen with snow."* Or something like that. Bill used to quote that at her when she was going through a bad patch with her writing: teasing her.

'Face your demons, girl,' she murmured and carried the heavy laptop to the long rectangular table under the windows. Shifting around on the wooden chair to get comfortable she pushed her lips out in a silent whistle and waited for the email connection.

It was unusual for her to feel so nervous but then, she reasoned, it was unusual for her to write to strangers about anything other than her work. For a moment her fingers hovered over the keypad. She took a long breath and started to write.

To: Megmath222@aol.com
From: Avrilbreen@sheepfold.freeserve.co.uk

Dear Meg Matthews, you don't know me but....

Chapter Thirteen

A Kitchen Table Movement: DES Action Is Born[13]

Richard's arm was heavy across Meg's waist. It was still dark outside, the wind battered splats of rain on the windowsill from the broken joint in the guttering that she kept meaning to ask Alice's prospective son-in-law to repair. The radio clock on Richard's side of the bed showed it was only seven and by its light she watched his lips move in and out with each rumbling breath, his shoulders and arms twitching restlessly. She leaned towards him and kissed his forehead.

'You ok, love?' He fell back into sleep without waiting for an answer.

She stroked his arm. The muscles under his skin were bulky and hard, a result of years of hauling the weight of his legs from bed to chair to wheelchair. She lifted his fingers in hers and held them against her cheek feeling the smooth calluses.

Yesterday, when Rachel had asked her about Richard's disability, Meg had skirted around the truth. Bad road conditions: an accident, she'd lost control of the car, she'd said. She hadn't mentioned the quarrel she and Richard were having at the time, one of many since Lisa had died. She didn't tell

---

[13] *DES Voices From Anger to Action.* 2008 © Pat Cody. Ch. 6

Rachel how close they had come to separating, each blaming the other for not realizing the depth of Lisa's depression. Or how once, just the once, Richard had blamed her for taking Stilboestrol when she was pregnant. He'd cried afterwards, promising never to say it again, knowing how she lived with that guilt; didn't need reminding.

But still they'd argued, bitterly blaming each other: as they had on that day.

She regretted not telling Rachel. 'Damn,' she whispered.

Richard shifted, moaning slightly.

'You uncomfy, love?' she asked.

'Been too long in the same position.' She could hear him grit his teeth as he tried to push himself onto his back. 'And bit of a pain in my shoulder.'

Meg slid from underneath his arm and dipped her head under the covers. She tugged at his hips.

'Just behave yourself down there.' She heard the grin in his voice.

'You behave *yourself,* Richard Matthews' she giggled, 'or I'll push the duvet back and leave you open to the elements. At least this way you stay warm.'

His legs, white, thin and useless were twisted at the ankles. She straightened them and reappeared alongside him. 'Alright now?'

They kissed.

'Mmmm, lovely.'

She lay back on her pillow. 'You were asleep when

I came to bed last night or I would have told you I had an email from another DES daughter. A woman from the boundary of Lancashire and Yorkshire, I think she said, called Avril Breen. Think she said she's forty six.' She turned her head towards Richard 'A writer, lives on the moors.'

Richard raised an eyebrow. 'Oh? On a farm?'

'Don't think so. Why do you ask?'

'With you saying about the moors,' he said.

'Just reminded me about the Foot and Mouth; they've had it bad up there with the sheep. I read they slaughtered cattle and sheep in their hundreds.'

Meg frowned. 'Awful.' She said nothing for a moment and then shook her head. 'No, I don't think she's on a farm; she said she lives in a cottage on her own. Sounds a bit of a loner,' she said. 'And ... like our Lisa ... she had cancer in her late teens ... had to have a hysterectomy and vaginectomy.'

'Oh.' She saw the trammel lines on Richard's forehead deepened. 'Any family?'

'Don't know, she didn't say.' Meg reached up and smoothed his frown with her thumb. 'She did say she had a fiancé at the time she was ill but he called off their wedding.'

'Rotten thing to do. Are you going to put her in touch with the others?'

'First thing this morning I'll write to her; I'll ask her if that's ok.'

'Right.' Richard kissed her hand. 'All this looking for women to become members of the group, and this public enquiry thing; promise me you'll let Jackie and Rachel do the majority of the work. They're younger than you and all this is new to them. Like I've said, we ... you've been here before and I don't want you getting in a state again.'

'I never thought before to try to form a group, Richard; it was always only our battle.' Meg tucked her head into his shoulder. 'Don't worry so much.'

'I'm not and I know that; and it's great that you've got them on board. Goodness only knows you've done it on your own for long enough. Just let them do all the physical stuff.' He ran his fingers through his hair. 'They're more than willing. Nice girls, I like them.'

'Only because they make a fuss of you; you're positively in your element.'

Richard smirked. 'Not lost the old touch then?'

Meg pinched him. 'You know you haven't, you old flirt. Now, let me get up, I've work to do.'

It was cold in the kitchen. Meg switched on the fan heater and drank her tea standing in front of it. The warm air rippled her nightdress and dressing gown.

Avril's story had upset her; too similar to Lisa's. She switched on the Today programme. *Thought for the Day* was just finishing. 'Good,' she nodded at the radio, 'I've enough thoughts of my own, thanks.' Pouring a mug of tea for Richard she took it upstairs. Before anything else today she would write to Avril Breen.

To: Avrilbreen@sheepfold.freeserve.co.uk
From: Megmath222@aol.com
Subject: DES

Dear Avril,
I'm surprised the interview was in the Cardigan Gazette. Carvoen, the village where I live and where the radio station is, is a long way down the coast from there. Glad you contacted me. Have attached the piece I wrote about Stilboestrol.
Two other women are now involved - since November we've been organizing ourselves. It'd be great if you would be a member of our group, if you could help in some way, even though you live so far away.

Warm Regards
Meg

Ps You mention you live on the Pennines — have you been affected by the Foot and Mouth? We're quite lucky in this area to have avoided it but some paths are still closed and tourism was hit quite badly last season. Also the farmers couldn't move stock so they suffered. It was a dreadful time for many.

To: Jacgay@yahoo.com. info@theconways
From: Megmath222@aol.com
Subject: DES.

Hi both,
Had an email from an Avril Breen - DES daughter –
lives near Huddersfield. I've attached her email
and website.
See you next week - one-ish?

Best Wishes
Meg

PS. Jackie - reply came through from my MP,
Stewart Jones. He doesn't think the agreement
between the UN Permanent Court of Arbitration
and the Cousteau Environmental Society[iii] would
apply to us. Helpful or what?!!!! Will write again
but think we're flogging a dead horse there.

Chapter Fourteen -February

It comes down to members, not the government that allows DES Action USA to keep going strong[14]

I'll see you later, then.' Jackie clicked off her mobile, took a swallow of coffee and stubbed out her cigarette. She tried to avoid looking at Hazel who was cleaning the window outside, her short grey hair flattened in the wind. She'd stopped rubbing at a corner of one pane and was peering in through the glass. Within seconds she was in the kitchen.

'Who were you on the 'phone to?' Hazel's voice was truculent as she squeezed the chamois leather dry and rolled it up. She pushed it into the plastic container and snapped the lid on, watching Jackie through the reflection of the window.

Here we go again: the Spanish Inquisition had nothing on Hazel once she got going. 'Rachel, then Meg; we were talking about Avril Breen, the woman from up North.' Jackie dragged her jacket from the back of the chair, the metal legs screeched on the black and white tiles on the floor.

'Why?'

'Why not?'

'Discussing strategy?' Hazel sneered.

---

[14] Quote: Fran Howell, Executive Director DES Action USA. See bio.

'What is your problem?' She didn't need this, why the hell had she told Hazel about the drug? Blame that extra glass of wine and her talent for talking too much. 'Quite frankly Hazel, it's got sod all to do with you anymore. I should never have told you about it in the first place.' She picked up a pair of suede ankle boots from near the back door and, leaning over, put her forefinger in the back of each boot in turn, pushing her feet into them. Her voice was stifled as she fastened the laces. 'You keep ignoring what I said. We're finished and we both know it.' She stamped her right foot to make her toes more comfortable. 'You have to decide what you want to do but you can't stay here.' Jackie's words hung in the air. 'I'm going out,' she said finally, lighting another cigarette.

'Where? Where are you going?' Hazel caught hold of her arm. Her hand was small but strong, and her fingers dug into Jackie's skin.

Jackie shook her off. 'If you must know I'm picking up Rachel, then we're going to Meg's. And later, Rachel and I are going for a meal.' This happened every time she made a move to go out. Grief, Hazel must be good at her job. Jackie had a flashing image of her standing over some poor bloody suspect at the police station.

Hazel followed her from the kitchen and through to the sitting room. 'You fancy Rachel, don't you? Go on, admit it.'

'Bloody hell, how many more times?' Jackie held

the cigarette between her lips, pushed her arms into the sleeves of her jacket and zipped it up. 'She's straight, she's a friend. Okay?' She wrapped her scarf around her neck and knotted it with a vicious pull. 'And if I was having an affair with all of Beddgaron and Carvoen, it would be none of your business.'

'Don't go.' Hazel looked as though she would cry at any moment. She stood between Jackie and the hall. 'Please, don't go. I'm sorry. I need ….' her face seemed to break up, become vulnerable.

In the long pause Jackie heard her own breathing, ragged and shallow, the low tick of the clock and a car go by outside. She smelt the sickly scent of the forced-grown carnations Hazel had brought home. She hadn't wanted the flowers. She didn't want the woman's apology; she didn't want the feeling of being in the wrong, of being guilty for hurting her. She told herself to stop being stupid: Hazel had tried this act before.

'For god's sake have some self-respect.' Jackie pushed past her and walked down the short dark hall towards the porch, pulling on her gloves.

Hazel got to the front door first. 'Wait.' her eyes flickered from side to side as though searching for something.

'I can't stand this anymore, Jackie said, 'I want you out. It's over; it's been over for a while.' Her voice softened, she knew how callous that sounded. 'We can still be friends.' She stopped herself from reaching out to hold the woman's arm; she knew it would be misinterpreted.

'No.' Hazel backed up against the door her arms outspread. 'I love you. We can sort things out.'

But there was a hard edge to her words and Jackie responded to it. 'The only thing I want you to sort out is when you're going to find somewhere else to live. Now, please move.' She waited but Hazel didn't move so she reached round her, flicked the lock and pulled on the handle, forcing the smaller woman out of the way.

Hazel followed her onto the pavement to the Peugeot. 'You'll be sorry.' Her voice was shrill.

The queue of people waiting at the bus stop further along the street watched curiously. Two women walking past the house, chattering and laughing, glanced at Hazel.

Her eyes narrowed. 'What the hell are you all laughing at eh? Go on,' she stuck her middle finger up at them; whirled around and did the same to the line of people, 'sod off the lot of you.'

Jackie kept her head lowered; this was awful. She dropped the tab end of the cigarette down the grid in the gutter, got into the car and drove away as fast as she could. In the rear mirror she saw Hazel watching her, her arms held limply by her side.

'I tell you Rachel, I'll finish up doing something I regret.' Jackie swung the car into Meg's drive. 'It's a nightmare.' She looked across at Rachel who had her eyes closed. 'I'm moaning again. Ignore me. You alright?'

'Yes, fine.' Rachel started, struggled past the fug of the headache. She hadn't heard a word of what Jackie had been saying. 'Sorry.'

'What is it? You heard from Stephen?' Jackie yanked at the handbrake and twisted round to stare at Rachel who flushed.

'No. I saw him; in town.' Rachel remembered the way her heart had leapt when she saw his tall, broad-shouldered figure; how she'd almost called out to him as though the chance encounter could change everything. For once he wasn't in a suit but in jeans and the Sonneti leather jacket she'd bought him for his last birthday. She'd hid in the doorway of M&S, frightened he'd see her. 'I feel stupid now.' She cursed herself for being so weak. Jackie would probably have faced up to him and what had she done? 'I followed him, Jackie'

She'd watched him walk, hands stuffed in the pockets of his jacket, head down as usual. It was as though he was oblivious to those around him but in reality she knew it was an unwillingness to meet eye contact with anyone just in case they tried to engage him in stupid (his word) conversation about the weather, cricket, sport: anything, when all he wanted to do was think his own thoughts. She tried to see past the handsome planes of his face, figure-out his expression but with his collar hiding his mouth it was impossible. It was his lips that always gave the game away: the upward quirk of inner amusement, the pulled-in corners of disapproval, the gentle smile. His eyes were always difficult to read, except when he was angry. And he hadn't looked her way. 'He went into that block of flats on Thomas Green Place.'

She saw the shock on her friend's face. 'I know, feeble or what?' She twisted her wedding ring.

'I'd probably have done the same,' Jackie said, 'if only to torch wherever he was living.' She scowled. 'But I didn't mean that. I meant, Thomas Green Place, it's a right dive. What the hell was he doing there?'

'I don't know.' Rachel fussed with her seatbelt, reluctant to let Jackie see the emptiness in her.

Jackie touched Rachel's cheek gently with the back of her hand. 'It's okay, kiddo.'

'I just wanted to see where he was living.' Rachel's voice thickened with tears.

'Well, I'd have wanted to hit the bugger with something, never mind see where he was living.' Inquisitiveness got the better of her. 'How did he look?'

He looked pathetic, Jackie,' Rachel forced the muscles of her face into a small smile, 'like he was lost.' Or was that wishful thinking? She knew it was, so why was she trying to gain sympathy for him from her friend? Perhaps because Jackie had taken against him so much it would be difficult if, when, they got back together?

'Well, let's hope he stays bloody lost, the dickhead. Don't you go feeling sorry for him. He's left you without a word for over three months. Have you forgotten Christmas? Good grief, Rachel, you go soft now and he'll mess you about for the rest of your life. That's if you do manage to talk to him again.' Rachel flinched. 'Sorry, love, he's a right bastard and if I ever see him, I'll tell him

."I know … I think but … but I'm stuck … I don't know what to do.' Rachel had established a daily routine in her life, completely different from the one with Stephen but the nights were another matter; she couldn't control her dreams and often, when she woke her face was wet with tears. 'Who was it said, *"The saddest thing in the world, is loving someone who used to love you?"* Rachel smiled wanly.

Oh for god's sake, Jackie thought, exasperated. 'Well, whoever it was must have been a soft cow,' she said instead. 'Look, if you like, I'll come with you to see him. Bit of moral support, sidekick, bouncer, assassin? Your call.'

The humour went over Rachel's head, she lifted her shoulders, 'I don't know.' Looking towards the house she said, 'see, Meg's waiting.' She waved. 'Come on, we've a lot to discuss. It might take my mind off things.'

'Let's hope so.' But Jackie doubted it: she felt like murdering Stephen.

Chapter Fifteen

...Who would be willing to help? What would be the next step?[15]

To: Avrilbreen@sheepfold.freeserve.co.uk
From: Jacgay@ yahoo.com.
Subject: Hi

Hi Avril, My name's Jackie Duffy. I'm a DES Daughter and I joined Meg's campaign with my friend, Rachel, who's not well at the moment so I'm writing to say hello from both of us.

Hazel walked into the sitting room, bottle of lager in her hand, and glared at Jackie. 'You ready to talk yet?'

Jackie's stomach flipped. Not again. Be careful, she told herself; don't set her off again. She didn't look up from her computer but couldn't prevent the muscles above her jaw line tightening. 'I can't say it any plainer, Hazel. We're through. There's nothing else to talk about.'

'You won't get rid of me that easily.' The words were defiant: her face all panic.

'We'll see,' Jackie said with forced calmness,

---

[15] *DES Voices From Anger to Action.* ©Pat Cody 2008 Ch.6 P. 62.

adjusting her reading glasses on her nose.

After a moment Hazel went out, banging the door behind her.

Jackie closed her eyes. She'd been clenching her teeth and now they ached. Her inability to make Hazel leave, the battle to force a love of literature into the listless minds of teenagers and the hot silence between her and her mother all joined together to make her feel that her life was lurching hopelessly on. Lighting another cigarette to replace the one that had burned away in the ashtray, she made herself concentrate. This was something she could manage.

Seeing all the research Meg's done we realised there has to be hundreds of women in this country alone affected by Stilboestrol. As you know the idea is to find a way to reach them, to build up a strong membership, to get greater public awareness. We've had a few meetings. I've attached a list of our ideas.

Upstairs Hazel was noisily opening and closing drawers and slamming the wardrobe doors, her swift footsteps, heeled down hard, made the light shade on the ceiling above Jackie move. She rubbed her temples; the tingling headache under her skin was becoming more insistent.

It was probably too much to hope Hazel was packing.

I know you live a long way from us but there must be something we can all do together.

She was probably being too pushy but sod it.

One thing – please place the enclosed appeal in your local rag. We've set up a group email account- joinus@aol.com
My mother lives near Manchester. Meet when I'm up that way? It was on our local news in January that the Foot and Mouth outbreak was declared over. Is it the same for you up there?

Jackie rubbed her forehead, warding off the pain. She knew she'd have to see her mother soon; she'd only just managed to wriggle out of the Christmas visit by claiming pressure of work. She remembered the tone of disbelief just before her mother put the 'phone down. It had gone to voice mail each time Jackie had rung since then. She'd have to go if only to check the old bat wasn't lying unconscious (or dead, the thought came involuntarily) at the bottom of the stairs. Visiting Avril Breen would be a good excuse to get out of the house if she did go up North. The thought cheered her. She typed the rest of the email quickly.

Let me know.
By the way, I've seen your website - fantastic!

My contact details are below. Feel free to ring/write/email.
All the best
 Jackie

Upstairs Hazel was still crashing about. Jackie stubbed out the cigarette, closed down the computer and, dropping her glasses onto the table, stood up, pressing down on her knuckles they cracked. She cursed her lack of prescience; it wasn't as if she hadn't been warned; she remembered the words Hazel's last lover, Christine, had flung at her. God, she must have been so relieved to be shot of her.

'If you've got friends now,' Christine had said, 'you soon won't have.' She chucked the last of Hazel's bags into Jackie's car boot. 'She's a vicious jealous cow.' She stood with her arms crossed, a tall thin woman with short blonde hair, dressed in a baggy jumper and jeans. Jackie couldn't see her eyes; they were hidden behind tinted lenses. 'You'll get the sulking, the snide comments - the lot - until one day you'll turn round and it will just be the two of you.'

'I'm sorry,' Jackie said, wondering what was meant by "the lot", 'I didn't know the two of you were still involved. She told me you'd left.'

'Left?' The woman gave a short bitter laugh. 'It's my house. I've kicked her out and I'm well rid.'

They watched Hazel walk through the garden of the large detached house towards them, a wide grin on her face. 'Let's go,' she said, without a glance at Christine.

Jackie felt the first twinge of apprehension.

'Good luck!' Christine turned away, 'you'll need it.'

'Oh, fuck off,' Hazel shouted. She climbed into the car and put a hand on Jackie's leg. 'Let's go home, lover,' she said.

How right the woman had been; only Rachel had stuck it out. Other friends, the few she had made through University (there was no one from her school days) had drifted quietly off the scene without Jackie even noticing until it was too late.

It wouldn't be as easy getting Hazel to move out as it was for her to move in.

Jackie went to the living room window and knelt on the arm of the black leather sofa looking out. People walked past the house chattering and laughing, the young mother across the road bundled her two children into her little red Ford and drove off, joining the steady stream of traffic taking the short cut through Sangford Terrace on the way to the sales in the shopping mall.

The front door slammed. Jackie jumped back holding aside one length of the vertical blind and watched Hazel walk down the street with only her thin denim jacket over a tee shirt, her head bobbing with each step, feet carefully placed on the pavement. She'd been drinking since lunchtime; Jackie's lips twisted, perhaps she thought the alcohol would keep her warm.

She went into the kitchen and poured water into a glass, drank it in one long gulp and studied the calendar on the wall. The days were dragging and the weather was typically unpredictable for this first half term holiday of the year, just like Hazel's moods. She couldn't stand much more of this.

Wiping her mouth with the back of her hand she rinsed the glass. Outside the corners of the back yard were clogged with dead leaves and the pots by the walls now held only soggy yellowed plants. The broken slates from last year's storm were still propped against the step near the gate, waiting for the council to collect. Three magpies landed on top of the yard wall, one after the other and then flew off, chattering harshly as the cat from next door appeared. Jackie banged on the glass. 'Sod off,' she shouted. It stared at her for a moment before picking its way slowly towards the gatepost.

Restlessly clicking her fingers Jackie followed the birds' progress above the roofs of the houses backing on to hers.

She wondered about ringing Rachel, then remembered she'd said she thought she was coming down with a bug. Meg? No, *she'd* mentioned in her last email that Richard was having a bad week. There was no one else. Who'd have thought she'd want to go back to work but anything was better than being with Hazel. Anywhere would be better.

Mooching back into the living room she ran her fingers along the bookshelves crammed with collection of biographies of various women; Jane Addams, Eleanor Roosevelt, Emmeline Pankhurst. She paused for a moment tapping the spine of her copy of the autobiography of Billie Jean King. It reminded her of Elton John's song *Philadelphia Freedom* and she hummed the first few bars before getting bored. Tedium, ennui, lethargy, lassitude. Even the word game didn't interest her today; nothing did. She was really fed-up, stymied. She picked up the packet of cigarettes, tapping it against her chin and thinking. Suddenly the thought came to her; that was it! She gave a snort of laughter; it must be a first, escaping *to* her mother's.

To: Avrilbreen@sheepfold.freeserve.co.uk
From: Jacgay@ yahoo.com.
Subject: Hi

Hi again, I wondered if it would be ok to call on you later this week. Please let me know if it'll be ok. Short notice I know but I've decided to visit my mother. I'll ring - if it's not convenient just say.
Jackie

Having made the decision Jackie couldn't wait. She packed quickly and threw the bag into the back seat of the Peugeot. Within an hour she was on the motorway.

At the first service station she pulled in and taking her phone out of her rucksack, rang Rachel. When the answering service connected straightaway she left her message. 'Hi Rachel, it's Jackie. Last minute decision: things are bloody awful at home so I've decided go to Mother's for the week. I know, I know, unbelievable huh? Anyway, killing two birds with one stone, I thought I might go and see Avril Breen while I'm there. I can't see any problems about the Foot and Mouth business now. I've taken some of the DES stuff we've been discussing; see if I can get her interested enough to help us….' The beeps sounded the end of the time allotted and cut Jackie off. She clicked the switch, debated whether she'd said all she needed and decided she had.

Scrolling up to find Hazel's name, she moved her thumb quickly over the buttons.

I wnt U out by the tme I gt bk - uv 7 days.

Then she left a voice message on her mother's 'phone.

Chapter Sixteen

...she definitely remembered taking something during her pregnancy with me. She could not remember what it was. All she knew was that the obstetrician had given her a medication to "help save the baby."[16]

Rachel woke to the beep of her mobile. Her head ached and she was still nauseous; damn seafood platter, she should have known; the Captains' Cabin wasn't exactly haute cuisine. She rolled onto her side and listened to Jackie's message. Sounded like there'd been another row with Hazel, it must have been bad for her friend to take off to Manchester.

She lay back against the pillows, focussing on the photograph of her and Stephen's wedding day, next to the one of her parents. It had rained, the hem of her dress had been wet and grimy before they'd even arrived at the reception but it hadn't mattered. She looked so young, hanging onto Stephen's arm and laughing towards the camera with a self-conscious tilt of her chin. Stephen looked smug, Rachel decided.

Or did he? Was he smug or only relieved the stress of the ceremony was over? Or just happy? After ten years she couldn't tell. She had a sudden

[16] Excerpt from - *DES Daughter: A True Story of Tragedy and Triumph: The Joyce Bichler Story* 1981 © Joyce Bichler Ch.2 p.34

understanding that she didn't know him anymore. Had she ever? When had she, they, stopped talking, *really* communicating? On her part she realised she'd taken him, his love and support for granted. It was as though having studied him, his character, his personality she'd decided she knew all there was to know; that having done her dissertation on him and gained her degree she forgot everything she'd learned: had just taken the consequent way of life it gave her for granted. And that, for a long time, the space between them had been filled with dead air: no shared words hovering, no implicit understanding, none of that synchronization of routines that other couples seemed to have.

Or maybe she was wrong, maybe it was like that for everyone.

She shifted restlessly against the churning of her stomach, striving to take even breaths but it didn't help; in a second she was out of bed and hanging over the lavatory, heaving up bile. Waves of the panic swept over her as she waited for the next involuntary thrust of her stomach; she'd always hated being sick. When she was a child her mother would hold her until it was over.

Sometimes, in the few seconds between sleep and wakefulness, Rachel forgot her mother was dead, the realization paralyzing her for a moment so much she felt pinned to the mattress.

Her life had imploded but carried on all around her; she saw that on the television, read it in the papers. Stephen was walking and breathing through his days, presumably with no thought for her. Had she misjudged indifference to be tact, adherence to duty for love? Had he ever loved her? She was sure he had. Once. When had it stopped? With which baby? The questions rattled through Rachel's head.

She felt isolated and scared of the future.

The loneliness had burrowed its way deep within her the moment Stephen had walked out. She'd never been on her own before, she'd moved straight from her parent's home to her married life. She hated being alone in the house. Yet she didn't want to go out either. It was as though she wore a label that announced her failure to have children and the breakdown of her marriage for all to see.

The retching stopped. She closed her eyes, daring to cautiously straighten above the splattered bowl of the lavatory. Wiping her mouth with a facecloth she carefully lowered herself to the floor and curled up, rocking silently with grief.

Chapter Seventeen

The first response of many (DES) mothers (on discovering that the drug may harm our children) is often panic and blind fear. Next is anguish about telling their child. [17]

'How's Richard?' Alice squeezed through the kitchen door and carefully closed it.

'Not too bad, he's sleeping now,' Meg said. 'The doctor called round again this morning.'

'Kidneys are a bugger,' Alice declared.

'Mmmm.'

Alice pulled a chair out from the table and, with a sigh of relief, lowered herself onto it.

'How's the group going?'

'Good ... really good,' Meg smiled. 'A few women have emailed. And Jackie gave her mobile number as a contact and she says one or two more have rung to talk to her, find out who we are and what have you. I couldn't ... well I didn't... get anywhere on my own. I think the more we are the better chance we have of the Government listening at last. Well, let's hope so, eh? It's worth a go. The main thing is finding other women.' Meg switched the oven off. 'You alright?'

'Mmmm, not bad.' Alice shifted around on the seat and grimaced. She sniffed loudly. 'Smells

---

[17] *DES Voices From Anger to Action* © Pat Cody.2008, Ch13 p164

smashing in here, love,' she said, 'I didn't realise you were busy.'

Meg buttered two scones and put them on the plate in front of her. 'Always bake on a Friday, Alice,' Meg said, careful not to let her friend see her smile; it was a conversation they had every week.

The big woman leaned down and scratched at the bandage on her leg. 'Bloody ulcer's playing me up again,' she moaned.

'What did your doctor say?'

'Same as usual, lose weight and rest. Bloody fool. How can I rest with everything I have to do?' She gave a short laugh. 'And what am I supposed to do while I'm resting? Minute I sit down my stomach thinks I should be eating.'

Meg nodded. She sat across the table from Alice and mopped the spilt tea in her saucer with a tissue. 'It's not easy, I know. Anything I can do to help?'

'No, lovey.' Alice bit on a scone and slurped her drink. Crumbs and drips from the cup ran down her cleavage and she absently rubbed her chest. 'Take no notice of me, I got out of bed the wrong side I think and I don't know why.' She grinned, revealing the gap in the top set of her large teeth. 'I really popped over to give you some news. Our Wendy's set a bloody date for the wedding.' She gave a loud guffaw and slapped her hand on the table. 'Fair took me by surprise; I never thought I'd get rid of her.' She stopped, gazed over at Meg, her voice quieter. 'I mean ...'

'I know, Alice, you must be so happy for her.'

'Oh I am, I am,' she said. 'It's fairly soon too - in May. She's - she's having a bairn.'

In the long silence that followed the clicking of the fridge freezer vied with the faint sound of commentary of horse racing from the television in the bedroom. Alice made the small lip-popping noises she always made when she was embarrassed or uncomfortable.

Oh dear god; the pain filled Meg's chest. 'That's wonderful, ' she said eventually, reaching over and patting her friend's large soft hand. 'Wonderful. When's the baby due?'

'August, she says.'

'Well, that'll be two celebrations we'll have this year.' She crossed to the worktop. Lifting the lid of the teapot, she peered in, willing the tears not to fall. 'More tea.' Despite all her efforts her voice was high-pitched, scratchy.

Alice shook her head. 'No thanks, pet.' She brushed scone crumbs off her bosom. 'I'll have to go in a minute: lot to do.'

'Will you want me to make the wedding cake? My present?' Meg put the cups and saucers in the dishwasher, desperately keeping her voice even.

'Would you? Wendy will be really chuffed if you do.' Alice pushed down on the surface of the table to help herself to stand. 'They're having a bit of a break next weekend. I wouldn't go anywhere this time of year but it's their choice, I suppose.'

'Tell her to have a good time from me.'

'Oh, I bet they do.' Alice laughed 'Even if they don't go out.'

'Alice Baker, behave yourself.' Meg grinned, recognizing her friend's attempt to lighten the mood.

'Well, she might as well have fun while she can. She'll be too tired after the baby ....' Alice stopped.

'It'll certainly be all go from the minute she gets back,' Meg said, pretending not to notice her friend's discomfort.

'It will and all. And now I'd better get back,' Alice hobbled over to her friend and hugged her. 'I promised to go with her to the Mall to that posh dress shop. Have a look what they've got, like.' She moved her eyebrows up and down comically. 'Nowt in my size, I'll bet. 'Lifting her top lip away from her teeth and tapping them she said, 'and I'll have to get my gnashers sorted as well.'

Meg laughed.

Watching Alice manoeuvre her huge bulk through the garden gate she called out to her. Ask Wendy to pop over and give me some idea what she wants for the cake.' She closed the door and stood with her back to it.

The memory of watching her daughter's face, when she was told she'd never have a chance to be a mother if she wanted to live, came back in a rush; the anguish in her eyes as they'd looked at one another had mirrored her own. Meg couldn't stop the automatic stab of resentment against Alice and Wendy.

Unfair, unfair, she chastised herself, tightly squeezing her eyes closed; Wendy had been a good friend to Lisa, she was entitled to a future. So was Lisa, she thought bitterly, but she didn't get one, did she?

Stop it, Meg clenched her hand, her nails digging into the palm. She took in a lengthy breath and peeped into the bedroom. Richard was awake.

'Mrs Foghorn gone?' he chuckled.

'Sorry, love, did she wake you?' Meg sat on the bed and stroked the back of Richard's hand. Seeing him lying with the duvet over his legs and his familiar broad shoulders pressing down the pillow she could almost forget his disability. 'How do you feel?'

'Fine.' He looked up at her. 'You ok, sweetheart?'

'Yes,' Meg said, 'Alice had some news; Wendy's having a baby.'

Chapter Eighteen

Widespread use of DES on pregnant women was halted in 1971, after a study linked clear cell adenocarcinoma, a rare cancer of the cervix and vagina, to those exposed to the drug in the womb.[18iv]

'Hi, is that Avril?' Jackie said, staring through the car window at a family getting back into their four-by-four carrying fish and chips. Her stomach rumbled reminding her she hadn't eaten all day. She switched the interior light on and peered at the clock on the dashboard: seven twenty. 'I'm on my way to Manchester. Wondered if I could call in for an hour sometime over the next week?' she listened for a moment, frowning slightly. The voice on the other end of the 'phone sounded hesitant. 'Are you sure that's okay?' Jackie said, conscious that, as usual, she'd jumped in with both feet; perhaps the woman had changed her mind about meeting and getting involved with the group. 'Look, if I'm being pushy just say, we can put it off. I mean if you're busy or something I can come another time. Or not at all?' After all, the woman didn't know her. She switched the heater on, to clear the build-up of condensation from the windscreen, while she listened again. 'Well,

[18] Quote from an interview with the mother of Jill Vanselous Murphy Washington Post: September 23, 2003

okay,' she fumbled in her rucksack for her diary and a pen, 'if you're sure? Great. If you can give me your address, I've got a map.' She scribbled it down on the back page of the diary. 'Lydfield's the nearest village?' She paused again. 'Track on the left, half a mile after The Granary pub,' she repeated the words. 'Right, okay, I'll give you a call.' She took the keys from the ignition. 'Yeah, I'm going to my mother's.' She grimaced into the 'phone. 'Ok, Avril, I'll be in touch. Bye.'

Jackie switched off her mobile and opened the car door. The whiff of hot fat from the fish and chip shop engulfed her. There was a queue outside the door, always a good sign, she thought. She would wait as long as it took to be served; she was famished. And, after all, she wasn't in a great rush to get to her mother's.

Chapter Nineteen

The ultimate impact of DES as a traumatic experience will depend on how the situation is handled by adults important to the developing child.[19]

Her mother's prolonged coughing woke Jackie from a restless sleep, just as it had in her childhood. Then, the bed seemed enormous. Now she lay on it with her arms over her stomach, elbows touching the wall on one side and the bound edge of the mattress on the other.

The room was still dark and Jackie felt rather than saw the outlines of her surroundings. The tiny window, the box-like shape in the corner that allowed for the stairs to rise underneath onto the landing, the small low door she now had to duck under. She'd given her head a right crack the last time she was here.

'It's a normal door,' her mother said, 'it's you that's gone gangly. Nobody else has a problem with it.'

'That's because no one else bloody goes up there.' Jackie knew her mother hadn't had visitors in years. She wouldn't be here herself, given a choice. As it

---

20   Roberta J Apfel, MD.,M.P.H. Susan M Fisher, M.D. *To Do No Harm: DES and the Dilemmas of Modern Medicine.* Ch.5 p.72 (see footnote *i*)

was she made the two hundred and forty mile journey twice a year under sufferance. Once during the summer holidays when, exhausted by trying to instil Shakespeare into disgruntled boys and thin look-alike teenage girls with their ponytails and too-old eyes, that even a visit to her mother seemed respite, the next, usually sometime over Christmas.

Christmases had been different when she was very young; her Dad had seen to that. Even now the wistful nostalgia was painful. She'd idolised her father with a fierce possessiveness that she knew made her mother feel excluded. His leaving should have brought them closer but it did the opposite. She could still picture the spite on her mother's face as she told Jackie he'd gone because he couldn't stand her demanding needs; that he'd walked out because of Jackie.

Jackie's face tightened. Even harder to take was Mary's assertion that Harry wasn't her father. Whether that was true or not Jackie never knew but her mother had sown the doubt; it was obvious she thought she'd had her revenge, had achieved a sweet settling of scores.

But Jackie made sure Mary knew she'd lost her daughter as well.

She couldn't remember when the inchoate sense that she was to blame for her mother's bitterness disappeared; when she'd stopped accepting the acerbic comments as something she deserved. She only knew they'd fought for years and her desperate need for love was finally replaced by dislike and she'd given up trying to understand.

A car passed the house, its headlights a sweep of light that travelled across the uneven surface of the woodchip wallpaper. Jackie moved carefully onto her side clutching the shiny dark green eiderdown to stop it falling off the bed.

She'd known from an early age her parents didn't have a marriage made in heaven. Their quarrels were noisy and vicious and she never saw them kiss or cuddle. Affection wasn't part of her mother's make-up.

She lost her battle with the eiderdown and it slid onto the floor: she pushed back the sheet and thin blankets. Shivering, she pulled on the old red towelling dressing gown, which stayed in the wardrobe between her visits, and then pulled back the curtains. Ice glazed the panes. She breathed on one, melting the myriad patterns. Rubbing the edges with her finger she widened the hole and peered out. In the blackness, faint light from two of the windows in the house opposite lay across the ground: glistening yellow rectangles. The dark shadow of a man moved along the road, pushing newspapers through letterboxes. There was no one else around.

Opening the door to the landing Jackie waited, holding her breath. The coughing had stopped. She felt her mother listening.

Stumbling on the narrow treads in her outsized

Scooby Doo slippers, Jackie went downstairs, angry that, yet again, she had let herself reflect on the unfathomable tie between her and the woman upstairs.

God above. Jackie stared around the cramped kitchen; a small Formica table, two chairs, a gas cooker with claw feet, and an old kitchenette with the opaque glass doors and the room was full. The pantry door stayed permanently open; forever trapped by the edge of a wall cupboard that a lazy council worker had fitted wrongly when the house was built in the nineteen fifties. She scowled. Damn Council should be sued; her mother was living in the dark ages here.

Jackie pushed past the table, dislodging the chequered cloth so the breadcrumbs and bits of food left from the previous day spilled onto the floor, and shoved a chair out of the way so she could get to the small fireplace. It was covered in grey ash dotted with tiny pieces of unburned coal. Jackie knelt down to extricate every piece, following an inbuilt routine. She crumpled newspaper, refusing to form the twists her mother made so meticulously and instead, pushed the balls of paper into the grate, covering them with oiled wood, the rescued bits

of coal and tiny new pieces out of the bucket. Lighting the paper she held a sheet of newspaper over the fireplace in the hope the backdraught would encourage flames. On one side of the page a photograph, a young couple posed self-consciously in the arch of a church, darkened as the paper was drawn in and then the image began to glow orange and smoke filled her nostrils. She pushed the paper into the fire and charred pieces flew up the chimney.

Condensation covered the windows and she wiped a tea towel over each pane. Lifting the lid of the old-fashioned twin tub pushed under the stone slab of the pantry she threw it in.

'You could have dried that in front of the fire, or stuck it on the rack.' Jackie's mother jerked her head towards the ceiling where a wooden contraption swung as she touched the rope that held it in place.

'It's dirty,' Jackie answered shortly, getting up from her knees. 'The fire's on the go now. I'll go and get dressed.'

'There's no hot water yet, the boiler won't have heated up.' Mary Duffy's voice was deep and crackled with phlegm, a forty-year legacy of smoking.

'I'll manage.' Jackie looked at her mother who stared impassively back at her. 'I'm going out.'

'Oh?' The exclamation was indifferent as Mary Duffy filled the kettle with cold water from a tap that shuddered with the pressure. She banged it down on the cooker and twisted the knob until the gas, popping rapidly, lit with a whoosh and drips of water spluttered and spat on the flame.

'I'm meeting a friend.'

'Oh.' Now there was an undercurrent of disbelief in her mother's tone. Jackie knew what she was thinking: she had no friends from her childhood; she'd been a loner. However hard she'd tried she'd always been on the outside of any of the groups in school. Once, believing her infatuation with one of the sixth form girls was reciprocated, she'd declared her love. Even now remembering the public humiliating derision made her cringe. Her life was unbearable after that and she'd left that school mid-term, stubbornly refusing to return despite her mother's fury. Forging her mother's signature Jackie enrolled herself at another school. She stayed for as long as it took her to pass her A-levels and, until the exhilarating freedom of university, developed an implacable manner that kept her peer group, and her mother, at a distance. Behaviour that sent Mary Duffy into rages that were staggeringly satisfying to watch.

Now Jackie couldn't resist the implied challenge. 'I've joined a group of women who want to get the problems that Stilboestrol caused, recognized. I'm meeting one of them.'

'What's that got to do with you?' Mary's shoulders tensed but she didn't face her daughter. She continued rinsing a beaker under the cold-water tap, her hand unsteady.

Jackie heard the antagonism. 'Oh, for goodness sake mother, you know full well what it's got to do with me.' She waited; talk to me, she thought. But the urge for confrontation plummeted as quickly as it rose and an unexpected sadness replaced it.

Wind gusted down the chimney sweeping a cloud of smoke into the kitchen, sprinkled soot over the hearth. 'You should get the chimney swept,' Jackie said, looking down at it.

'Too expensive.' They were on safer ground now.

'You know I'll pay.' When Jackie walked towards the stairs there were two clean footprints where she'd stood, surrounded by a thin layer of black speckles. Her large slippers were now grimy.' I don't know when I'll be back. It'll probably be late. Will you leave a key out?'

Mary Duffy nodded. When her daughter left the kitchen she folded her arms stiffly across her waist. And when she heard the creaking of the bedroom floor above her face crumpled and she wept.

Chapter Twenty

You can't change your genes, or the toxic exposures you or your parents faced, but knowing about them can spur you into taking the actions needed to protect your health[20]

'How are you feeling now?' Meg came into the darkened bedroom with two cups of tea.

'Better,' Richard pushed against the mattress and sat up. 'Open the curtains will you, love, let's get some daylight in here.'

'It was only while you slept.' Meg moved the telephone to one side and put the cups down on the table next to the bed and hurried to help, piling the pillows around him. 'Ok? The doctor said it'll take a day or so for the new antibiotics to start working.' She drew back the curtains and squinted against the brightness into the back garden where the wind spun the washing on the rotary clothes dryer. 'Bit breezy but it's quite a nice day … sunny.' She came to sit on the side of the bed and took hold of his hand. 'Are you sure you don't want a couple of those tablets he left you for the pain?'

'No, I'll be ok, save them for tonight.' He screwed his face as a sudden spasm stabbed his kidneys.

---

[20] Fran Howell. *Voice* 119 Winter 2009

'You've got your sleeping tablets for then, ' Meg reminded him.

'Well, perhaps I will then. It does feel quite bad.'

'Your 'quite bad' means it's awful.' Meg poured water from the jug by the bedside into a glass and tipped two tablets into the palm of her husband's hand. 'Here, take these,' she said in mock severity, 'I'll expect some gardening to be done tomorrow, if this weather keeps up.'

Richard chuckled. 'Slave driver!'

She leant forward and kissed his forehead.

He held onto her for a moment. 'You're still beautiful, Mrs Matthews.'

'And you're still that cocky Teddy Boy my dad disapproved off.' She kissed him again. 'I'll sit here and read until you feel like having a sleep.' She took her tea, sat on the small green velvet chair in the corner of the bedroom and picked up her book from the floor where it lay open. 'No talking,' she commanded.

'Sorry to be a nuisance ….' For a moment Richard looked wretched.

'Don't be an idiot.'

'What a great bedside manner you have, Nurse Nightingale.' He managed a grin and closed his eyes.

'All you deserve, you fake,' Meg retorted. She watched him until the tablets took effect and soft snores parted his lips.

Before long the book lay in her lap and she too slept.

The nightmare returned. Richard yelling at her, her yelling back, hating him. The monotonous rhythm of the wipers. The swish of the tyres ploughing through flooded roads. The raw anger making her press harder and harder on the accelerator. Watching the needle on the speedometer moving steadily towards maximum speed.

And then the scream of the engine, the squeal of brakes …louder and louder.

Chapter Twenty-One

... my research (in 1993) found there had been at least 14 cases confirmed in the UK. And DES Action UK has become aware of further cases diagnosed since 1993.[21]

Avril Breen was restless. There was little else to do indoors so she went outside, pulling on the large brass handle to close the door. She leaned against the wall of the stone porch of her cottage and shoved her hands up the sleeves of her thick cardigan, hugging herself, her breath turning to pale mist. In the distance Lydfield crouched between river and canal in the valley. The village was in shadow, blotted out by the flashes of the weak sun on the surfaces of the waters. She was distracted by movement on the track leading up to the cottage and watched as a car stopped half a mile below and a tiny figure emerged from the driving seat. A woman stared up towards the cottage.

Avril caught her lower lip between her teeth. It was a long time since anyone had visited. The cottage had been her refuge for more years than she cared to remember and she avoided inviting people, even friends. And now she'd let herself in for this, a stranger coming into her home. A stranger, who in

---

[21] My DES Story – Jane Kevan - a trustee and member of DES Action UK. See bio.

her own words, had said she was bloody pushy. If she was that astute to realise that, why hadn't she taken the hint that Avril really - really, she emphasised to herself - didn't want her to come up here to talk face to face about the drug.

Stop it; she told herself, you started this particular ball rolling now deal with it.

She went back into the warmth of the long low building. Cooking was always a solace in her occasional phases of agitation and the large kitchen was filled with the aroma of chicken and red pepper soup. She was glad she'd taken the trouble to drive down to Lydfield bakery and buy bread. Spreading the chunks thickly with butter (bang goes the diet for another day) she wiped both sides of the knife on the edge of the butter dish and closed the lid.

The rumble of the car travelled in the clear cold air, the noise of the engine got louder. Avril threw another log on the fire checked the lock on the macaw's cage and pushed a slice of apple through the bars which the bird delicately took off her. 'Good boy,' she murmured.

He balanced the fruit on his perch and held it with his claw. 'Good boy,' he repeated, jerking his head up and down.

'I'll let you out later,' Avril promised, 'when our visitor's gone.' The macaw lifted his bright blue wings slightly away from his body and stared at her. 'Yes, show-off, I know you're beautiful.' She smiled, admiring the contrast of feathers. 'But it might surprise you to know not everybody likes birds. 'He began to tear at the apple.

Avril closed the door to her study; she didn't want Jackie to see the books she'd removed from the shelves in the living room, not yet, anyway. Once she'd had sussed out what kind of woman she was she'd judge whether to tell her what she wrote besides the thrillers and plays. After all, even though her alter ego had earned her a good living for over twenty years, she was still someone she kept secret. She looked around; the cottage was tidier than it had been for ages. 'Right, here goes.'

It was like *Emmerdale, Jackie thought. W*rong county but near enough to the border not to matter. Or did the old rivalries of Lancashire and Yorkshire still exist? Jackie shielded her eyes with her hand against the brightness of the sky, staring past the fields separated by crumbling stonewalls to where the outline of the cottage broke the silhouette of the hill. Thin smoke gusted from a large chimneystack that jutted out from the gable end. 'Fantastic,' she murmured, envying the woman who lived there: coveting the privacy.

Taking a last draw on the cigarette, she squeezed the end of it and, getting back in the car, dropped it in the ashtray. Without fastening her seatbelt she set off again. The Peugeot trundled up the track in first gear, startling sheep in the fields on the other side of the tumbled walls and occasionally dipping so far onto one side or the other that Jackie thought the car would roll over. At the top of the hill she followed the wall to the left and stopped behind an old green Metro outside the cottage.

The woman at the door was exactly how she imagined Avril Breen would look; the wide mouth smiling her welcome was echoed by the laughter lines around her eyes as she held reddish - grey hair away from her face with the back of her hand. There was no reticence.

'Hi, Jackie? Any problems finding the place?' Now it was happening Avril was determined to make the best of the situation.

Her voice was a subdued mixture of Yorkshire and Lancashire accents, unlike the harsh Manchester twang Jackie's mother deliberately stressed, as though needing to remind Jackie of her roots for some reason.

'None at all, thanks.' She smiled gazing around the surrounding countryside. 'Fantastic views too.' The gorse-covered hills on either side of the cottage rose smoothly and plateaued out onto the moors under the vast expanse of pale sky. Sheep nibbled the stubby grass, occasionally raising their heads to look around and bleat: the sound travelling in the still air. The fields sloped down towards Lydfield in an assortment of shapes and sizes, the mixture of greens and browns blending into a misty dark blue over the suburbs and city of Manchester. 'Wonderful!' Jackie marvelled and then, her voice sobering, 'good to see sheep roaming free again.'

Avril grimaced. 'Yes, that lot only came out from the farm last week and they're a tenth of what used to be around.' She pulled her cardigan tighter around her and shivered. 'You wouldn't have wanted to be here last summer, the smoke and stench from the culls was awful for months.' She stared towards the moorland. 'A lot of the local farmers went bust,' she glanced at Jackie. 'Was it bad where you live too?'

'Perhaps not as bad but, yeah, it affected farmers and tourism; a lot of the countryside was out of bounds.'

'It'll take a long time for a lot of people to recover.' Avril turned towards the cottage. 'Still, it's all over now, fingers crossed. Come on in, there's a good fire on the go and you're just in time for lunch.'

'It's a lovely place you have.'

Ivy covered parts of the grey stone cottage hunkered down on pitted cobbles, its slate roof crisscrossed by glossy lines of moss. On either side of the arched porch eight small windows in deep-set casings ran the whole length of the building and sported pale lemon curtains.

'I think so. I bought it from the grandson of an old farmer who'd let the place go to rack and ruin before he died.' Avril waved vaguely towards the end of the building. 'This was a sort of barn; the actual farmhouse was over there: it was so derelict it had to be demolished. Luckily I bought the land it had stood on. It actually has planning permission for a build but I don't ever see me doing anything about that.' Avril shivered. 'Let's get inside.'

A World of our Own played quietly in the background. Jackie wandered around the room, admiring the oak beams and the large iron and stone fireplace where logs crackled and flamed. She examined watercolours of streams and woods until finally she stood in front of the portrait in the alcove. It was clearly Avril when she was younger and it was beautiful: sexy. Jackie was captivated, she couldn't remember the last time she had seen anything so sensuous.

A piercing shriek from a far corner of the room startled her and she turned swiftly. A bird, a parrot, she thought, was clambering around a large cage, scraping its beak along the bars. 'Hello,' she said and was thrilled when it repeated the word. 'A parrot?' she called towards the clattering in the kitchen where Avril was dishing out the soup.

'Macaw, Mr Macawber.'

'Does he bite?'

'Only my agent, Natasha.' Avril laughed. 'They hate one another. Mr Macawber shat all over her Hermes handbag once when she mistook his climbing frame for clothes hooks. They went for the bag at the same time and he bit her.'

Jackie grinned. 'Oh, you naughty boy.' She didn't chance going nearer.

'I'll let him out later if that's okay.'

'Yeah, no problem, I don't even possess a

handbag. Rucksacks yes, handbags no.'

Avril chuckled again.

Jackie made a few clucking noises at the macaw, which ignored her and then she spotted a shelf of books in the opposite alcove to the portrait. She ran her fingers across each one, reading the titles. 'Are all these yours?' A stupid question, she realised at once; each had the woman's name along the spine.

But Avril was polite enough to answer in the affirmative and not even in a sarcastic tone. 'Yes.'

Jackie took one out and read the blurb on the back cover. She skimmed through a few pages: it was good, a modern day thriller, main character a woman in her late forties apparently: unusual in itself. She put it back in its place. There must have been about twenty similar looking novels in all. At the end of the shelf there was an empty space. Peering at the shelf she could see book-shaped marks in the dust.

When Avril appeared with the two bowls of soup Jackie half-turned, her hand resting where the other books had been. 'You've written a lot. I'd like to read one, if that's okay?'

'Borrow what you like.' Avril struggled to keep her voice neutral, silently cursing because she'd forgotten to dust.

'Are there others?'

'No, that's the lot so far.' Well it wasn't a lie, Avril told herself; the last in that particular series was published over a year ago and she wasn't intending to write any more about the woman detective. 'Hope you're hungry?' she smiled, 'this is one of my made up recipes. See what you think.'

'That was gorgeous.' Jackie sat back in her chair and wiped her mouth with the kitchen roll Avril had produced as napkins. 'Thanks.'

'Easy to make and easy to heat up when I'm too busy to cook.' Avril gathered the crockery and took it into the kitchen, reappearing with a large basket of fruit in one hand and a plate of cheese and biscuits in the other. She put the food on the table. 'Help yourself.'

'Thanks,' Jackie took an apple and cut it up. She sliced off a piece of Edam and took a bite, indicating towards the book she'd chosen. *'Twelve Hours to Die.'* she read. 'Have you always been a thriller writer?'

'Mostly,' Avril hedged, 'I've written other stuff as well.' She changed the subject. 'Years ago I wanted to teach English, like you.'

Jackie groaned and rolled her eyes.

'Yes, well, that's what I thought I wanted to do at the time.' Avril refilled their glasses. 'Shall we sit over there?' she gestured towards the fireplace. 'It's warmer and more comfortable. Bring your food. I'll let Mr Macawber out.' She crossed the lounge and opened the cage before sitting on the settee.

Jackie followed, keeping a close eye on the bird,

and sat on a chair balancing plate and glass. 'So when did you actually begin to write?'

The bird flew across the room and settled near Avril's shoulder, nibbling her hair. 'A long time ago; about two years after I found out about the drug; for all that time, I refused to talk about it to anyone,' Avril said. 'I found this place, shut myself away; feeling like a freak.'

'I know that feeling,' Jackie said. 'But I've been surprised how many women have come forward ... all with different stories, but all with the same thing in common... DES. And it seems most of them have never talked to anyone about it before.'

Avril nodded. 'My doctor persuaded me, eventually to have a few sessions with a councillor. She suggested I wrote down how I felt. I realised I enjoyed writing and that I was actually good, so I carried on. At first I wrote short stories and one act plays. Didn't make anything from them; just bits of prizes with competitions, things like that. I needed some sort of income so I got a part time job cataloguing archived stuff at the library in the village which suited me; I could keep myself to myself. One day the librarian asked to write a piece for the local Ramblers on Stackrock, a local walk, and when I was researching it I found out about a murder that had taken place there years ago. That's how I began with my Jenny Allott books.' She turned and wafted a hand towards the shelf. The macaw followed the action, refusing to let go of the strand of hair. 'I was very lucky; second agent I sent my first novel to accepted it, thank goodness; I'd almost ran out of money, thought I'd have to sell up. But here I am … still here.'

The logs in the grate shunted and sent up a flurry of sparks and flames that played on the faces of the women.

'Don't you get lonely up here?' Jackie asked finally. 'I mean it's beautiful, a lovely place to live but it's quite isolated, isn't it?'

Avril pursed her lips and gazed into the fire. Smoothing Mr Macawber's wing feathers she said, 'I'm used to it; it's how I've chosen to live. I have book signings, book fairs, requests to read at literary festivals, that sort of thing. I was at Hay on Wye a couple of years ago. And I visit friends when I can. Family sometimes, not often,' she pulled a wry face, 'too many memories there.' She stopped. The silence stretched between them. Avril wondered what it was about this woman that made talking about herself so easy. 'Some of them haven't let go of what happened to me, especially my parents; I love them to bits but they make me feel like I'm still some sort of victim.' Oh no, she was going to cry. She blew her nose and then said firmly, 'I'm not … I'm not a victim. Do you ever get that reaction?'

'It's different for me. Before Rachel and Meg, no one ever knew about my connection with the drug, except for my mother. So I never talked about it,' Jackie said, 'the only one I would want to discuss it with is her and she point blank refuses.'

'Why?'

Jackie pulled a face. 'Long story, I'll tell you sometime.'

The idea that there would be another time didn't bother Avril as much as she thought it would; perhaps contacting Meg Matthews was the best thing she'd done in a long while.

Chapter Twenty-Two

"We are all deformed," she says quietly. "But nobody sees our handicap. We walk down the street and people think we are normal. But we are not."^{v 22}

It was already almost dark outside. *Calling me Home* faded away into a haunting echo. The fire settled and the chunks of wood shifted and flared. Avril got up to throw on another log. 'I just love Judith Durham's voice,' she said. 'Coffee?'

'No thanks, I really should be going,' Jackie said. 'I meant to go earlier so I could get down your lane in daylight.'

'I've got to go out in a bit; if you wait I'll lead and help you to navigate the potholes. Or you could come with me?' Avril said, on a sudden impulse. 'I promised to go to see the rehearsal of one of my plays with a drama group in the theatre in Lydfield. It's being performed in a couple of weeks. I think you'd enjoy it.'

'I should get back.' Even as she said it Jackie knew she would take up Avril's offer. She'd had quite enough of her mother for today; if she left it late enough she would be in bed before Jackie got back to the house. 'But yes, ok, why not. I'd love to.' It

---

²²   DES *Voices From Anger to Action.* 2008 © Pat Cody Introduction: *How It Began* p.5

would be interesting; she loved theatre of any kind. 'And I will have that coffee, thanks.'

'Good. A friend from the village, Georgina, is directing the play: she works for the Royal Venue Theatre in Manchester. She's directed a couple of my other plays in a small theatre in the city and she's good.'

'That was brilliant, I really enjoyed myself.' Jackie forced herself to speak normally; well she hoped she sounded normal. 'You were right; Georgina seems able to get the best out of people.' She was shaking and it wasn't with the cold wind that eddied around them. 'I really liked her.' An understatement: Jackie had been breathless with the force of the instant attraction that had sparked between her and the tall good-looking woman.

She stood with Avril on the steps of the small theatre. The square facing them, with its war memorial in the centre, dominated the village. Streetlights showed the high street splitting into two on either side, hemmed in by two lines of old three-storey buildings, a mix of shops: groceries, delicatessens, charity, tourists tat, and houses. At the far end of the village a church, raised up from the road and surrounded by a graveyard, was an angular shadow against the clear frosty sky. It was very quiet on the street, there wasn't a soul around, but from behind curtained windows came the muted noise of televisions and music.

'Drink?' Avril wrapped her long multi-coloured shawl around her shoulders and tucked her arms inside. 'The Crown's just down on the left, it's only small, bit old-fashioned but it sells real ale.'

'Great, let's go. I can chance a half.'

Five minutes later they were sitting on large wooden benches alongside a blistering hot fire at the end of a long low-ceilinged room. Their only companions were two old men with flat caps and ruddy faces slumped in chairs nearby and a couple propping up the bar and chatting to the landlord.

'The others should be in shortly,' Avril said, 'it's their favourite haunt. And I want a chat with Georgina about a couple of things.'

Jackie held up her glass; the beer glowed with the light of the fire behind it. A thrill of anticipation ran through her at Avril's words. 'Great,' was all she could say, thinking, wonderful, brilliant, fantastic. Her face burned, it wasn't from the heat of the fire.

'They're all good friends of mine. We often meet here for a drink and a natter.'

'Only friends?' Jackie couldn't resist asking.

Avril surprised herself with her next words. 'There's no one there I'm interested in other than as friends. In fact,' she said, 'there's been no one for years … not since my fiancé, Bill.'

'Bill? Was that the Bill who painted your portrait?' Jackie asked, curious. 'William Durwood? I noticed the signature. Meg said you mentioned he was an artist in one of your emails.'

'Yes.' Avril flushed.

'It's good. How old were you?'

'Eighteen. We got engaged at Uni. Stupid really, we were far too young.' Avril took a long drink before continuing. 'He couldn't cope with,' Avril paused, 'with what happened. He left and I haven't seen him since.'

'Charming!'

'He was actually. The family hated him for what he did ... probably still do.' But that had long since lost its effect on her; after all, he had been her first lover and a secret part of her still treasured that. He'd adored her, she knew that. 'He was just too young to cope with what happened to me.'

'And you weren't?'

'I had no choice, he did.' Please shut up, Avril thought, she didn't want to feel the old acrimonious despair again; she'd gone beyond that.

The pub door opened. Avril looked around, hoping for a diversion, hoping to see the actors crowding in but it was only another old man, face glowing from the cold, unwinding his scarf from around his neck and shuffling towards the bar.

After a couple of moments she said, 'Earlier you said something about a partner? Hazel?' Avril had seen the looks that had passed between Jackie and Georgina.

Ex ... or about to be. Whatever we've had between us has come to an end.'

'I'm sorry.'

Jackie pulled a face. 'It's no problem.'

They drank in silence for a couple of minutes.

'Will your mother worry if you're late back?'

'No.' Jackie plucked at imaginary bits on her jeans and brushed them away with a sweep of her hand. 'We don't get on.'

'You said she won't talk about the drug?'

'No,' Jackie tilted her head back and studied the ceiling. 'She won't even acknowledge she took it.'

'Your father?'

'Left years ago. He was okay; we had great fun. Every year we'd go to Blackpool to see the illuminations. I started being ill after he'd left us. I was in and out of hospital with stomach pains and bad periods for years. She shrugged. 'When I was in my late teens I started seeing a gynaecologist for my endometriosis; had a couple of small ops. Eventually he discovered the connection with Stilboestrol. I tackled Mum about it.' She pulled a face. 'Probably went about it in the wrong way; could have been more tactful, I suppose. It's not one of my strong points, tact,' she acknowledged. Avril smiled. Even though she'd only just met Jackie she could quite believe that. 'I was angry she denied it.' Jackie held her lower lip between her teeth. 'I see my visits to Mum as a penance for not liking her; we're like cats forever prowling round each other.'

'That must be awful. Even though I don't see my mum very often we chat on the 'phone. She's easy to talk to. It's a bit different with Dad. He's not the most talkative of men but I know he loves me, and he's good with Mum. He looked after her when she went through a rough patch … after we found out about the drug.' Avril leaned forward and looked steadily at Jackie. 'I'd like to be part of the group.'

'Fantastic!' Jackie was pleased; in just the few hours since they met she felt they could become friends.

'Listen; if you like you can stay over at mine tonight. It's too late to be travelling across the moors anyway.'

'I couldn't impose.'

'Don't be daft,' Avril didn't feel the usual qualms about having her privacy invaded; she liked this plain-speaking woman. 'Go on, it'll be no trouble, there's plenty of room.'

'If you're sure?' Jackie was tempted, knowing it would give her a chance to find out more about Georgina.

'Yes, I am.'

'Well then, thanks, I will.'

The pub door opened with a swirl of cold air and the group from the theatre hustled noisily in. Immediately the quiet cosiness of the room vanished and was replaced with jubilant vibrancy.

Jackie felt her stomach clench as she caught glimpses of Georgina amongst the group and heard the infectious laugh. She watched as the woman bore down on them shrugging out of her thick red cape and running her fingers through her curly black hair. 'Want another?' she smiled. They locked eyes.

The feeling of being jolted by electric currents made Jackie sit up straight. Even Georgina's voice was enough reason to fall in love with her. She managed to croak, 'thanks.'

'Please.' Avril said.

'I'll join you in a minute if that's okay?' Georgina looked at Jackie.

'Of course.' Jackie moved to one side on the

bench. For a moment the two women kept eye contact. Then, as though satisfied, Georgina nodded and turning, called across to the bar, 'I'll get these.'

Jackie watched as she walked away. She took in a long breath.

To: Avrilbreen@sheepfold.freeserve.co.uk
From: Jacgay@ yahoo.com.
Subject: Hi

Hi Avril,

just got home. Thanks for letting me stay over.

Think Mr Macawber is great - can't believe how much he can talk (and swear, ha ha.)

I always wanted to write but I'd never have the guts to leave a steady income for something I might not be good at. You must have been very sure of your talents.

Something's ticking over in my mind. Can I give you a ring sometime? I've had an idea.

Please give Georgina my regards

Chat soon
Jackie
Ps. Just going to watch the closing of the Winter Olympic Games.

To: Jacgay@ yahoo.com
From: Avrilbreen@sheepfold.freeserve.co.uk
Subject: Ref Hi

Hi Jackie,
Glad you enjoyed yourself- change for me too.
I'm very proud of Mr Macawber, he's good company. The people I bought him from showed me how to train him. Love, trust and rewards (with food -much like his owner!!!)
Had an idea as well after you'd left. Wonder if we're thinking on the same lines. Give me a ring; I'm in every evening this week.
Anyway, must get on with some work. Georgina told me to tell you to please keep fingers crossed for next Wednesday.
Avril

PS Hope you enjoyed the ceremony.

Chapter Twenty - Three -March

DES- The effects on male offspring are still being studied, but there is reasonably consistent evidence of increased testicular cancer and testicular abnormalities in DES sons. The full range of health effects in the offspring has probably not been documented, and attention is now being focused on DES grandchildren. What is already a tragedy may be still unfolding across generations[23]

The heat of Meg's house hit Rachel at once; she could feel the sweat on her hairline.

Jackie prised off her shoes and put them on the mat, next to Rachel's. 'How's Richard? You said on the 'phone he's been ill?' She took Rachel's coat from her. 'Where shall I put these?'

'Here, I'll take them,' Meg said. 'He's much better, thanks, but he's in bed at the moment.' They'd both been awake most of the night but she was glad she had refused to listen to Richard when he had tried to persuade her to put the meeting off and have some rest herself. The last thing she needed was another day to just drift by with nothing to occupy her mind; she felt as if she could climb the walls as it was.

'What was it, 'flu?'

'No, a kidney infection, he gets them now and

---

[23] Public Health Classic: DES Daughters By Dick Clapp posted by The Pump Handle on Oct 9, 2012

then: they clear up with antibiotics but they take it out of him.' Meg took their coats and went into the bathroom to hang them over the shower rail. She poked her head around the doorframe. 'Go on into the living room. Coffee's on a tray on the little table. Help yourself, I'll just check on Richard.'

After a few moments she reappeared. 'He's asleep.' She closed the lounge door quietly and took the cup Jackie handed to her.

Rachel shook her head at the offer of a coffee. 'No thanks, wouldn't mind a glass of water though.'

When Meg returned Jackie said, 'you look worn out.'

'I'm alright, combination of no make-up and lack of fresh air.' Meg sat down.

There was no need to say anything else; they could both see by her bleached face and puffy eyes that she had barely slept.

'It's this bloody awful weather,' Jackie said, going along with the pretence.

'Apparently it was the wettest February since nineteen ninety,' Meg said, looking towards the rain-smeared window. 'Dismal.' Her face clouded for a moment, then she clapped her palms on her knees and leant forward. 'Anyway, never mind all that ... Avril, Jackie?'

'Yeah, Jackie said, 'keen to help. In fact she ... we had an idea. I'll tell you in a minute. Let's just get everything else out of the way first.' She grinned, anticipating their reaction; hoping they'd be as excited as she was when they heard what it was. Taking her glasses and a notebook from her bag she said, 'have we heard from anyone else?'

Rachel sighed, exasperated. Meg looked at her and lifted an eyebrow. Rachel shrugged. Jackie was being infuriatingly secretive about something; "wait 'til we get to Meg's," was all she'd said on the way. "It's worth waiting for".

'Yes,' Meg opened her folder. 'First things first; exciting news.' She took her glasses off the top of her head, positioned them on her nose and reached down the side of the armchair, pulling out a square of paper. 'I spoke to a woman from Birmingham over the weekend; she has a cousin in America.' She began to read aloud. 'She says ... although action groups around the world are not affiliated they will support groups like us, if we'd like them to.' She took off her glasses. 'Obviously I knew about them but because I was really only fighting to get Lisa's case recognised I never thought to contact anybody in other countries.'

'So we'll do that? See how they run things?'

Yes, I think so,' Meg said. 'And in the meantime I think we should get on with what we're doing here.' She paused, fiddling with her glasses again. 'The notices we sent out to the 'papers have had some results; there are more women like us than I ever knew.' She skimmed through her notes. 'You saw I answered that message from Margaret, the woman in London whose daughter was affected? I told her we'd be in touch after our next meeting.'

'Want me to contact her?' Jackie waited, pen poised.

Meg nodded. 'If you would, please; just to see if she just wants to get involved; she seemed a bit wishy-washy about how much she wanted to help. She said they both work full time and thought we'd got the Health Department already on board.'

'Chance'd be a fine thing,' Rachel's mouth wasn't the only thing that felt sour this morning; she was feeling distinctly crabby.

'Email from two sisters, from Pontefract,' Jackie continued. 'They've been battling on their own for recognition for years and they're keen to join in with whatever we're doing. I copied it, and my reply, to the group address.'

'Oh yes, I saw that. And I've had a letter from a man. He says he saw the notice you emailed to his local paper, Rachel. Great to see ideas come to fruition eh?

Rachel smiled; it had been a flash of inspiration. She drank the water, feeling the cold travel down her throat, soothing, cooling. 'What does he say?'

Meg put on her reading glasses and pulled an envelope from her cardigan pocket. 'I'll read it out. He didn't put his address on it and he doesn't want to be involved but he says he just wanted a DES Son's point of view to be acknowledged,'

'Fair comment,' Jackie said.

Meg unfolded the piece of paper.

Hi,

I was exposed to Stilboestrol.

I've been married for over seven years now and we haven't been able to have children. I've felt guilty. Being infertile, I'm the one who's responsible for not being able to have a family. I blame it on my exposure to DES.

When I was fourteen I began to have problems peeing. Eventually it got so bad I had to go into hospital to be catheterized. I stayed in that first time for almost a week. (I didn't realise that it was odd for a bloke to have the opening of the urethra on the underside of the penis- bit embarrassing for a boy of that age to find that out, I must say) Since then I've been in hospital a few times for investigation for cysts which turned out to be with epididymis cysts (they usually go on their own). The last time, earlier this year, the cyst was bigger and painful and I'm not afraid to say I was scared stiff - thinking it was cancer.

Well, I've surprised myself. I just wanted you to know how I feel and to speak for other men like me. I've written more here than I've ever told anyone (except my wife). It felt easier than talking face to face with someone. I feel it's done me good but I wouldn't want anyone to know who I was.

Good luck with your group anyway.

All the best

x

'Hell's bells.' Jackie sat back. 'We didn't think about ... well, I didn't anyway.'

'We should,' Meg said, 'we should have thought about the DES sons.'

'I know,' Rachel said, 'but it's not too late; we can put out emails ... messages to reach them.'

'Shame he doesn't give his name but I can understand why,' Jackie said, 'perhaps they'll be others that will.'

They were quiet for a moment, each lost in their own thoughts.

'I was thinking we should be starting a register for the group?' Jackie eventually said.

'It' a good idea. Need to ask their permission though: data protection and all that.' Meg stood up. 'More coffee? Would you like another glass of water, Rachel?'

'Please.' The sick feeling was subsiding, not before time.

'Hang on a minute first, Meg,' Jackie said, 'there's something we want to ask you.'

Meg sat down. 'Sounds serious?'

'It's to do with the group,' Rachel said, hoping Meg would like the idea.

'We've thought of a name. Actually it's an acronym.' Jackie leant forward and clasped her hands. 'We thought it would be good to call the group Lisa, L.I.S.A. ... it stands for the Legislation for the Investigation into Stilboestrol Association.' She paused, apprehensive. Suddenly it sounded crass. 'If you don't think ...?'

Meg held a breath, puffed it out gently. 'I think,' she said, 'I think that's a beautiful thought. Thank you,' she said, 'thank you ... both of you.'

'It was Jackie's idea really,' Rachel said, relieved. She hadn't realised how concerned she was that the idea would be distressing, like they were meddling in the privacy of Meg and Richard's grief.

'I'll get those drinks.' Meg hurried into the kitchen, her emotions all over the place. Waiting for the kettle to boil, she swilled out the coffee pot and tried to chase down what she was feeling; sadness mixed with a quiet pride, was the best she could identify, and an ever-growing comradeship with the two young women in the other room. What a wonderful, thoughtful thing to suggest. She'd tell Richard as soon as he woke up.

Chapter Twenty-Four

But the story doesn't have to have a sad ending. Now you know this information and you are going to tell your friends and they will tell their friends. Daughters will talk to their mothers, grandmothers and aunts about this part of their medical background. Word will get out, so it really isn't ending. ...

And the story goes on...and on...and on.[24]

'I think that's all for now,' Jackie said, 'we've covered the lot.' She checked her watch. 'Right, about Avril: I hope you don't mind, Meg, but I asked her to ring us here, this afternoon.'

'Okay,' Meg said slowly. She wondered what was coming next. 'Curiouser and curiouser, eh Rachel?' Rachel turned up the corners of her mouth in the semblance of a smile.

'I told her around four o'clock. It's twenty to now, so I've just got time to explain.' Jackie paused. The idea she and Avril had been bouncing of one another over the last fortnight was exciting but now she wondered how the other two would feel. 'You know Avril writes plays?'

'Of course, I saw some scripts on her website,'

---

[24] *Some stories simply do not end ... ever* (Blog – under *Women of a Certain Age* posted 4th November 2011 ©*Lodinews.com, Lodi, CA*)

Meg said, already getting an inkling of where this was going. 'And you said in your last email that you went to see a rehearsal.'

'Yeah,' Jackie said. 'In a local theatre; an amateur group's performing it. They were good. Well, Avril's suggested she writes a play about Stilboestrol.' She hoped the long silence with which her news was greeted was through surprise rather than dissent.

Meg and Rachel exchanged fleeting looks.

Rachel sucked in her lower lip 'Before she rings, Jackie, can *we* talk about it?' She was annoyed; why hadn't Jackie thought to ask her and Meg when Avril first mentioned it. They didn't even know the woman. 'Personally I don't know that it's something we should do; we've only just started our campaign and we've got enough on our plate with that. A play would only be a distraction.'

'We needn't do anything: it would be Avril writing it,' Jackie said, twisting around on the settee to face her. Rachel was looking down at her hands, threading her fingers together, a hank of dark hair hiding her eyes. There was a sheen of perspiration across her top lip. 'What's wrong, Rachel?'

'I just think we should have discussed it between us,' she swept her arm around to encompass Meg and herself, 'first, that's all.'

'I have to agree with Rachel in a way, Jackie, it does take us right away from what we agreed to do,' Meg said, 'I'm really not convinced ....'

'Anyway, wouldn't putting on a play about it make

it appear to be fictional,' Rachel added, 'something made up; not to be taken seriously?'

Damn, Jackie thought, she'd handled this all wrong. Still she persisted. 'Written as a factual drama it would tell an audience what a dangerous thing Stilboestrol has been and still is,' she said. 'Think about it, out in the public arena it would get more attention: it would mean more people would know about it.'

'Would anyone want to see it anyway?' Rachel said, 'it's a very dark subject?'

'Don't you remember that comedy we saw last year at the Playhouse with Year Twelve?' Jackie said. 'The one about the boy with testicular cancer: it was moving and yet it was funny. We laughed but it certainly got a discussion going afterwards.'

'Hmm,'

Jackie saw the stubborn set of Rachel's mouth: she'd seen that expression before at work whenever the Head had tried to bulldoze them into something that was more to facilitate the school budget rather than for the good of the pupils. Rachel could put up a good argument. She felt herself deflate, the rush of enthusiasm gone.

The streetlight outside the bungalow flashed on and then off, before it stayed lit; a dull muddy-yellow colour that cast shadows in each corner of the room. The water in the radiator gurgled as the central heating clicked on at the same time.

Meg stood up and switched on a couple of table

lamps. She'd seen the disappointment on Jackie's face. 'It's not that I'm totally against the idea ...'

'Well, I am,' Rachel broke in, hanging on to her hostility; Jackie made the thought of a play sound almost like fun. As though writing a play about Stilboestrol was something inconsequential.

Meg carried on, '... but I do wish you'd said something before you asked Avril to ring us about it. You haven't given us much time to discuss it, that's all.'

'I'm sorry.' Jackie wished she could have a cigarette but Meg's house was a no smoking zone. 'You both had so much on your plates; I thought it easier if we ... Avril and me ... could put our heads together first so I would be able to...'

'Bulldoze us into it,' Rachel said.

'No, present the idea better.' Surprised by the harshness of Rachel's words Jackie said again, 'I'm sorry, I know I can get carried away sometimes but ...'

Rachel snorted. Stop it, she told herself, stop being such a miserable cow.

'I'm only trying to get as much publicity as possible.' Jackie suddenly felt defensive. She couldn't believe it; she and Rachel hadn't quarrelled before but it looked now as though they were on the verge of a row. 'What exactly is it you object to, Rachel: my talking to Avril first or the idea of a play?'

'Both, if I'm honest,' Rachel said. They sat in silence. Rachel rubbed her hands over her face. 'Oh,

I don't know, it's just all too much.'

'Okay,' Meg said, 'let's not fall out about it. Rachel, how about we listen to what Avril says? Then if you still are against the idea we drop it, yes?' She could see both of the young women were distressed. 'Right, let's not wait for Avril to call, let's ring *her*. Rachel? See what she says, hmmm? Then we'll talk about it.'

Rachel pressed her fingers against her eyes. 'Okay.' The darkness was calming and she was reluctant to move her hands.

'Use our 'phone.'

Jackie scrolled down the address list in her mobile and picked up Meg's telephone.

'Put it on loudspeaker so we can all join in,' Meg suggested, 'it'll be easier that way.'

Jackie nodded as she pressed buttons. After a couple of seconds she said, 'hi Avril, it's me....'

Chapter Twenty-Five

'... I didn't cry anymore. I suddenly felt stronger and able to handle what was coming. At least now I knew what to expect. The monster had an image – it was an image of cancer and of surgery, but I was determined to survive. I had finished crying for now.[25]

'So,' Avril said, 'that's about it. Let me have your stories ... what's happened to you. Then I'll write a draft to you for your approval. There's nothing else you need to do,'

Jackie saw Rachel bridle. No one in the room spoke. They could hear Avril breathing softly into the receiver, waiting.

'We'll need to discuss it between ourselves first, if you don't mind, Avril?' Jackie said.

'Sure.' Avril thought they already had. 'Look, if it's a problem...'

'No , it's not ....' Meg looked deliberately at Rachel, 'I think it could work. If you could just run through it again, Avril?'

'Sure. Four voices ... monologues ... each telling their story ... interspersed with short anecdotes or something like that: like I said, similar format to Vagina Monologues. I know you haven't seen that

---

[25] Excerpt from - *DES Daughter: A True Story of Tragedy and Triumph: The Joyce Bichler Story*© Joyce Bichler Ch4 p 60

play, Meg, but Jackie said she and Rachel have so they can explain it to you afterwards.' They heard the rustle of papers. 'I've spoken to Georgina Lees, she's a first rate director who usually works for the Royal Venue Theatre in Manchester and directs at Lydfield theatre as a favour to me.'

Rachel raised her eyebrows and pulled her mouth down in a scathing gesture.

Jackie ignored her and concentrated on listening to Avril.

'She says she's got four good actors we can get on board. Jackie's seen them in action, haven't you?'

'Yes, and Georgina's a great director,' Jackie added, unable to help herself, 'and a really nice woman.' For 'nice' read 'delectable, gorgeous, fantastic '; she barely controlled the grin as the word leapt unbidden into her head.

Rachel gave her a searching glance but said nothing.

'They're just right for the parts,' Avril said, 'even if they are amateurs. And there are enough in the company for any extra parts. And they won't want paying, there'll be no need for special costumes and the theatre will be happy just to have the takings for the overheads. There's a regular audience; it's one of the few entertainments in Lydfield and well supported. If the play goes any further than that, we'll talk costing then.'

'Suppose there's always sponsorship?' Jackie suggested, striving to lighten the atmosphere. This should have been such an upbeat discussion; why the bloody hell was Rachel being so obstructive?

'Yep, loads of places for help, 'Avril agreed. 'For now let's just take it one step at a time. But after the first run,' Avril said, 'who knows? I've contacts in various places.' She hoped that didn't sound like boasting. The playwright in her had immediately seen how each woman's story could be represented for maximum effect and Georgina had agreed. The more she wrote down ideas for this play the more convinced she was that it would succeed; that it would bring Stilboestrol right into the public arena. 'It's all stewing, albeit slowly. I didn't want to go too far with it before I had your approval.'

There was that silence again, loaded with so much doubt. Perhaps she and Jackie were wrong, maybe this wasn't such a good idea. Avril perched on the back of the settee and looked out of the windows. Small snowflakes fluttered down, a few clinging to the glass before melting. In the distance the corners of the darkening fields still held the last of the drifts, now covered by a crust of grey. She watched Mr Macawber tear the inside of a toilet roll to pieces and throw it around, a satisfied croak each time he tossed his head. She could hear low mutterings at the other end of the telephone.

'Can you give us a few minutes?' Meg asked eventually, ' bit of breathing space?'

'Sure, shall I ring back?' It was a no-go, she could feel it. Ah well, no skin off *her* nose. But it was a shame.

'Please,' Meg said.

They heard the receiver click.

'Right,' Jackie said, 'can we talk about this?' she spoke directly to Rachel. 'Please?'

Ten minutes later they were back on the line to Avril.

'We've got some questions,' Rachel said, her tone clipped.

Avril could sense the antagonism in Jackie's friend. 'Great! Fire away, then.'

'Our stories, could we just write down the facts?'

'Sure, I'll interpret them as I read them;' April spoke with care, 'add my own emotions to them.' No, that wasn't right. 'I mean I'd write as I would feel and then run it past each of you. See what you think ... if it's alright.'

'How soon would you need them?' Rachel wasn't going to let the antipathy go, even if it did make her feel miserable. She refused to look at Jackie. She knew she was being awkward but couldn't stop. 'We've got plenty of other stuff to do, so we haven't much time for this.' Actually she had all the time in the world but she ignored the little voice that reminded her of that fact.

'Well, it's early days.' Avril heard the reciprocal curtness in her own voice. She paused and carried on in a more neutral tone. 'Jackie says you've done some research, Meg?'

'Yes, I was going to ask if you wanted to use some of that.' Meg was relieved there would be little for her to do other than send the stuff to Avril. With Richard as he was she had more than enough to cope with at the moment.

'If you could let me have some of that I can start collating everything.'

'Will do,' Meg said.

'And then let me have your own stories when you can.'

'But we would need to know what's happening,' Rachel said, 'right from the beginning.'

'Of course, I've already said I don't intend carrying the whole burden of the play by myself. I want you on board from the start. It would be brilliant if you could come up here to any of the discussions between everybody who's involved, the read-throughs and especially the rehearsals if it takes off.'

'If,' Rachel murmured. Oh god, it was as if she couldn't help herself.

Avril heard her, recognised again the antipathy, refrained from answering it. 'Look, this is something you started; I wouldn't dream of not consulting with you at every stage. I haven't got enough knowledge about Stilboestrol to do that anyway.'

'What about the women who've contacted us?' Meg said. 'Shall we ask if they'll give permission for their stories to be told? Oh, and we have had a letter from a DES son... could we include something for the sons?'

'No problem; brilliant; I could weave anything into the script.'

Rachel put her hands on her head. Fingers locked she moved her scalp back and forth. The movement eased the tension in her head. 'Okay,' she said eventually, 'in that case ... and as long as the aim is to let the audience know this is a real issue involving women ...'

'And men,' Meg reminded her.

Rachel nodded. '... who are trying at the same time to get on with their lives,' she said slowly, 'I'm in.' She was thoroughly embarrassed, she'd acted in a childish, surly manner. Even feeling ill was no excuse.

'Great,' Jackie released a long breath.

'And me,' Meg stood to draw the curtains, 'I'm in too.'

'Right,' Avril said, 'so I can get on with it?'

There was a chorus of yeses.

As soon as she heard Avril put the receiver down Meg said, 'Well, I never thought we'd sort that. You sure you're alright with it, Rachel?'

'Yes, I'm fine.' Rachel pulled a wry face. 'I just thought we might be biting off more than we could chew.'

'I never expected we'd be involved in making a play about DES when we first got together.' Meg said, 'but I think it'll be exciting. We should have a glass of something to celebrate.'

When Meg had left the room Rachel turned to Jackie. 'Sorry I've been such a grumpy cow.'

'You don't look right, you know' Jackie said, relieved that the awkwardness had passed but still concerned that Rachel seemed totally out of sorts. 'That bloody Captains' Cabin has a lot to answer for.'

'Perhaps you need to get back to the doctors?' Meg suggested, coming back in holding a bottle and some glasses. 'Non-alcoholic, I'm afraid.

'I'm driving anyway,' Jackie stood to help her pour. 'Meg's right, Rache, you should go to the docs, you know.'

'Umm, perhaps I will,' Rachel said. She wouldn't, she'd had enough of doctors to last a lifetime without going back for a trivial stomach upset. 'Anyway, let's not spoil the moment.'

'So, we're all agreed,' Jackie lifted her glass.

Rachel couldn't stop herself throwing out one more concern. 'As long as Avril doesn't take over and do her own thing.'

'You heard her; she said she'll be led by us.' Jackie said.

'And I think if we can get the message over it will do our campaign no end of good,' Meg added.

They clicked their glasses together. 'Cheers.'

'I think it's a fantastic idea,' Jackie persisted, anxious for them both to agree.

'Fantastic, 'Meg murmured.

Rachel hesitated then relented. 'Fantastic,' she

said.

'Fantastic,' Jackie repeated firmly.

They looked at one another and laughed. 'Fantastic!'

Chapter Twenty-Six

All the DES Action groups have met with difficulties in getting awareness from their medical providers and health departments. [26]

To: Jacgay@ yahoo.com
From: Avrilbreen@sheepfold.freeserve.co.uk
Subject: Ref telecom

Hi Jackie,

Blowing a gale here - blocked in with snow and a load of sheep in the garden that should have gone down to the lower field ages ago. Who they belong to I've no idea.

Brilliant that Meg and Rachel were finally ok with the play idea. What was the problem?

Thought of a few titles this morning - Silent Devastation, A Waiting Time Bomb, My Trauma, A Silent Trauma or A Quiet Trauma?

Emailed Meg to say I got all the stuff she sent.

As it's a difficult theme, grateful if any of you have any anecdotes to share

Avril

x

---

[26] *DES Voices From Anger to Action* 2008 © Pat Cody Ch. 12 p 151

From: Jacgay@ yahoo.com
To: Avrilbreen@sheepfold.freeserve.co.uk
Subject: Hi

Hello Avril,

Can't watch anything to do with the 9/11 anymore-depresses me too much, thinking what people can do to one another.

The play - great titles, I'll put my thinking cap on re anecdotes.

No sign of Hazel moving out - bloody awful atmosphere -need to do something about it.

Not sure what the problem was re the play. Rachel's been ill for a few weeks now – food poisoning/virus? And shitty husband problems. And Meg's husband's been ill. Think they were worried about taking too much on.

Piles of homework to mark - groan, groan - and I've been putting it off by watching a reality show about Ozzy Osborne and his family. Absolutely mad, absolute rubbish but sooooo funny ... couldn't tell half off what Ozzy said for all the bleeps.

If you need digging out give us a ring. Look after those sheep!!

Love Jackie

Jackie cradled her coffee mug, holding its comforting warmth against her cheek and re-read the agenda for the next meeting.

Register of members: progress of permission for

*details of addresses etc. to be kept on record.
Emphasise to all who inquire that the group is
membership supported- we will rely on contributions
from members and friends to support our work.*

Jackie put the mug down on the pile of exercise
books she'd been marking earlier and lit another
cigarette from the tab end of the one she'd let
almost burn away in the ashtray.

50 flyers printed: discuss where to distribute

*Record of letters sent and received - as hard copies
as well as emails.*

*Funding. Accountant found who will deal with our
accounts (if we have any!) (He told me to emphasise
donations are tax deductible and that everybody
knows we will make our financial statements
available to the public).*

She leant back and blew a series of smoke rings
then flopped forward and peered at the screen,
grimacing as she read the next listing.

*Progress.   Replies from emails sent. As above
Accountant found/ Bank account set up/ Solicitor
(Jones and Coleman) approached for representation
if needed.*

Not much else so far: initial response to the first
group's letter from MPs had been disappointing to
say the least. She picked up a single sheet of cream
paper with the red portcullis logo at the top on one
side and the MP's name in large bold letters on the
other and read it again, searching for the slightest
sign of empathy. A surge of anger returned as she

picked out phrases.

… only 10,000 women were exposed to Stilboestrol in the UK …. A programme to find these women would create anxiety …. "

Jackie snorted. 'As opposed to the health worries they already have without knowing why?' she said aloud, throwing the letter on top of the folder and crushing her half-smoked cigarette in the ashtray.

It was the concluding words of their MP that riled her the most… I hope this reply was helpful. Insensitive bastard! Jackie jerked back her chair and typed the last item on the agenda.

The play: ask if any of the women who've contacted us would to tell their stories

A car horn made her jump. Hazel? She waited but there was no following click of a door or a key in the lock of the front door. Breathing a sigh of relief she turned back to the computer, scrolling down the emails until she found the one from Georgina.

To: Jacgay@ yahoo.com
From: georginalees@btinternet.com
Subject: play

Hi Jackie,
It was good to meet you, we must keep in touch?
Was she reading too much in that last remark?
Agree with Avril's idea of the monologues - think it will be very effective. I'd like the stage simple, `
Regards Georgina

Regards? Jackie leaned back in her chair and pressed her fingertips to her temples. She gazed around the room. The artificial flames of the gas fire curled blue and yellow around the smooth imitation coal, the slats of thin light through the window-blind showing up the film of dust along the wooden mantelpiece. Regards? Yup, perhaps she was being too hopeful. She typed:

AOB. Anything else that comes to mind, as a last thought.

She worked standing up to print out three copies and clicked back to her emails, earmarking a couple from friends to be read later and deleting five junk mails. Hitting on the 'sent' folder she began to automatically delete outdated messages. It was then she noticed the cursory email with no subject title.

To: Avrilbreen@sheepfold.freeserve.co.uk
From: Jacgay@ yahoo.com.
Subject:

Avril,
Changed my mind. Still in love with Hazel. Don't contact me anymore.
Jackie

Chapter Twenty-Seven

None of the doctors I have seen were really educated about DE, and for the past six years I felt I was in the dark and alone to deal with this frightening phenomenon ... You are working a miracle every day you send out information about DES ... breaking the silence and denial..[27]

Jackie cursed and wrote quickly.

To: Avrilbreen@sheepfold.freeserve.co.uk
From: Jacgay@ yahoo.com.
Subject: Ignore last email

Avril, the last email was NOT from me.
Hazel finally gone too far.
Will explain soon
 Jackie

Her fury propelled her up the stairs. Going into the spare room, where Hazel had slept since Christmas, she stuffed everything she could find into the rucksack and, when that was full, she brought plastic carrier bags from the kitchen and filled those.

---

[27] DES Voices From Anger to Action 2008 © Pat Cody Ch 15 p. 187/8

When she was sure there was nothing left of the woman in either bathroom or bedroom she went downstairs.

Unable to keep still; she paced from fireplace to window, glancing every now and then at the computer and taking angry drags on her cigarette. The room became a fug of warmth and smoke.

One hour, three coffees and four cigarettes later she heard the sharp twist of the key in the lock of the front door. The combination of caffeine and nicotine made her tremble as she listened to the swift footsteps on the stairs and the crash of the bedroom door on the wall. A sick chill settled in her stomach while she waited for the scene she'd avoided for the last three months.

When Hazel bounded downstairs she was still in her uniform. 'What the hell's going on?'

Even from across the room Jackie could smell the alcohol; she must have gone straight from the station to the pub. She pointed to the computer for Hazel to see the emails on the screen

'So?' Hazel folded her arms.

'You had no right to touch my computer, let alone access my emails.' Jackie had never raised a hand to anyone in her life; living with a violent parent had cured her of that. But she knew that if she went near Hazel she would slap her. 'I want you to get out of my house. Now,' she said.

Her stillness seemed to unnerve Hazel at first and then she smiled as though she could sense Jackie's apprehension. Slowly she unbuttoned her jacket, then her blouse. 'You don't mean that.' She let the clothes drop to the floor, her breath quickening, the tip of her tongue curled on the edge of her top lip. 'You're just cross with me and you know what that does.' She unfastened her bra, her small breasts swinging slightly with the movement. Undoing her trousers she stepped out of them. There was strange deliberateness in her actions, as though she was preparing for a fight rather than being sexually enticing.

Jackie took three paces, picked up the clothes and shoved them at Hazel. The hook of the bra scratched the corner of the woman's mouth. 'Get out! Get out now or I'll throw you into the street just as you are.'

'You'll be sorry you did that.' Hazel touched her mouth, licked her lips, face thoughtful. Her expression changed as Jackie turned on her heel and went into the hall. 'Don't go.' Hazel grabbed the back of Jackie's jumper. 'I'm sorry,' she said. 'Honestly. It was a stupid thing to do but you know how jealous I get. I love you. Listen ... we can sort things out, can't we?'

'No,' Jackie said. 'When I come back I want you gone.'

Hazel didn't move but her body tensed, took an aggressive stance. Jackie spun round, made for the kitchen.

'No you don't.' Hazel clutched at Jackie again.

'Get off.'

The smaller women ducked under Jackie's arm and slammed herself against the door looking frantically around.

'Move.' Jackie heard the fear in her own voice, swallowed her panic, it lodged, a lump in her throat

'No.' Hazel's expression shifted. She lunged at the nearest worktop and grabbed the bread knife.

Oh my god; Jackie sidestepped and yanked open the door. Jumping down the step, she ran across the back yard and through the gate into the narrow lane, feeling for her keys in her pocket. Turning the corner at the end of the terrace she ran back up the street towards the Peugeot. Hazel was already waiting at the front of the house, dressed only in her pants but still carrying the knife. She dropped it to the ground and leapt at Jackie trying to wrench the keys from her. The sensation of Hazel's cold bare skin as she clung to Jackie brought a sweep of revulsion over her. Steeling herself against the touch she grasped Hazel's arms and pushed her away. Then she yanked the door open and fell into the car. 'Oh god.' She fumbled with the ignition and handbrake and, stamping on the clutch, rammed the car into gear. The engine turned, faltered and then started. Jackie twisted the wheel and the car lurched away from the kerb, the open door swinging violently.

In the rear view mirror she could see Hazel running in bare feet along the street. She saw her stumble, almost fall. Then she heard the hoarse shout. 'Bitch,' Hazel screamed, 'bitch!'

Silent Trauma

Chapter Twenty-Eight

I wish we did not live in a society that tells us we are nothing without our own biological children. Because I know this is not true ... The glass is half full, not half empty... and it might even be overflowing. Please know that your worth comes from within[28]

It seemed to Rachel that the room became still and hushed.

'How long has it been going on?' she gripped the edge of the sink behind her, her hands cold, clammy and willed herself to stay upright, to push away the darkness that threatened to close in.

Stephen mumbled a reply.

'How long?' she screamed. 'Two years? You've been having an affair for two years.'

They locked eyes.

Stephen moved towards her. 'Sit down Rachel, you look ....'

He had the nerve to look concerned. 'Don't touch me, you bastard. Don't you touch me ever again.' She swayed, her fingers caught the rim of a saucepan on the draining board and, grasping the

---

[28] *DES Voices From Anger to Action* 2008 © Pat Cody: *How it Hurts: the Effects if DES ON Daughters.* Ch.2 p.30, *DES Daughter, Utah*

handle flung it at him.

It hit him full in the face and he sank to his knees, a stream of blood flowing from his nose and down the front of his shirt and tie. His best shirt and tie, Rachel noticed with bitter satisfaction, watching it soak into the white material.

'You stupid cow.' Stephen doubled up, hand cupped over his nose. 'Get me a fucking towel or something.'

Rachel stared at the red drops forming a pattern on the cream floor tiles. She turned and, picking up the dishcloth ran it under the tap and crouched to wipe them away. 'You're dripping all over the floor,' she said with forced calmness. 'Please don't.' She used long sweeping motions so the blood was a pink arc between her and Stephen. 'Lean over the sink.'

'You're sodding mad.' Blood seeping through his fingers Stephen pushed past her to grab a tea towel.

'You're right,' Rachel said, 'I am mad; mad to think I was ever in love with you, mad to believe you loved me. Now get out of my house before I use that ...,' she nodded towards the saucepan which had skidded up against the back door leaving a series of tiny chips in the stone tiles, '... before I use that again.'

'Our house,' Stephen sneered as best he could through the ever-reddening cloth. 'Our bloody house and I want my share of it.' Before he'd finished speaking Rachel was crawling swiftly across the floor towards the saucepan. He half-ran, half-staggered towards the hall. 'Bloody mad cow,' he shouted.

The crash of the front door rattled the kitchen window frame. Upstairs in the bedroom, Jake barked.

The sun slanted across Rachel's face from the window, a pale thin sun, but it felt warm for March and she was reluctant to move. Her crying had been explosive and painful. Now she was exhausted.

The house was quiet, distant traffic rumbled on the by-pass; where was it all going? The thought flickered through her mind before she lost interest. Staring up at the kitchen clock she forced herself to focus. She'd been crouched on the floor for over an hour.

It was Saturday. He must have called on his way to the golf course. The golf club. How had she not known? She'd seen the woman ... girl, Rachel corrected herself; she was no more than a girl; she'd seen her behind the bar at the golf club ever since they had become members two years ago. It hadn't taken him long to make a move.

The floor tiles were cold. It felt like every joint in her body had seized up. She dragged herself up and balanced for a moment before hobbling to the downstairs lavatory. Hand flat against the wall she lowered herself onto the seat.

Pregnant. The word was so loud it was almost as though she could see its repeated imprint on the door in front of her. Pregnant. Pregnant. Pregnant.

Washing her hands she stared at her reflection, her eyes swollen to slits, her mouth a tight line. She remembered what he'd said when she'd protested she wasn't in the slightest bit interested in golf. "It'll do you good," he'd said. "Take your mind off things." Well it had certainly worked for him.

Rachel turned the soap over between her palms. When she dropped it onto the basin, she saw it was squashed into finger shapes. Still watching herself she dried her hands on the sleeves of her blouse. 'She's married too,' she said out loud, the recollection of the last time she'd seen the girl came back to her with such a shock her skin tingled. She remembered the thin gold band and her own resentment on seeing the unmistakable roundness of early pregnancy under the thin tee shirt as she'd reached up to get a glass off the shelf above the bar. A belly filled with Stephen's child!

The doorbell rang. Then rang again: a long insistent clatter. Rachel heard the letterbox creak open. 'Rachel? Rachel, are you there? It's me Jackie,'

Chapter Twenty-Nine

...I'd automatically think, can't wait to be pregnant ... The hard truth would then flash into my mind, reminding me that I was dreaming. No, that won't happen to you. Not ever![29]

'We made love two days before he walked out.' Rachel shredded the sodden tissue clutched in her fist. Jake rested his head on her knee. She stroked his long silky ears. 'Two years, Jackie.' The sob turned into a hiccup, 'and I hadn't a clue. And now she's pregnant,' she wailed. 'How could he, after everything that's happened. How could he?' The question hung in the air. She listened to the pounding of her blood in her ears.

'Because he's a bastard and thinks with his cock!' Jackie came through from the kitchen holding two glasses and with an envelope tucked under her arm. 'Post's come,' she let it drop onto the settee and held out one glass. 'Here, drink this.'

'What is it?'

'Brandy.' Jackie studied her friend; she looked ill.

'That's Stephen's.'

'All the better then. Don't argue; you obviously need it.' Jackie sat on the floor next to the dog. And

---

[29] Excerpt from - *DES Daughter: A True Story of Tragedy and Triumph: The Joyce Bichler Story*© Joyce Bichler 2008 Ch.8 p94

so do I, she thought, the image of Hazel with the knife still vivid. 'Now, tell me exactly what happened.' She listened, rolling the glass between her palms while Rachel talked. Eventually she spoke. 'Unbelievable.'

Jake pawed at Rachel and whined. She reached over to rub her fingers under his chin.

'What are you going to do?' Jackie asked.

'I haven't got my head round it yet.'

'Course not, stupid question.' Jackie knelt up beside her. 'I haven't been much of a mate to you lately, have I?'

'After the way I behaved at the meeting I'm surprised you're here now.' Rachel managed a shame-faced smile. 'I was so awful: I don't know what was wrong with me.'

'Well, I have to say I did think the Aliens had landed and invaded my friend Rachel's body, 'Jackie grinned, 'but I shouldn't have done anything before I'd talked to you and Meg. It was just that I had the idea of the play on the way home.' Not to mention being desperate to keep in touch with Georgina, Jackie acknowledged the thought. She finished her brandy. 'And, strangely enough, when I emailed her about it, she'd had the same idea. I think we both were carried away.'

'I was being stupid. God only knows what Avril thought of me.' Rachel blew her nose and straightened up.

'She'd understand. I know she felt she was a bit

full on with it all. I think you'll like her when you get to know her properly.'

'I'm sure I will.' Since the meeting Rachel had tried to unravel why she had reacted so forcefully against the idea of a play. She'd justified her instinctive dismissal of it: that it was so awful a subject that no one would want to see it, but underneath she knew she was jealous. The instant friendship that had sprung up between Jackie and Avril became suddenly obvious to her and she'd been angry and upset that yet another part of her life seemed to be shifting under her feet. However much she tried to tell herself she was being pathetic, it made her realise how much she'd relied on Jackie's support.

As though she could read her mind Jackie said, 'we'll always be mates, you know, whatever.' She smirked. 'We are far too intelligent to fall out over trivialities.'

Rachel laughed, 'well, one of us is.' Suddenly serious she said, 'everything gets to me these days,' she said, 'and I know it sounds like an excuse but I can't seem to pick myself up.'

'Understandable, with what that bastard's put you through.' Jackie sank back on her heels and shoved Jake's hindquarters, encouraging him to stop leaning against her. She stood up and drained her glass. 'Another?'

No thanks, I don't really like brandy.' Rachel put the untouched drink on the floor. 'You have one though.'

'Sure?'

'Course.'

When Jackie returned Rachel said, 'I am so fed-up with talking about my problems.' She pushed aside the mental picture of Stephen and his lover: it was too painful. Like the future. Whenever she thought about that, a mass of fears filled her head. 'Let's talk about something else, shall we?' she said, opening the envelope. 'I'm in need of a good laugh, the film on at The Taliesin is supposed to...' Her voice faltered.

'What is it?'

Rachel didn't speak, nausea swilling around her stomach and threatening to rise. She gazed mutely at Jackie, the sheet of paper quivering in her hand as she handed it over.

'Rachel?' Jackie took the letter. 'What is it?' She skimmed the page. 'What does it mean?'

Stephen's stopped his pay going into the joint account.'

'He can't just do that, surely' Jackie said.

'Rachel moved her head; it seemed he could do anything he wanted. How had she ever thought she knew him? When she spoke Jackie could barely hear her. 'How could he? After everything else he's done, how could he?' She stared at Jackie. 'What am I going to do?' The bile that flooded her mouth was sour. Without thinking she took the glass of brandy Jackie that held out and took a large gulp of it. 'I'm only getting half my pay now, what happens when it stops altogether? Sick pay won't even begin to cover everything.'

'You get yourself a solicitor and you bloody fight him for some maintenance. '

'How can I? On what grounds?' The fear refused to subside; it filled every cell in her body.

'On the grounds you're his wife and he's been playing away from home. You're not going to let him get away with it.' Jackie read the letter again. 'This says you have to go into the bank as soon as possible.' They could at least have had the decency to ring Rachel first. 'Why the hell didn't they tell you Stephen had stopped his salary going in? Why let it get to this stage?' She read out, '"not enough funds to cover the direct debits." Inconsiderate idiots.' If Stephen was standing in front of her right at this minute she'd kill him. Rage coursed through her. 'Ring them,' she said. 'Ring them now and make an appointment. I'll come with you.' She sat on the cream leather settee next to Rachel and put her arm around her. 'And at the same time I'll transfer some money in from my account to tide you over.'

'No, I'll use my savings.' What little there was. She couldn't allow Jackie to do that; her pride wouldn't let her.

'No arguing.'

'You're a good friend but no,' Rachel squeezed Jackie's hand. 'I'm sure it'll get sorted. Somehow.' She didn't know how, but somehow.

'It will be if you see a solicitor and pretty damn

quick. So, ring the bank and make that appointment and then get on to your solicitor.'

Rachel put the telephone down. 'That's it then, they'll both see me tomorrow: the bank in the morning, solicitors at three o'clock.'

Jackie stood up. 'I think you could do with a bit of fresh air.' She pushed herself off the settee and held out her hand. 'Come on, we're going for a walk.' At the mention of 'walk' Jake bounced around the room, his long tail rhythmically hitting the furniture.

'Oh no, I don't want to go out.' Rachel protested over the top of his barking, holding her hands to her hair. 'I don't want anyone to see me looking like this.'

'Put some slap on,' Jackie studied her, ' and a hat; you look like Bob Geldof.'

'Well, thanks a lot.' Rachel managed a laugh.

'It'll do you good.' She finished Rachel's drink; the warmth of the alcohol in her stomach was invigorating. 'Come on.' She went to get a hat and coat for Rachel from the cupboard in the hall. 'These do?' she asked.

'No, he bought those for me last winter.' Rachel was peering into the mirror on the wall. 'Oh God, look at me! I'd much rather stop in, Jackie.'

'Jake needs to let off some steam by the look of him. Come on, we can go along the river; there'll not be many people about today.'

Rachel sighed. 'You won't give up, will you?'

'Nope.'

'You win. There should be a black coat at the back of the cupboard and I'll wear my woolly hat if I really have to go.'

'You do. We do.' Jackie fastened her jacket. 'Like I said, sweetie, put some slap on and let's get out.'

Chapter Thirty

"Tell your children" and "Ask your mother" are two DES Action slogans[30]

They huddled into their coats against the chilly wind. Jackie was right; they'd met no one so far on the path alongside the river. Bloated by the constant rains over the winter the water flowed swiftly, high on the banks, sometimes overflowing so that the two women were forced to negotiate trails of mud, which Jake joyfully paddled through until his legs and belly were caked.

'Do you want to turn back?' Jackie said finally, an ache in her pelvis lurked, auguring real pain. 'That dog'll need a bath.' They were holding onto one another, balancing precariously on stones in the middle of a large puddle. 'This is a bit daft now. And we've been out a while: it'll be getting dark in another hour.'

Rachel turned around and leapt towards a drier patch of earth. 'About time,' she said in relief,' I thought you'd never suggest it.' Still, it felt good just to be out of the house, she thought. She waited for Jackie to catch up with her and they linked arms and walked along the path, each absorbed in their own thoughts. 'How're things with Hazel?' Rachel said in

[30] DES Voices From Anger to Action.2008 © Pat Cody *Breaking the Silence: Testimony from DES Parents* Ch.13 P164

the end.

Jackie hunched her shoulders deeper into her jacket. 'I'm sorting it.' She'd decided not to tell Rachel what had happened earlier; she was ashamed to admit that Hazel scared her sometimes; after all, she stood head and shoulders above the woman.

'She's no good for you.'

'I know.' Jackie pressed Rachel's arm closer to her side. 'It's all bollocks this relationship business.' She gave an ironic chuckle. 'How about we become celibate sisters and live together in your house?'

'What and leave your place to Hazel?' Rachel put her head to one side, pretending to be considering Jackie's proposal.

'Well, it's either that or you give yours to Stephen.'

'We could make it a condition they have to live together.'

'With a bit of luck they'll kill one another,' Jackie said. 'It'd solve a lot of problems.'

''They would too; Stephen's always hated her ... ever since the first time you brought her to our house.' Rachel said. 'I bet he hates me now. I can't believe I threw that saucepan at him, I think I broke his nose.'

'Serve him right.' Jackie stopped and faced her. 'You deserve better.'

'Do I? I don't know. I've been a pretty miserable failure of a wife.' Rachel's face crumpled. 'I can't believe he's been so cruel.'

'But he has,' Jackie said. 'He has, and the more you remember that the stronger you'll be. He's not worth it, love, and whatever he says about wanting the house, or even half his share of things, you tell that solicitor to sodding fight for everything you can get.'

They began to walk again.

'You're right; but ...'

Jackie interrupted, 'I am. No buts. Do as your Auntie Jackie says, expert on all relationships ... not!' she said, turning her mouth down in a self-mocking gesture. 'No, really, love, do what you want. I don't mean to be so bossy. Just do what you think is best for you. If you truly want Stephen back, fight for him ...even if he is an out and out waste of space. No ... no,' she shook her head. 'Sorry, I didn't mean that.'

Rachel gave a short laugh. 'Not much, you didn't. And I'll be damned if I'll make it easy for him ... or her.' She watched two mallards struggle through weeds up the banking on the far side of the river. 'But it might have been different if I'd managed to hang on to one of the babies.'

'I've told you before; it's not your fault.'

'I know ...' Rachel's voice trailed away. 'It's just ....'

'You can't take the blame, Rachel. Let me tell you something; you think you've failed because of what's happened but you haven't ...'

'I just wish ....'

'You wish things were different?'

'Yes.'

'Well, years ago, so did I. All the time: when my Dad walked; when my mother refused to take me to the doctor's to find out what was wrong with me; when she wouldn't talk about Stilboestrol,' Jackie paused for breath, 'when I've been crippled with pain from the endometriosis. And you know what? It didn't make one bit of bloody difference. So forget it, it's not your fault. And that's all you have to remember.'

'Will you come in for a cup of tea? Or a drink?' Rachel pushed open the gate to let the dog into the garden and looked up at the house. With no lights on it was dark and unwelcoming.

'No, I won't, thanks. Like I said, I've things to sort out.' Jackie stopped by the side of her Peugeot, one hand on the roof as she leant to unlock it. 'I'll call for you tomorrow?'

'No, honestly I'll be alright on my own.'

Jake bounded towards the front door and barked.

'If you're sure?'

Rachel nodded. 'I've got to do this on my own.'

'Okay but remember, the offer of the money stands, just let me know.'

'I'd rather not.' Rachel was embarrassed; it was usually Jackie who was strapped for cash. She'd never really had to worry about money before. Now the thought of it resurrected the worry. 'If I did take you up on it I'd pay it back with the usual rate of interest.'

'Crap!' Jackie said crisply.

'Succinct and to the point as usual, my friend.'

They laughed; one forced, one genuine.

'Night then.' Jackie settled into the driver's seat.

'Night.' Rachel opened the front door and immediately switched on the hall light.

'Ring anytime.'

'Yeah, thanks.' Closing the door behind her she shut the dog in the kitchen, ignoring the mud he was scattering around the kitchen, and went to the top of the stairs. She gathered up Stephen's clothes and carried them down and through the house and out into the back garden.

Then she found a box of matches.

Chapter Thirty-One

I think it's important to realise that DES did shatter myths/paradigms, particularly the thalidomide paradigm of all harmful effects of exposure show up immediately (as in birth effects) – DES story shows there can be multiple, latent harmful effects that manifest years later.[31]

Jackie tapped her fingers on the steering wheel and watched all the house lights being switched on. 'Please get some backbone, kiddo, 'she murmured. It seemed to her that the guilt from losing the babies had made Rachel particularly weak when it came to Stephen and his moods. She was going to need all her strength for this next fight.

The low whistle and draught of air blowing into Jackie's face when she pushed open the front door of her own house took her by surprise. She dropped the keys on the back of the chair in the living room and looked round. Everything appeared to be normal but there was something wrong. It was too quiet. And freezing cold.

The promised pain in her stomach and lower back was a reality now; she knew it would get worse as

---

[31] Quoting Marion Vickers: DES Action Australia

she got nearer the date of her next period; it always did, but this last month she felt it had never entirely gone away. She tried to relax the muscles in her stomach. When the latest spasm subsided to a dull ache she walked with slow wary steps into the kitchen.

The back door was wide open. It was dark now, except for the occasional light from the upstairs windows of the line of houses across the back alley. A train on the line behind the industrial estate on Stamford Road rattled by, a dog barked, a man and woman laughed as they walked unseen past the back gate. Jackie shivered, closed and locked the door.

Turning slowly she noticed the draining board cluttered with crockery and cutlery. The knife was not on the table. Was it still on the pavement outside? Or not?

The pulse in her throat raced as she crept back through the living room. She tilted her head, sure that Hazel was somewhere still in the house, waiting. Waiting with the knife? Jackie gritted her teeth and refused to acknowledge the small voice in her head that urged her to leave. Prising off her shoes, she forced herself up the stairs, stopping and listening at every creak of the treads. When she finally reached the landing she realised she couldn't let go of the banister: the bedroom doors were ajar, the bathroom door was closed and she was afraid to move. She pressed a hand to her waist. Hazel could be waiting for her behind one of them, knife raised. All she could hear was the hollow drip of water in the lavatory cistern. 'Hazel?' her voice was hoarse as though she hadn't used it for ages. 'Hazel? Are you up here?'

The ends of her fingers tingled as she gently

pushed the door to the spare room. The rucksack and bags were still on the bed. The door caught on something and stopped. Jackie forced herself to look. One of Hazel's shoes, left out in the frenzied packing, lay, sole upwards on the floor.

The room was empty. She let a small breathy laugh escape.

But her scalp tightened when she hesitated outside their bedroom. Half - expecting to see Hazel hiding, she peeped through the line of vision between the hinges before stumbling against it in shock. The wardrobe door swung open. Empty hangers lay around the floor. Her clothes were shredded and strewn about. Drawers upturned, spilling out their contents. Her pillow and the duvet had been slashed open and feathers, disturbed by Jackie's presence, floated in the air. One blade of an open pair of scissors was stabbed into the carpet.

Jackie backed out, whipping round when she heard a tiny noise, a moan. It came from the bathroom. 'Hazel?' Jackie put the heel of her hand on the door and pushed.

Hazel was slumped on the floor, still undressed, her head at on odd angle resting on top of the lavatory bowl, her eyes half closed, her fingers loose around the large carving knife. At her side lay a bottle of whisky and a small brown bottle, five white tablets spilled out; Jackie's own tablets; the pain killers the specialist prescribed for her endometriosis; strong pain killers.

The front of Hazel's shirt was covered in the vomit that was also sprayed over the blue floor tiles. The smell was stomach churning.

'Stupid bitch. Stupid, stupid bitch.'

Kicking the knife away Jackie put her hands under the woman's armpits and turning her face from the stench, hauled her up until she could hold her by the waist. Hazel flopped like a rag doll, whimpering. 'Put your fingers down your throat. Come on.' Jackie yelled, pushing the back of Hazel's head down towards the lavatory.

'Fuck off.' She waved her arms, feebly hitting out at the air.

'Fingers down your throat or I'll do it.' Jackie swung her around to get a better look at her, sliding on the splattered vomit. Hazel's face was pale, glistening with sweat and her eyes rolled in their sockets.

When she finally focussed on Jackie they were dark with hatred. 'Fuck off,' she mumbled before her knees collapsed again.

'Oh, sod it.' Jackie balanced them both over the side of the bath and, grimacing, shoved her own fingers into the woman's mouth. Hazel gagged and shook her head, trying to free herself. Jackie followed the movement, pushing further against the back of the throat. There was another shuddering heave and the contents of Hazel's stomach spewed over Jackie's hand and down the side of the bath.

When it was finally over they slid to the floor. Hazel began to cry, holding on to Jackie, her face pushed against her breast. 'I'm sorry, I'm sorry.'

Shuffling back on her knees and wiping her hands on the front of her trousers Jackie reached into her jacket pocket for her mobile. Flicking it open, she jabbed at the buttons. 'Ambulance,' she said.

Chapter Thirty-Two

DES: Still around in 1987 and - OOPS! - 10 times too strong!!! (A) recall notice appeared in Australian national daily newspapers on 30 November 1987. As we commented at the time, any strength of Stilboestrol is too strong![32]

'You're a friend of Hazel's?' The elderly couple in front of Jackie could almost have been twins, both small and round with glasses and grey hair. The woman's thin lips were pursed in puzzlement. 'Jackie, you said?'

Jackie nodded. Her eyes were gritty with exhaustion. She rubbed them with her knuckles and stretched her back against the hard plastic hospital chair she'd been sitting in for most of the night. She'd perched for hours, her stomach knotting with tension and pain, on a similar chair amongst the pandemonium of the waiting area of the accident and emergency department. Squashed between drunks she'd felt the underlying hostility from the people around her and the tense efficiency of the staff, watchful in the centre of the chaos of bustle and raised voices. The man on her right, violently challenging anyone who came near him, was

---

[32] DESPATCH: Newsletter of DES Action Australia 57 Winter 2012

eventually taken away by the police and the one on her left swayed increasingly, backwards and forwards, until he fell onto the floor to be ignored by everyone.

Jackie was worn out, partly from lack of sleep but more so from the constant stomach cramping and had neither energy nor patience for the antagonism that emanated from Hazel's parents. 'That's right, Mrs Hewitt.' She'd been waiting for them to arrive since she'd 'phoned them late into the night, expecting they would drive from London straightaway but they'd been oddly reluctant and it wasn't until the third telephone call that they'd agreed to come.

'Hazel never mentioned you.' The mother's tone was dismissive.

Jackie looked up at the woman. Dressed in a belted fawn raincoat and maroon cloche hat she was an identical older version of her daughter. Jackie shrugged, 'there's nothing I can to do about that.' She was tempted to tell her exactly what her relationship with their daughter had been but held back. She moved her head from shoulder to shoulder, stretching her neck. 'Look, I've explained what happened. If you want to know anything else the doctor who's been looking after Hazel is Doctor Vellupillai. Ask at the desk.' She nodded towards the table in an alcove off the corridor, 'they'll get him for you.'

'Don't know what all the secrecy's about.' Hazel's

father spoke for the first time. Jackie was aware he'd been studying her suspiciously.

'There's no secrecy. I told you, she overdosed; she took some tablets with whisky.'

'Yes, but you haven't said why.' He demanded, the roll of flab spilling over his collar jiggled when he jerked his chin upwards. 'And you haven't said why, if you were at her house, why you didn't stop her.'

Jackie's control finally snapped. 'If you'd listened, I told your wife. It's my house. Hazel lived with me at my house.' She shot him a furious look.

It was as if he hadn't noticed. He pulled his top lip in, nibbling on the ends of his moustache. Suddenly he said, 'you're one of them, aren't you?'

'I beg your pardon?'

'A lezzy, butch, a queer?'

Jackie took in a long breath of air. 'Whatever.'

'What? You lived with Hazel and you're ....' Mrs Hewitt looked at her, eyes sharp behind the lens of her spectacles.

'Gay,' Jackie nodded, 'or, as your husband so succinctly put it, 'a lezzy, butch, a queer. And, by the way,' she paused for affect, 'so is your daughter.' She enjoyed their dumbfounded expressions. 'So now you know, I'll be off. I would have thought you'd have been more concerned with going back in to see your daughter rather than discussing my sexuality.'

They'd spent barely five minutes by Hazel's bedside. Uncertain what to do she'd waited outside the small side ward and was just about to leave when they'd marched out of the room and begun firing questions at her.

'Jackie?' Relieved, she heard Rachel's voice and footsteps. 'Sorry, love, I only just got your messages, have you been here all night?' She hugged Jackie. 'You okay?' She held Jackie at arm's length and gazed at her. 'I thought at first you were going to tell me the pains had got worse and you'd been admitted. When I realised it was Hazel ... what happened?' Becoming aware of the antipathy coming from the couple standing in front of her, she wrinkled her forehead. 'Who...?'

'Hazel's parents,' Jackie said shortly.

Rachel held out a hand that was ignored. Hazel's mother fussed inside her handbag, clipping it shut without producing anything. She shuffled her feet, her sensible lace-up shoes squishy on the tiled floor. The man concentrated on stuffing his flat cap into the pocket of his matching tweed jacket before glaring at her. 'Are you another one?'

'Another what?' Rachel looked from him to Jackie.

'He wants to know if you're gay ... a lesbian.' Jackie's tone was laconic. 'I think, *they* think it's catching.' She almost giggled when she saw Rachel's face take on a look of complete bemusement.

Rachel looked from one to the other. 'What?'

'They can't believe Hazel's gay, that we were partners.'

The man's face was puce. 'She was ... normal, when she was at home.'

Jackie laughed but Rachel now flushed with anger; who did these people think they were? 'I think you'll find that your daughter has never been normal. She is the most difficult unbalanced woman I have ever met. And she has a violent temper. If you don't know that, then you don't know your daughter.' She put her arm around Jackie. 'Come on, love, you've done your bit for these people. Let them take over now.'

'We just want to know why she did this. What did you do to her?' he called after them.

Jackie stopped and swung round but all she said was, 'Nothing, I did nothing to her except to tell her she was impossible to live with but I suspect you already know that. I honestly do hope she's okay but I don't want to see her ever again. I'd be grateful if you'd pick up her things from my,' she emphasised the word, 'my house … sometime soon. The address is on her notes. Let me know when you're coming for them.' Linking arms with Rachel she kissed her on the cheek as they turned to leave. 'That'll give them something to think about,' she muttered, 'let's hope they'll be only too glad to insist their innocent little daughter goes home with them before she's completely corrupted.' she grinned at Rachel, then stifled a yawn.

'Let's get you home to my place for now.' Rachel pressed Jackie's hand. 'You look knackered. Just be glad it's all over and done with.'

A young doctor came towards them reading a sheaf of notes. He looked up and smiled, despite the dark shadows under his eyes.

'Doctor Vellupillai.' Jackie smiled back, a flash of memory; the quick efficiency of his movements, the revolting sounds of gagging from Hazel as they pumped out the contents of her stomach, coming back to her as he nodded recognition. 'I'm going home now.' She tossed her head back, indicating the two people. 'Ms Hewitt's parents,' she said. 'They're anxious to talk to you.'

'Bye then,' he said, straightening his shoulders and lengthening his stride.

'Poor kid, he looks knackered.' Jackie looked back at him.

He'll have his hands full with those two.'

'I know.' Jackie hung back for a second or two. 'Do you think ...?'

'No,' Rachel pulled on her arm, 'not your problem any more.'

'You're right, thank god,' Jackie smiled wearily 'Come on let's get out of here.'

To: Jacgay@ yahoo.com.
From: Avrilbreen@sheepfold.freeserve.co.uk
Subject: All OK?

Hi Jackie,
Everything ok?
Avril
x

To: Avrilbreen@sheepfold .freeserve.co.uk
From: Jacgay@ yahoo.com.
Subject: Re: All OK?

Hi Avril,
Yep, sorry about the drama. One of Hazel's stupid games. Anyway she's gone now. Much relieved. Will tell you about it sometime
Jackie
x

Chapter Thirty-Three

We are now calling for a public health enquiry to understand:

What action has been taken? What knowledge the government has had at various stages? How decisions were taken to address the needs of this group?

How many people are still affected? What future requirement there may be outstanding in order to ensure people's lives are improved and protected?[vi33]

'So you don't think I should say anything to Rachel when they arrive?' Meg fidgeted with the thick floral curtains then sat on the broad ledge of the bay window and stared out at the avenue. The privet hedges around the garden dripped wetly on the winter grass, the sedum heads were a dark rusty brown and the chopped off branches of the rose bushes had yet to start sprouting new life. It wasn't raining now but it was still depressing.

'I really wouldn't, love.' Her husband spoke from behind his newspaper.

'It sounded such an awful argument; the man was shouting and she sounded so upset. I feel so

[33] DES ACTION U.K NEWSLETTER NUMBER 26 NOVEMBER 2006

ashamed, Richard; I just drove off.' Meg remembered the angry voices; it made her feel queasy.

'What could you have done, Meg? If she was arguing with her husband she'd have been mortified if you'd turned up at the door.'

'Perhaps.' Meg tried to think how she would feel if it was her and Richard. Only he never shouted at her, he hated arguments. Except for those few months after Lisa died. She shut out the memory.

'You went back to check if she was alright,' Richard said firmly. 'You went back, Meg, you didn't just leave it. And when you got there you saw Jackie going in the house, didn't you?'

'Well, yes.' She recalled the relief mixed with the sense of shame that she had done nothing.

'You're getting worked up for nothing, love.'

'What if she saw me?''

'Meg, stop it.' Richard lowered the paper and looked over his glasses at her, exasperated. ' Stop fretting. If they want you to know anything one of them will tell you when they get here.' His forehead crinkled. 'Is that all that's bothering you? You've been really jumpy lately.'

'I'm fine.' She couldn't, wouldn't tell him of the fear that had haunted her over the last few weeks, fear that returned each time he was ill, the worry tinged with guilt. 'And you're right,' Meg smoothed down the wayward clump of hair at her crown. I'm fussing over nothing.'

'Yes, you are. Now, shall I make a brew?'

'I'll do it.' Meg dropped a kiss on the top of his head and went into the kitchen. But her stomach still felt hollow. She trusted Richard's judgement but he hadn't been there; he hadn't heard the yelling, the language. Whatever he said, she'd have to tell Rachel she was there.

She brewed the tea and, restless, wandered back into the living room. 'Music?' she said, 'bit of Holst? '

Richard took his glasses off. 'Lovely.' He could see she was still upset. 'Wait and see if anything's said, Meg?'

'Perhaps,' Meg said eventually, selecting a CD. 'I know you're right,' she closed her eyes listening to the opening bars, 'it's just that I've become quite close to both of them.' She turned quickly towards him. 'Fine,' she said, 'I won't interfere.'

'I didn't mean ...' Richard's protest ended as her lips were planted firmly on his.

'I know,' her voice was muffled against his face. He could feel her smile. 'Why do you always know best?'

'Just a talent I have,' he said, coming up for air. 'Now where's that tea?'

But when they arrived Meg saw the weariness in Jackie and the layers of despair and fear under the veneer of Rachel's smile.

Jackie nudged the living room door open. 'How're

you, Richard?'

'Fine,' Richard dropped his newspaper on the floor and tilted his head back to look at them. 'Come in, come in.'

'Hi, Richard,' Rachel peered over Jackie's shoulder. 'I love this,' she indicated the Hi-Fi, 'one of my favourites.' Despite her efforts to appear normal, the tremor in her voice betrayed her.

'Saturn; The Bringer of Old Age,' he joked, 'think Meg's trying to tell me something.' He hid a fake yawn. 'And being an old codger, I think I need a lie down.

They watched him skilfully manoeuvre off the settee and into his wheelchair and moved aside so he could leave the room. 'See you in a while.' He touched Meg as he passed her.

'I'll bring your tea in, in a minute,' Meg said. 'Sit down,' she glanced from one to the other of the women; they were both pale. 'Tea – Brandy – or there's wine?'

'Brandy would be good.' Jackie nodded briefly

Rachel sat on the edge of the settee. 'If it's red I'd love a wine.'

'It is.'

'Great.'

They were talking in low tones when Meg carried the tray in. Jackie took it from her and put it on the occasional table between the armchair and the settee.

'Hope we didn't chase Richard off,' Rachel said.

She'd seen the glance between him and Meg and knew, by leaving the room; he was being tactful about something. Her headache throbbed.

'Not at all, I'm glad he decided to have a rest, it'll do him good,' Meg handed out the drinks. 'There's something I need to tell you Rachel.' Her voice was almost inaudible as she sat opposite them. 'I called round to your house last week. I was in Beddgaron and I thought I'd just say hello.' She licked her lips. 'But when I got there I heard shouting. An argument.' She cleared her throat; she couldn't tell what Rachel was thinking: her face was expressionless. 'I didn't know what to do.' She looked down. 'I left; I thought it was none of my business.' She pushed her hands into her cardigan pocket and wrapped it around her. 'But I was worried so I came back,' she said, 'then I saw Jackie arrive and you answered the door.' She glanced at them both. 'Once I knew you were alright, Rachel, I left again.' Neither of them spoke; Jackie opened her mouth as though she was going to but after a sideways look at Rachel, she pressed her lips together. 'I feel awful,' Meg said. Rachel looked dazed, brittle. 'I knew I should have knocked, made sure you were alright.'

There was a long pause before Rachel said, 'it was Stephen.' The thought of Meg hearing the words that they had hurled at one another was mortifying. 'There would have been nothing you could have done. He came to tell me he has a lover and she's having a baby,' she said flatly. 'No, don't,' Rachel held out her hand as Meg seemed about to cross the space between them. 'Don't, Meg, please, no pity, I couldn't stand it,' she tried to smile but the next words came out as a thin wail. 'I have enough self-pity without anyone else feeling sorry for me.'

Jackie gave Meg a comforting smile, shaping her lips into a silent, 'don't worry, it'll be okay.'

Grateful, Meg closed her eyes, acknowledging the support.

The music played quietly in the background.

Eventually the hiccupping gulps stopped. 'Sorry,' Rachel gave them a weak smile. 'I kept saying to myself he'll come back, this is as bad as it gets, hold on. But it just gets worse.' She took in a great shuddering gulp of air. 'She's pregnant and I'm not.' The despair was raw in her voice. 'She ... they'll have a baby and I won't. I can't stand it.' There was nothing either of them could say. She wiped her eyes. 'I'm alright, really. I'll be fine.'

'You will be; you're strong.' Meg remembered the months Rachel had sat with her mother at the hospice, knowing she was dying: never allowing herself to cry until she'd left her bedside. 'Look, I made a curry earlier. I could boil some rice in ten minutes?' Rachel and Jackie exchanged glances. 'With Richard in bed I'll be glad of the company.'

'Well, ' Rachel blew her nose, 'that would be nice.'

Jackie needed no persuasion. 'I'll nip to the

supermarket and get a couple of bottles of wine..'

'No, don't bother; we've got some in the kitchen.'

'Then I vote we leave the meeting for another day.'

Jackie carried the tray into the kitchen. The others followed.

'You shouldn't be lumbered with my problems,' Rachel said, pulling out a chair. 'We haven't known one another that long. You must think I'm completely dysfunctional.'

'Nonsense,' Meg said. She filled a saucepan with water and put it on the hob. 'It's not your fault and I'm glad you felt able to confide in me. Besides, one of the reasons we got together was to help and support one another.'

'I know but that's different, that's because of Stilboestrol ... not my messy personal life.'

'We all have messy lives one way or the other.'

'Do you, Meg. Do you feel your life's messy?' Jackie opened the bottle of wine Meg handed to her. She and Richard seemed so positive about the future despite what had happened. Yet, there was something she couldn't put her finger on.

Now, Meg said to herself, tell them now; tell them the truth. Tell them how, every time Richard is ill you're terrified of being left alone with the guilt. How selfish that sounded.

'I have the feeling today that something's wrong,' Rachel said, 'and I don't think it's just that about hearing me and Stephen.'

The water began to bubble and steam. Meg poured the rice into it and stirred. 'Perhaps I haven't managed to hide things as well as I usually do.' She rested the spoon on the edge of the saucepan and, without turning around, waited for one of them to ask.

'If it's too upsetting just tell us to mind our own business.' Jackie began to pour the wine. 'Rachel?'

'No thanks, I'll stick to water.' Rachel said, fumbling for the right words to say to Meg. 'I think we'd both like to help … if we can.' She glanced up at Jackie who closed her eyes in a slow blink of agreement.

Meg sank onto the chair opposite Rachel and picked up the glass Jackie put in front of her. 'I've been meaning to tell you for a while.' She spoke carefully. 'You're always so sympathetic about us; about me and Richard, about Lisa, about the accident. You need to know the truth.' She looked at both of them. Hesitated. 'The accident was my fault. We were arguing. We were always arguing.' Her eyes were blank. 'Bitter, nasty quarrels: blaming one another for not seeing what was happening to Lisa. We almost split up afterwards … after she died. We'd waited so long to have her.' The pain swelled inside her, made it difficult to take in air. 'She was so precious … such a bright bubbly little girl. When she grew older we were close, we could talk about anything. *You* must know what I mean, Rachel; I saw you with your Mum.'

Rachel gave her a tentative smile and nodded, even though the memory hurt. 'Yes.'

Jackie flinched; Meg wouldn't have meant to stress the comparison between her relationship with her mother and what Rachel had had with hers.

'But when we found out she was ill, she changed,' Meg continued, 'she shut herself off from us. It was a bad time. They said there was no proof Stilboestrol had caused the cancer. We tried so hard to get her to talk; to us, to the doctors ... we even asked her to talk to her friends but she became so angry, furious with us for even mentioning it; she didn't want anybody to know.' Meg blinked rapidly. 'She was ashamed.'

Jackie looked around, reached over to the kitchen roll and ripped a sheet off and gave it to Meg.

'Richard found her, you know,' Meg whispered. 'We'd had the letter with the date for her operation. She was even quieter than usual. She'd been out the evening before ... with some of her friends we thought at the time.' She swallowed through the tightness in her throat and forced herself to continue. 'But when we spoke to them at the funeral we found out they hadn't seen her for ages. She'd come home really late, drunk. We didn't say anything; we thought she wanted us to leave her alone; to deal with it herself. We were wrong.' The embers of their bitterness flared in Meg for a second and then settled. 'She hardly said a word the next morning. We encouraged her to stay in bed.'

She struggled for the right words to carry on, then simply said, 'After she killed herself we were in limbo for ages; we didn't know what to do. Then the rows started. I hated Richard.'

Neither of the other two women could stop the shock from showing; they exchanged glances.

'That day he'd persuaded me to go out for lunch and then for a long walk. We used to walk a lot in those days, always had. When Lisa was little he used to carry her in a chair thing,' she wafted vaguely in the direction of her shoulder.' On his back, you know.' Rachel nodded. Meg sniffed and straightened.

'We sat on a bench at the side of the reservoir, trying to work out how to handle things. We came home later than we meant to be.

'She was already dead when Richard found her. I blamed him for suggesting we went out.' Meg closed her eyes, the image of Richard screaming out their daughter's name as he held onto her legs, trying to take her weight; so vivid it physically hurt.

'Oh my god!' Rachel put a hand over her mouth.

Meg had to escape that memory; it brought too much hurt. She stood and busied herself getting out plates and forks for the meal. Absently stirring the curry in the saucepan she said, 'Before; when she was first diagnosed, we tried so hard to find out why it had happened. There were no answers. Then, months later, we heard of another young woman. We found out that her consultant had written a paper on it, warning other doctors and specialists to look out for that kind of cancer in girls. He said, he stressed, that it was unusual: clear-cell adenocarcinoma, is usually only found in post-menopausal women. I spoke about it in the interview if you remember?'

Rachel nodded slowly. 'I remember.'

Jackie didn't speak; however much she tried she couldn't help comparing Meg's anguish with the obstinate rejection of the facts in her own mother.

'He said it was happening in teenage girls like Lisa ... who had been exposed in utero to maternal Stilboestrol treatment. That meant me.' When the bubbling of water in the saucepan stopped and the noise turned to a low hiss, Meg emptied the steaming rice into a sieve and poured boiling water over it. She looked out of the kitchen window, remembering the bright white pain that had shocked through her at the realisation. 'My doctor prescribed it ... and I took it. I caused my daughter's cancer. Me.'

'No,' Rachel said fiercely, 'no, you didn't.'

Meg put the plates on the table. 'That's how I felt. Still do some days. Richard's said so many times that I shouldn't do but it's difficult when you're a mum. Guilt seems to be something you give birth to at the same time you have the baby. Knowing that what I'd done when I was pregnant, that I'd taken the drug that caused the cancer in her, was unbearable. I know I was horrendous to live with. The doctor gave me tablets. I didn't want to take them but then I thought the damage of any drugs had already been done; it was only me they could hurt now. Anyway, they didn't help, I was either walking around like a zombie or I was shouting and swearing at Richard. And before long he began to shout back. Everything went downhill from then on.' She sat down; forgetting what she was supposed to be doing.

'One day, that day, we were in the car and we were arguing. I'd insisted on driving even though the weather was atrocious. I think we'd been to town; I can't really remember. We were on the back roads and there was black ice. It began to rain, and going round a corner the car slewed. Richard shouted at me to slow down. I was furious. I remember putting my foot down harder on the accelerator: thinking I'd show him he couldn't tell me how to drive.' Meg stopped abruptly. 'I don't remember exactly what happened; I dream about it though. So, it's my fault he's in a wheelchair … and it's my fault Lisa had cancer.'

'No!' Jackie slapped rice on each of the plates and spooned curry on top. 'No, it's not, Meg; everything you've just said goes back to one thing only. You're not to blame … it's that bloody drug… that's the thing that's caused so much grief. So much has happened to each of us and the one thing that started it all was the drug.'

'It just gets me down sometimes, the fact that no one will listen; no one will take any responsibility.'

Meg said. She struggled to find the right words. 'It's the layers and layers of false statistics and ignorance that hide the truth. Sometimes I think we'll never succeed.'

We will,' Jackie said, 'you'll see. We will.'

They kept the conversation light while they ate but none of them had much appetite and they pushed the food around on their plates.

'Sorry, Meg,' Jackie leaned back in her chair, 'it's a super curry but I'm not very hungry.'

'No, nor me. Have you both had enough?'

Rachel nodded. Meg put the lid back on the serving dish. 'Richard'll probably eat the rest later.'

They helped her to rinse the dishes, their reflections merging and separating against the blackness of the night through the window. None of them said much.

Jackie closed the dishwasher. 'That's the lot.'

Meg was pale, her features somehow blurred. 'Shall we go in the living room?'

It was comforting, sitting in silence. They didn't need to talk: they'd said enough. It felt to Jackie that they'd moved on; shared something other than the campaign. Now they were equal in this friendship.

Chapter Thirty-Four - April

"I knew about the cancer but never, ever, was I told that I could have fertility problems," said Jill Vanselous Murphy ... DES took my right to have children. It took the rights of thousands of women."[34]

'I had a bit of a cold just after Christmas and then in February I was ill with food poisoning. But otherwise nothing major.' Rachel could hear how calm her voice sounded but she knew she could burst into tears at any moment. She rolled her wedding ring round her finger.

The doctor studied her through thick spectacles, tapping his pen on the surface of his desk. If he didn't stop she'd grab it off him and stick it up his bloody nose, which, she noted with fascination, sported the largest wart she ever seen. She fixed her gaze on it, trying to look impassive, waiting for the right moment to escape. If she'd known Doctor Harris was on holiday, she wouldn't have even dressed, let alone left the house.

---

[34] *The DES Legacy: Children of Women Given the Hormone DES Decades Ago Now Cope With Their Own - and Even Their Children's Health Problems* by Leef Smith Washington Post Tuesday, Sep 23, 2003

This doctor was older, probably partly retired she thought, watching him turn to read her notes on the screen making small 'hmm-hmming' noises.

Rachel transferred her stare to the large family photograph on the wall; Doctor Harris and his wife had triplets. They would be at least six years old by now. His wife was at the hospital clinic the same time Rachel had attended when expecting her second baby, just before she'd miscarried. She closed her eyelids, willing the tears to stay unshed.

'Mrs Conway?' From the way he spoke it was as though it was the second, even the third time he'd said her name. When she opened her eyes he seemed very small, like he was at the end of a telescope. He coughed, cleared his throat. 'I said how are you sleeping?'

There was a droning in her ears. She wondered how much to tell this man. The nights were the worst; thoughts of Stephen and his pregnant girlfriend tormented her. And, however hard she tried to ignore it the prospect of being alone for the rest of her life haunted her.

'Not so good,' she said.

'I think you could be suffering from depression, Mrs Conway.'

'No.' Tell me something I don't know. The reason was lying on the kitchen table: Stephen had made it quite clear in his letter that if she didn't start divorce proceedings, he would. Nice of him to give her the option, she'd thought at the time, screwing the paper into a tight ball and flinging it across the room.

'I could give you something for it but I wondered if Doctor Harris has ever suggested counselling?'

She'd wondered when that would be mentioned. She stared around the room before answering. The shelves, filled with reference books, gleamed, and the walls, the colour of putty, reflected the vertical slats of morning sunshine. The examination couch was covered with a broad clean layer of blue paper. She ran her finger over the cheese plant next to her; it was dusty. 'I've had one session, a while ago, after my ectopic pregnancy. I've had four miscarriages as well,' she said, feeling strangely detached. She felt the coldness of sweat on her top lip. 'I'm sorry ....' She was aware of the droning sound changing into a loud whooshing; the plant wavered and the room darkened before she lost consciousness.

When she came to, she was on the floor, with the practice nurse kneeling by her side.

'Oh fuck,' she thought.

'Ah, back with us,' the doctor said. Between them he and the nurse helped Rachel up onto the couch. 'When you're feeling up to it there are a couple of tests I'd like to do.'

An hour later she walked slowly to her car, unlocked it and got in. She closed the door quietly, leaned back in the seat without attempting to put the key in the ignition and stared blankly through the windscreen.

She didn't remember driving home. In the hall she took off her coat, turned sideways in front of the long mirror in the hall and ran her hand over her stomach.

How could it be? She was still having periods ... well of a sort. The state she'd been in it was no wonder things were all over the place. The doctor's words came back to her.

About twenty weeks.

Oh god!

Chapter Thirty-Five

Urgent need remains for long-term investigation of health of DES daughters, sons, mothers, and grandchildren[35]

Jackie watched the young woman from across the street as she struggled with the key to her front door, three Asda carrier bags hooked over her arm. From inside the red car, parked haphazardly in front of the house, the baby's cries were reaching a crescendo. The toddler had escaped from her car seat. Rummaging through the remainder of the plastic bags she'd found a bar of chocolate and was ripping off the wrapping. Jackie smiled. She'd never wanted kids herself but found them quite entertaining. At least until they were in their teens, she thought hastily, picturing what she thought of as the gormless faces of some of her students.

The news that Rachel had just given her filled her with both delight and concern for her friend. 'Have you seen your own doctor?' she asked finally. 'Are they sure? I mean, you don't look pregnant, you've lost loads of weight; you're like a rake.'

'That's because I haven't been eating much lately.

---

[35] "'Timeline: A history of diethylstilboestrol" DES Cancer Network Website 2001

I am pregnant, Jackie.' Rachel emphasised each word, her fear coming out as irritation. 'I can't believe it. I can't believe I didn't know ... it's so bloody unreal. I've not managed to get this far before.' She fought the panic. 'But I have to go into hospital. And this isn't how it's supposed to be. After all this time, this is not how I wanted to be having a baby. On my own.'

'Are you going to tell him?'

'No.' Rachel said. 'No.'

'He might want to come back.'

Rachel had an instant picture of Stephen with her and the baby, quickly replaced by the image of his heavily pregnant girlfriend. 'Well, he can sod off.'

Outside, the young mother's shouts and the howls of the little girl drowned out the crying baby. There was a series of doors banging and then the noise was muffled.

'Your choice, kiddo.' Jackie shrugged.

'I'm not going to tell him. He'll find out soon enough,' Rachel said. She blew her nose. 'I've an appointment with the consultant on Wednesday. Doctor Harris thinks a cervical suture would prevent losing the baby.'

'A what?'

'It's like a stitch,' Rachel said. Because I have what they call a weak cervix ... like,' she searched around for an explanation, 'well, put simply, to keep the baby in the womb.'

'Ah,' Jackie said, 'I get it, a stitch in time?'

'Idiot.' Rachel gave Jackie a tremulous smile. 'Anyway, I'll have to stay in hospital for a few weeks ... for rest and to be monitored.' It was something she faced with a mix of apprehension and relief. 'Will you look after Jake?' The dog, sprawled across the rug, lifted his head at the mention of his name and then closed his eyes and flopped back down.

'Of course I will, no problem,' Jackie said, 'anything. You'll be a fantastic mum,' she hugged Rachel, 'with or without that bloody dickhead of a husband.'

Chapter Thirty-Six

DES was given to pregnant women for the prevention of miscarriage, and injuries to their offspring did not appear until years after the initial exposure to the drug. DES was taken off the U.S. and Australian market in 1971, but continued to circulate in the world marketplace for several years thereafter. [36]

To: Avrilbreen@sheepfold.freeserve.co.uk
From: Megmath222@aol.com
Subject: DES.

Dear Avril,
I've sent you a copy of the recording of the programme I did for Radio Carvoen, together with other bits and pieces I have here.
Must go, I have a wedding cake to finish decorating.
Hope you are keeping well.
Meg

Meg had forty small red fondant roses to make for Wendy's cake.

She gazed out into the garden where Richard was

---

[36] DES ACTION U.K. Newsletter Number 28 November 2008

sitting very still in his wheelchair, snuggled under a mound of blankets despite the mildness of the day. Although neither of them had said anything about Wendy's wedding she knew instinctively how he was feeling. As the day grew closer both of them were struggling to block out the painful reminders of what they would never have.

Turning to the kitchen table she began to knead the blood red cochineal into the fondant icing.

Chapter Thirty-Seven - May

DES daughters often have structural changes in their reproductive system that make it difficult for them to conceive or carry a pregnancy ... Every pregnancy of a DES daughter must receive high-risk care, as their risk of miscarriage or premature delivery is higher.[37]

'Right, I'm off now.' Jackie picked up the chair and stacked it with others near the door of the ward. 'I'll ring tomorrow lunchtime to see if there's anything else you need for me to bring: more nighties, pants, books,' she glanced at the sour-faced nurse standing at the door and pointedly studying a watch attached to her bolster-like bosom, 'file in a cake?'

Rachel moved slightly on her pillow, trying to focus on the nurse. 'Fool,' she grinned, slurring the word.

'Well, she frightens even me.' Jackie whispered. 'Look at the hairs on her chin. I reckon she's a bloke in drag.'

Rachel's chuckle was followed by a sharp intake of breath, 'Ouch, don't make me laugh.'

'Sorry.' Jackie shrugged into her jacket, checking her pockets for her car keys. 'Have you done the

---

[37] www.cdc.gov/des/consumers/about/effects_daughters.html

letter for Avril?' she asked, casually looking at a younger nurse who had just walked in. Nice tits *and* a uniform, she thought, smiling as the young woman glanced up and smiled back at her.

'Yes.' Sleepy or not Rachel had followed the exchange; her friend was obviously recovering from all the trouble with Hazel. 'It's in the top drawer in the kitchen. I meant to give it to you before I came in. Have you written yours?'

'No. No, not yet, I will. And you're sure you'll be alright if I go to Avril's at the weekend? I could have taken Jake with me to Avril's you know, she said it was ok.' Though how the macaw would have reacted was anybody's guess, she thought. 'But your Dad said he'll be here Friday afternoon so I'll get some groceries in, take the dog to the house and wait for him there.'

When Phillip Lewis had rung her, her initial reaction had been to wonder how he had her number. It was only when he mentioned Stephen that she'd realised Rachel's husband was behind the call. Jackie tossed her car keys from one hand to the other. Well, she'd make sure he knew all the facts before she left. 'You'll be alright seeing your Dad?'

'Yes.' Rachel's voice drifted away. After a moment she roused herself. 'Stephen had no right to interfere.' She'd struggled to stay calm when Jackie had first told her that her father was coming over from Crete and her blood pressure had soared; she didn't want or need him to be here, the contact between them had been sporadic and awkward over the last year. She could feel the rapid beat of the pulse in her neck and concentrated on taking in long slow breaths; it's okay, baby, it's okay. 'But I can't tell him not to come, I suppose.' She screwed up her eyes tightly and then opened them. 'Tell Avril she can use as much or as little of what I've written as she wants ... anything to get people listening.' She knew she wasn't as enthusiastic as Meg and Jackie about the play but it didn't matter. Now she had no room for anything other than concern for the life she was carrying.

Jackie recognised that her friend didn't want to talk about her father anymore. She smoothed Rachel's fringe off her forehead. 'You're really warm; sure you're okay?

'I'm fine.'

'Okay,' Jackie said. 'I'll tell her. And don't worry, between her and Georgina it'll be a rip-roaring success.' God, even saying Georgina's name gave her the hots. She couldn't remember the last time she'd felt like this. 'Now rest, do as they say,' Jackie indicated with her chin, 'especially King Kong over there,' she said in a conspiratorial voice. 'And don't let her give you a bed bath.'

'Shush,' Rachel pulled the sheet up over her mouth to hide her laugh. 'Go, go,' she waggled a finger at Jackie.

'I've gone. See you tomorrow,' Jackie blew a kiss, 'take care.'

Rachel listened to the click of Jackie's heels as she walked away. 'Don't worry, I will,' she rested a hand on her stomach. 'Whatever else happens, I won't let you go.' She refused to listen to the small insistent voice of fear.

Chapter Thirty-Eight - Whitsun -May

(Endometriosis) - DES Daughters are at increased risk from this painful chronic disease. They often have anatomical complications such as ... (a) ...narrowing of the cervical canal that may increase the likelihood of retrograde menstruation. Other anatomical malformations common to DES Daughters may also increase the risk[38]

'Nice place to eat alfresco,' Jackie said, putting the tray of drinks and two sets of serviette-wrapped cutlery onto the long wooden tables. Stepping over the bench she sat down. 'Especially on a day like today.'

'Yeah, The Granary's my favourite place to eat. The Crown doesn't do food.' Avril waved in the direction of the village. 'I sometimes go to The Fountain Head, the other side of Lydfield, but I prefer it here. The food's better.' She took a long gulp from the glass of Guinness. 'Ummm.' She put the drink down and wiped the line of foam off her top lip, raising her voice to be heard above the noisy group of hikers arriving at the pub. 'More walkers than ever around now,' she nodded towards them. 'The ban put a stop to everything last year.'

'Yeah, it's good to see things getting back to normal. I passed loads of ramblers coming over the

---

moors road,' Jackie said.

'Georgina likes to walk; we go over to Dovedale sometimes when we're trying to thrash out a script.' Avril watched Jackie 'She asked after you last night by the way,' she added, 'said she might pop over to the cottage later.'

A flicker of nervousness ran through Jackie. 'That'll be nice,' she said. Nice? Breathing deeply, she thought, wonderful, great, perfect.

'Yeah, she's got some brilliant ideas for the stage set.'

'Oh.' Jackie flushed. 'Oh yes, she emailed me with a couple of ideas.' And you obviously got the wrong idea, idiot, she berated herself. 'Did you manage to read Rachel's account by the way?'

'I did, I read it last night; sounds like she's really been through the mill.'

'She has, yes.' Jackie took off her jumper, dropped it on the bench and rolled up the sleeves of her white shirt. 'She's had a lot to deal with. Still has, now that she's pregnant again, in hospital for god knows how long, and that bastard of a husband's going AWOL on her.' She turned her face towards the welcome warmth of the sun and closed her eyes.

'You said. It's a shame.' Avril pushed away her own memories of rejection in the silence that followed. Eventually she asked, 'how does she feel about the play now?'

'Better, I think ... well as far as I can make out, anyway. At least she was okay about writing stuff down for you. As I've said before, she sometimes keeps things to herself; I didn't even know until recently that it was because of DES she kept miscarrying, you know.'

'It's a difficult thing to talk about; you know that as well as anyone. It's so personal. Until I heard about you lot I just shoved it to the back of my mind and tried to get on with my life.'

Jackie tilted her head and looked sideways at her. 'Did that work for you?'

Avril gave a short laugh. 'Not really but it's been the only way I could cope.'

A young girl came out of the pub carrying two plates. Seeing Avril she nodded and weaved her way through the other tables, empty except for a couple sitting at the one nearest the pub entrance. 'Two lasagne?'

'Thanks Kirsty.' Avril unwrapped her knife and fork from the paper serviette.

'No probs, chips and side salad in a mo.' The waitress put the meals on the table; the cheese sauce bubbled in the dish. 'Mind, the plates are hot.'

'Thanks.' Avril waited until the girl had moved away. She cut the pasta into squares, watching the steam escape. 'As I see it, this play will be good for all four of us.'

'Yes.' Jackie slid her lager back and forth on the table, leaving streaks of wetness where condensation from the glass dripped onto the wood.

Another girl appeared with the bowls of salad and

chips and Avril helped herself to some chips and chose a small plastic sachet of vinegar from a bowl on the table. 'Legislation for Investigation into Stilboestrol Association is too much of a mouthful for the title of the play, though,' she said, ripping open the packet with her teeth. The strong sharp tang made her eyes water.

'Still think *A Silent Trauma* the best so far.'

'Good. Have you written anything yet?' Avril asked.

'Not much.'

'Did you bring what you'd done?'

'Bits.' Jackie poked at her food with her fork. All at once she wasn't hungry.

Avril put her own fork down. 'Is it the business with Hazel?'

'What?'

'Whatever's bothering you ... because something is, I can tell.' She rested both elbows on the table and leaned forward, cupping her chin in her hands. 'I haven't known you long Jackie but I can see there's something wrong. Is it Hazel? You haven't told me what really happened.'

'It was bloody awful.'

Avril picked up her fork again and scooped up some lasagna. 'Want to talk about it?'

She was a good listener. Except for the occasional murmur and movement of her head she didn't interrupt.

'And the stupid part of it all is that I feel guilty about what happened,' Jackie said finally, ' I know I could have handled the whole thing better.'

'How?' Avril asked, 'seems you couldn't have done things any differently, except to stay with Hazel and pretend everything was okay.' She chewed thoughtfully before looking straight at Jackie, 'and in the long run, that would've done neither of you a favour. Sounds to me that the woman is so unstable that whenever you ended it she would have reacted in the same way ... or worse, it could have been you that got hurt, physically hurt, I mean.' She pointed at Jackie's plate with her fork. 'Eat, it's delicious.'

Jackie began to eat. 'I shouldn't have let things get as far as they did; it was finished month ago.'

'Hindsight's a wonderful thing.'

'Yep.' Jackie watched a young couple stroll past the pub, the man pushing a pram, the woman linking him. Looks ideal, she thought, but who's to say what goes on when the front door closes on the outside world? Stop it, she told herself, why shouldn't some things be just what they seem? 'Think I'm a bit down,' she said and grinned. 'Not a clue why on such a gorgeous day.' The smile didn't reach her eyes.

They sauntered along the lane that led to the turnoff for Avril's cottage. The faint chug of a tractor vied with the distant bleat of sheep and the drone of insects in amongst the gorse. Above it all they heard a high-pitched cry.

'Look!' Avril pointed; a sparrow hawk circled above them.

'That's so impressive,' Jackie breathed, shading her eyes and following the sweep of wings. 'Makes you feel totally insignificant.'

They watched until the bird dipped towards the moor below the skyline and then they turned up the rough track. Finally Jackie said, 'I haven't written my … account yet,' she negotiated a large rut of dried mud, 'because I don't think there's a lot to say.'

'I'm sure there is.'

'I've had bouts of endometriosis … a couple of operation …bloody painful periods for years since I was a young girl.' Jackie shrugged self-consciously. This is worse than talking about the business with Hazel, she thought. I feel ashamed. Humiliated, mortified demeaned. She played her word game to calm herself. Avril had stopped and turned towards her. 'That's all,' she said at last

'All! From what I've read, it's one of the most painful and debilitating things any woman has to put up with.' She studied Jackie. 'Why do I get the feeling there's something else?'

'It's nothing to do with DES.' Jackie picked a blade of grass and chewed the end of it.

'Do you want to talk about it?'

'Not particularly.' She spat the grass out.

'So just write what you want to about the

endometriosis; how you feel, how it's affected you,' Avril said, 'there must be thousands of women in this country that can identify with that.'

Jackie turned to look down towards the village: the faint chatter of the people in the garden of the pub, mingling with the occasional cries of the sheep was carried on the light breeze.

Chapter Thirty-Nine

Thousands of daughters grapple with (other) kinds of effects of their exposure, in far greater number than the 1 in 1,000 who develops cancer. Many of them feel to some degree "different" from other women[39]

Jackie shivered. 'There *is* something else.' She faced Avril. 'It's just that I've never, ever talked about it; let alone thought about writing it down. It's awkward.' To say the least, she thought. She pulled her jumper on, muffling her voice. 'I was born with a genital abnormality, no external labia, and other stuff. That's about it.' Her face was flushed as she emerged and she didn't look at Avril. 'But I was told a long time ago it was nothing to do with the drug.' She changed her tone of voice to a bland Middle English accent and quoted, "babies are born with genital abnormalities with no known cause," according to one doctor. So there it is, as my mother always says, I'm a freak with no known cause.' Her low laugh was resigned. 'When I was teenager I heard her tell someone I was an Aphrodite. Obviously she meant hermaphrodite but for years I thought she was liking me to a Greek goddess. Stupid cow.'

Avril waited a few seconds before tucking her arm

---

[39] *DES Voices: From Anger to Action:* Pat Cody.2008 Ch.2 p26/27

through Jackie's. 'Come on, let's get home.'

They were slightly out of breath when they arrived at the cottage and sat on the wall gazing across the valley where gathering clouds cast light and dark shadows on the fields.

'There's a lot more to you than just that,' Avril finally said, 'just as there is to all of us.' She picked at the leaves of the blackberry bushes trailing over the top. 'You know that, Jackie; you're a strong woman. Write down *how* it's affected you, especially your relationship with your mother. It'll help. And we can use it by threading your feelings through all of the characters.' She paused to gather her thoughts. 'Look, just because they said it had nothing to do with the drug how can they prove it? You've been affected in other ways. You don't have to write down anything you don't want to but that … that difference in you … has made you feel something. So use that emotion within anything else you say.

'When Bill broke off our engagement I was angry for a long time. At him, at what had happened to me, the bloody pharmaceutical industry: even, and I'm ashamed to admit it, at my Mum.'

Jackie pressed her lips tight.

Avril noticed. She flicked the leaf away and looked at Jackie. 'Eventually I decided there was more to me than being a victim of that bloody drug, however much it has harmed or changed me physically. So I picked up where I left off before … before it all happened and I started writing. I made things right with my mum and I made sure I kept in touch with the rest of the family and my friends. The only thing I haven't done, can't bring myself to do, is get involved with a bloke.' She held her top lip between her teeth. 'I couldn't face that. And not just because of what happened, the operation I mean. It's because I never stopped loving Bill.' She gave a quick glance at Jackie and shrugged. 'Oh, I've been out with one or two blokes over the years but on my terms. And no sex.' She stopped. 'Too painful; I only have part of a cervix ... so, for me, it's too painful. And I've never told anyone that before.'

Jackie carried the two mugs up the steps at the back of the house to the wrought iron table set amongst the mass of shiny-leaved rhododendron bushes, followed by Avril with the macaw in his cage. She set him down on the path. 'He likes to be out in the fresh air,' she said, poking a chunk of apple through the bars and watching the bird sidle towards it and take it from her. Without looking up she said, 'it's difficult for all of us, you know, we all have things we'd rather keep private but sometimes we have to stand up and be counted, whatever the cost.'

'I've spent a lifetime keeping that part of me secret.'

'But you've had partners?'

Jackie shrugged. 'Not that many. Anyway, I always like to think the women I've been with didn't care.' Except Hazel. She'd mocked her about it towards the end of their relationship. Jackie knew in that instant it was over. She rested her elbows on the table and cradled the mug of coffee against her cheek. 'When we found out we'd had the same idea about a play I was so excited. And I know it'll be brilliant. But I never even thought about,' she grimaced, 'my funny fanny.'

Despite herself Avril gave a shriek of laughter. 'Your what?'

Jackie stared at her and then grinned. 'My funny fanny, that's what I've always called it.' She began to laugh and soon both women were convulsed.

Eventually the screeching of the Macaw ended their laughter.

'Oh dear god.' Avril wiped her eyes as her giggles subsided, her mascara leaving smudges under her eyes. 'I'd better take him in; he'll be having a breakdown. I don't think he's heard such a racket before.' She stood.

Smiling, Jackie linked her hands behind her head and looked up at her. 'D'you know, I haven't laughed like that for yonks.'

The leaves of the rhododendrons rustled. Above the garden, on the moors, the stunted trees permanently bent towards the West, leant further over and the tall tussocks of stiff grass and brambles shivered in waves in the rising breeze as the sun dipped away below the roof of the cottage.

Having taken in the macaw, Avril reappeared at

the back door, oven gloves over her hands. 'You do realise, don't you Jackie, that if we're going to make people listen we need to tell the whole story of our lives?' Jackie opened her mouth in protest. 'No, not about your, ' Avril giggled, 'funny fanny, we'll leave that out but it's essential we portray the characters as strong, as living normal lives as much as possible, despite the various ways Stilboestrol has affected them.'

'I agree, absolutely essential.'

'I'll help you to write your story, if you like?' Avril said.

'No, I'm okay; I'll do it.'

'Great.' Avril went back into the kitchen.

Jackie heard the oven door open and close; there was a waft of cheese and garlic and her stomach rumbled in anticipation. She felt more relaxed than she had for ages. And then she remembered about Georgina. She ran her fingers through her hair, spiking it up and checked her shirt. She knew it! There was a stain still visible where the vinegar from lunchtime had splashed. And another she couldn't identify. She rubbed ineffectually at the mark. Bugger it; she'd change after they'd eaten.

'You know, no one has written anything about DES in this way, not in this country anyway,' Avril called from inside the kitchen. 'And from what Meg says she's been banging her head against a brick wall for years and got nowhere. We've kept quiet long enough; people need to know, Jackie. The play will make sure they do.'

Closing the back door, Jackie shivered, glad to be inside again; she'd forgotten how the temperature dropped so suddenly in this part of the world. She tapped her fingers across the row of novels. She picked out one and began to read the blurb on the back. 'Okay if I borrow a book to read in bed?'

'Sure,' Avril called above the clatter she was making in the kitchen.

Jackie tried to put the book back but it wouldn't fit. She took out a couple more to make a space and saw there was a paperback wedged behind them. She pulled it out and studied it. The suspicion raised by the name of the publishers, D*imples.co.uk* was confirmed by the cover; a woman's hand holding a large bowl of cherries (the nails, the longest Jackie had ever seen and painted the same colour as the fruit), was the give-away. Erotica. She opened it and began to read...

I popped the chocolate-covered cherry into my mouth and sucked on it until the coating of sweetness vanished and I rolled the fruit between my lips, never taking my smouldering look from his sexy brown eyes. He leaned towards me and teased my lips apart, scooping up the cherry with his tongue. I wasn't about to let my prize go so easily. I thrust my tongue into his mouth, searching. Sucking one last time on those luscious lips I tilted my head backwards, letting my long blond hair swing gently, brushing my bare shoulders.

'Mmmm, chocolate,' he murmured, his palms circling my breasts. My nipples stiffened.

'Chocolate cherries,' my voice was husky. 'I have another cherry somewhere if you'd like to look for it.'

He didn't need a second invitation ...

Jackie couldn't help it; she gave a snort of laughter and, closing the book, read the title. Sexy Dishes by Lucy La Bia. Oh my god, she thought, with a wide grin.

Hearing the scuff of Avril's boots on the kitchen floor she tried to push the book back but the row became dislodged and half a dozen thrillers fell off the shelf.

 When Avril appeared with two plates of pasta, Jackie was juggling to catch the rest. She half-turned, looking over her shoulder, 'I'm sorry, I ....'

Avril's eyes followed the action until she spotted the book Jackie was holding. 'Oh,' she said, 'hang on, I'll help.' Hurrying, she put both plates on the table.

'I am sorry,' Jackie said again, 'I was just looking.' The image the first page had produced wouldn't go away and the laughter was bubbling to the surface.

'So I see.' Avril's voice was neutral. She bent to pick up the books on the floor.

'What did you think of it then?'

'Lucy Labia?' Jackie couldn't help it; she smirked, 'the author's called Lucy Labia?'

'Actually it's pronounced La *Bia*,' Avril kept a

straight face. 'I think it sounds rather French.'

Something stopped Jackie mid-splutter. 'Oh no,' she said, 'it's you ... you wrote this?' she held the book out, 'this is your work?'

'Yes,' Avril put on a mock-proud face. 'It's all my own work.'

'Oh,' Unsure, Jackie kept a straight face.

Avril laughed and punched her lightly on the shoulder. 'And Lucy La *Bia's* earned me a lot of money.' A pause. 'A hell of a lot of money. Don't knock it; you should try writing stuff for your lot.'

Jackie gave a shout of laughter. 'Yeah, right. I suppose I could call myself Nola *Bia.'*

They left the crockery to drain and went back into the large front room. Glasses of wine in hand they sat in the chairs by the fireplace. Jackie curled her legs under her, basking in the warmth of the flames and sipped her drink. Unable to curb her curiosity any longer she asked, 'how did you start?'

'What? Writing?' Avril deliberately misunderstood. She grinned.

'You know what I mean.' Jackie paused, blundered on. 'I mean, why, after all that's happened to you. Why would you want to write erotica?

Avril's smile subsided. She took a while to answer. When she did the words came from somewhere deep inside her, a long-ago decision dredged up. 'Because I could, I suppose,' she shrugged. 'In a way it was defiance. I felt I was salvaging how I used to see myself when I was young before ... as a sexual human being. Does that sound as arty-farty to you as it does to me, now I've said it?

Jackie shook her head. 'I suppose the women whose books I have read, Fiona Cooper, Anais Nin, would say something similar: claiming oneself as a sexual human being.' She took a gulp of her wine. 'After all, what is it Nin says,' she paused, thinking. '"*It's all right for a woman to be, above all, human. I am a woman first of all.*"[40] Think that's it.'

'Exactly.' Avril refilled their glasses. Much to Jackie's relief she laughed. 'The first story I wrote was called *Ice Creamed and Jam Tarts*. Excruciatingly bad, it's embarrassing just thinking about it.' Above the rim of her glass the laughter lines around her eyes deepened. 'It was only supposed to be a one off but I won a competition in a magazine. Unbelievable when I think back, it was so bad.'

'Yeah but ... I mean ... Lucy La *Bia*?'

'Better than Clitoris (Avril pronounced it Clitooris, lengthening the 'o') Belle-Chose, which was my first choice after I'd been through a Chaucer phase.' She gave Jackie a sly look. 'Which I think is on a par with Nola *Bia*.'

They shrieked with raucous laughter.

There was a slight squeak of brakes and the clunk of a car door. 'That'll be Georgina.' Avril pushed

[40] (from The Diary of Anaïs Nin, vol. I, 1966)

herself off the chair.

Jackie ruffled her hair, gave a quick glance into the large mirror on the wall. Shit, she'd forgotten to change her shirt.

To: Avrilbreen@sheepfold.freeserve.co.uk
From: Jacgay@ yahoo.com
Subject: Hi

Back home safely.
Thanks for your hospitality – and for sharing the secrets of your pseudonym with me – ha-ha!
 Nola
 x

To: Jacgay@ yahoo.com
From: Avrilbreen@sheepfold.freeserve.co.uk
Subject: Ref Hi

You are very welcome.
Glad you're home ok.
Really enjoyed the last few days.
 Lucy La Bia's days are numbered!!!!

 x

To: Jacgay@ yahoo.com
From: georginalees@btinternet.com
Subject: Hi

Hi Jackie,
It was great to see you again. Perhaps we can get together for a longer chat next time you're up this way?
Love
George x

Love George! And a kiss!

Chapter Forty

DES ... is one of the earliest examples of an endocrine-disrupting chemical causing direct harm to the women exposed and trans generational effects in their offspring   A recent summary of the effects in daughters of women exposed during pregnancy noted significant increases in breast cancer, infertility, preterm delivery, stillbirth, early menopause and higher grade cervical abnormalities, among other adverse effects. [vii].[41]

'I'm thinking of killing off Lucy,' Avril said, as much to get a reaction out of Natasha, her agent, as anything but as soon as the words were out she realised how much she meant them. 'I'm bored with her now ... actually have been for a while.' There was an ominous pause at the other end of the telephone. Avril opened the curtains to let the morning sun into the room. Mr Macawber was biting the bars of his cage, ready to come out. She opened the door and he hopped over to his play area, bouncing from branch to branch, lifting first one toy with his beak and then another.

Finally Natasha spoke. 'Since I've taken you on you'd made your name writing thrillers and the Lucy

---

[41] Public Health Classic: *DES Daughters* By Dick Clapp posted by ***The Pump Handle*** on Oct 9, 2012

erotica. Over the past twelve months you've been writing scripts for a local amateur group that doesn't even pay you and I've told you before, it's taking you away from your proper work.'

'I enjoy the playwriting.' Avril watched Mr Macawber shredding a leaf of the cheese plant that had been presented to her as a thank you gift from the Lydfield Players.

'I wouldn't be doing my job if I didn't say something,' Natasha continued.

Avril knew she was right but it didn't stop the irritation. She could picture her agent swinging from side to side in her chair, slender legs crossed, designer glasses pushed on top of her head, hair immaculate. Avril could even hear the rhythmic beat as the woman tapped her pen on her teeth, a poor replacement for the cigarettes she used to chain smoke. Avril waited. The speed of the tapping had reached a crescendo. She'll damage those expensive caps if she's not careful, Avril thought.

'Actually, I've been thinking of writing another play,' she said; she didn't say she was already in the process of writing the script.

A strangled choking sounded in her ear. 'You're spreading yourself too thin.'

Avril gazed down at herself and grinned; standing, she couldn't see her feet for her breasts. 'I wish,' she laughed. Sobering she said, 'look, Natasha, it's a story that needs to be told. Nothing like it's been written in the UK before. I've been meaning to talk to you about it.'

'*Dimple's* are on my back. They want the next Lucy.' Natasha's voice was even more strident.

That statement encouraged a whole host of response, Avril thought, but didn't use one of them; Natasha was notorious for her lack of humour.

'Well tell them what I've said then: no more Lucy.' The macaw shook his feathers and flew across to Avril, landing on her hand. She tucked the telephone under her chin and, taking out a brazil nut from her cardigan pocket, gave it to the bird. 'I'm sorry Natasha; I truly don't want to write another Lucy La Bia book ever again. I did tell you months ago when *The All Night Man* was published.'

'But they're so popular.'

'Not with me. Not anymore,' Avril interrupted. 'This play, the one I'm trying to tell you about, might be the most important piece of writing I do. Look Natasha, come up here, get away from Manchester and breathe fresh air for once. I think we need a good talk.'

'You'll have to make sure that parrot's in its cage if I do.'

'Macaw,' Avril corrected automatically. 'Of course.'

'I have a window on Thursday of next week,' the agent now said, 'we'll sort things out then.'

Avril put the 'phone back on the receiver. 'Bit scary, burning all your boats at once,' she murmured. Whistling under her breathe she watched to make sure the macaw was behaving and then went into her study and picked up Rachel's letter again.

Dear Avril,

This is my fifth pregnancy and I am struggling to describe how I feel -exhilarated, frightened - I'm all over the place.

I've tried to describe things as objectively as possible but it's difficult.

Jackie's probably told you I'm separated from my husband, Stephen. We were married in 1990. We began trying for a family right away and were thrilled when I became pregnant.

It didn't last long. At twelve weeks, I lost the baby and then had two further miscarriages, both at about three months.

In nineteen ninety - eight, I had my third miscarriage.

I also have something called 'sticky blood' syndrome which causes blood clotting and can bring about miscarriages. There is no proof that this is linked to my being a DES daughter but the possibility is there, as exposure to DES is known to increase the risk of autoimmune diseases.

I lost my last baby in February of last year and have been off work for over twelve months. Not sure I'll go back ever.

At the beginning of April I found out I was sixteen weeks pregnant - a huge shock – but a good one. So far everything's okay - all I can do is follow doctor's orders and stay on bed rest. It's frustrating and every bone in my body aches but I'm determined to stick it out.

I'm not angry with the family doctor who prescribed Stilboestrol to my mother and I certainly don't blame her. I couldn't have wished for a more loving mother. She died eighteen months ago - I miss her very much.

But what does makes my blood boil is that pharmaceutical companies continued to make DES for many years after it was known not to prevent miscarriages and that it could cause cancer.

It also seems there's always been a complete lack of political will to do anything at all about the DES legacy in the UK, only an assertion that any discussion should be between Des Daughters/ Mothers and the companies. The consensus also seems to be that it's an issue that belongs in the past. And that the medical records of the mothers are 'probably untraceable' - (hmmm? I wonder why? - or is that just me being paranoid?)

DES and its side effects won't be history for some time. Many women are still living with the damage it has caused and there will be others who don't even realise what's causing their health problems.

And what about the third generation? When I think about that I fear for my baby.

I am so glad that I heard Meg, that day on the radio and I am glad you are writing about this. I'm sorry too about my initial reaction to the play. My only excuse is that I was going through a bad time.

I hope what I have written helps.

Best regards,

Rachel.

Avril slid the letter into a plastic folder marked DES script. Including her own she had all four stories now, as well as the letter from the DES son, and had already planned the format of the play.

And she wanted the group to see it coming together as soon as possible.

Chapter Forty-One

...The contrast between the original promise of DES, to create life, and its actual devastating effects suggests an explanation for the subdued, even paralyzed, responses of practicing physicians in the terms to the responses of patients – in terms, that is, of trauma.[42]

'I'm not still angry with you.' Rachel said, refusing to look at her father. She fixed her gaze on the daffodils he'd put on the small table at the bottom of her bed.

You are.' Phillip Lewis moved the flowers but

she still wouldn't turn towards him. 'Look, I came as soon as I found out what was happening.' Uncomfortable with the awkwardness between them he glanced around. The woman in the next bed was snoring, the baby in the cot at her side thrashed restlessly against the firm swathes of sheets.

'You came because of Stephen. Because he rang you. What did he say?'

'He said he was worried about you, about the baby...'

'The baby's nothing to do with him,' Rachel interrupted. She lifted her hand from the bedcovers at his look of surprise. 'Oh, it's his alright but it's

---

[42] Roberta J Apfel, MD.,M.P.H. Susan M Fisher, M.D. *To Do No Harm: DES and the Dilemmas of Modern Medicine* Ch.7 p.109

nothing to do with him; I don't even know how he found out about it. He left me,' she said fiercely as her father tried to speak. 'Okay?'

'Okay. I didn't know the full story until I got here,' Phillip said. 'Jackie told me everything and I'm sorry. I'm totally in the picture now. I could knock his block off.'

The old-fashioned phrase and the fierce expression on the face of her father, usually such an undemonstrative man, made Rachel smile slightly. 'You're in a queue,' she said.

He returned the smile, looking slightly embarrassed by his outburst. 'But,' he said, 'I think you're still angry because I left after your mother...' He didn't finish the sentence.

Rachel plucked at bits of cotton on the blanket

but still didn't speak. Her back ached and she looked at the clock on the wall, she had another hour before she'd be allowed to sit up.

'Give me a break, Rachel.' She looked sidelong at him. 'I'm sorry. We should have talked more, I suppose, but I couldn't stay in Beddgaron,' he said, 'not once your mother ...' he stopped again. 'With all the memories in that house.'

'The house I grew up in; our home. Mum loved that place,' she said. 'You couldn't wait to get away. You went without a backward glance.'

'I didn't. But I couldn't stay. And your mother loved our apartment in Crete just as much as the house in Pentre Road. Besides you had Stephen.'

'Then.' Rachel pulled the bedcovers higher.

'I don't know how to make things better between us.' He looked old, tired despite the tan: the whites of his eyes were bloodshot and there were more lines on his face than she remembered. He'll be seventy now, she thought with a stab of guilt. She hadn't rung him on his birthday.

'There've been faults on both sides, Dad, let's leave it at that. I can't cope with any hassle at the moment.'

'Of course,' he said, 'I'm sorry.' The woman in the next bed snorted and woke herself up. Phillip rose stiffly. 'I'll have to go anyway ... see to the dog.'

'Is he okay?'

'Right as rain,' he fastened his jacket. 'He's a beautiful dog. Well,' he hesitated, tapping his fingertips on the covers before leaning forward and kissing her clumsily, 'rest now. I'll be back in the morning.'

'Thanks,' Rachel closed her eyes so she didn't have to see him leave, or see the way his shoulders stooped as he walked away. He'd been a distant figure in her childhood, someone who hovered on the side-lines of the relationship between her and her mother, apparently unwilling to be part of it. Now she had a sudden unwelcome thought; what if he'd resented her in the past as much as she'd resented him for the last eighteen months?

Chapter Forty-Two

In 1976 ... I had a smear test which came back 'suspicious' ... more tests ... led to my being diagnosed with clear-cell adenocarcinoma of the vagina. I had a hysterectomy and partial vaginectomy in December 1977. The consultant ... suspected that the cancer was caused by DES. After a miscarriage and then six years before becoming pregnant again, my mother (was) advised her to take some tablets 'to make sure she didn't lose this baby'... My consultant found my mother's records .... They showed that my mother had been given Stilboestrol (DES)[43]

Meg sat on the wall at the far end of the grounds of the hotel, watching the sun dip below the horizon of the sea. The clouds that had threatened rain were now gathered in a long thin line of blackness between sea and space, splintered in places to reveal the brilliant reds and gold of the dying sun. Above and further east the sky was pearlised pink and silvers.

'Takes your breath away, doesn't it?' A large hand rested on Meg's shoulder.

Meg always marvelled how quietly Alice could

---

[43] Quote: Heather Justice – DES Daughter and member of DES Action UK see bio.

move for such a big woman. 'Mmm, wonderful,' she said, putting her own hand over her friend's fingers but not taking her eyes off the sunset. 'Glad the rain held off. Wendy looked so beautiful. I'm pleased nothing spoiled her day.' But still she felt worn-out and hurting.

'Even managed to hide the bump,' Alice chuckled. 'Surprising what a large bouquet can do.'

'Nothing to be ashamed of, Alice, that baby will be born into a loving home, you can tell John idolises her. I hope they'll be as happy as they looked today.' Meg swallowed. 'A baby is a blessing.'

'I know, love, I know. It's been a grand

day. Everything's been perfect. John's parents have been great, helping out with the finances and stuff. I couldn't have put on such a spread for Wendy on my own.' With a slight groan and a creaking of the strong - boned girdle she'd insisted on wearing under her new blue dress and jacket Alice settled herself on the wall next to Meg. She patted Meg's thigh, 'and the cake was the most splendid thing I've ever seen. You're a very clever woman Mrs Matthews. 'They watched the ever-changing sky in silence. The boundary wall of the hotel marked the beginning of rough scrubland that spread to the edge of the cliffs. Meg could hear the slap of waves on the cliffs below and the rustle of the light breeze through the grass. The band stopped playing in the large reception room and through the open windows she heard laughter and chatter rise over the chink of glasses. From the kitchens in another part of the building there was the jangle of crockery as the hotel staff cleared the remnants of the meal away. 'Everything was perfect,' she said. 'You did really well, giving Wendy away.'

'Yes,' Alice nodded slowly, her double chin wobbling. 'I was a bit worried about that. She nudged Meg. 'But I was bloody glad to get that sodding hat off, it was so tight it gave me a bloody headache.'

Meg didn't say anything but she could still see the faint outline of the hatband on the broad forehead of her friend. 'You looked lovely,' she said. And meant it.

'And you love. And Richard was so handsome in his new suit I thought John's mother was going to ravish him on the spot.'

They laughed. Then they turned to one another, the laughter dying on their faces.

'Lisa?' Alice said.

'Sorry,' Meg said, 'take no notice.'

'I was watching you in there,' Alice gestured towards the hotel with flick of her thumb, 'you don't have to put on a brave face with me, you know that.'

A gust of stronger breeze brought the music towards them again. Elton John's voice floated around them: *Can You Feel the Love Tonight*.

Meg's eyes smarted: through the blur of tears the sun was a sliver of red, throwing a last sheen across the water. 'I had to get out of there; I didn't want to spoil things. All day I've been trying not to think.' She straightened her shoulders. Now it was over she didn't need to keep up the pretence. The bleakness was still there but, to her relief, the heat of her anger was dampening down; the shock of its sudden onset, as always, frightened her. 'You've always been there for me, Alice. All those months when Richard was in hospital, when I was too frightened to drive... all the times you took me to see him.'

'Such a long time ago, love.'

'I don't forget. I'll always be grateful you know.' Alice shook her head. 'I mean it,' Meg said, 'if it wasn't for you I'd have given up.'

'No you wouldn't. Richard needed you. You two live for one another.'

'And I almost got us killed,' Meg closed her eyes. 'And look what happened to him.'

'He doesn't blame you.'

'He should. 'They sat together in the darkness. Each remembering that dreadful time; Meg reliving her fears the day her husband came home from the hospital..

She'd held her breath as she pushed the plug into the socket and switched it on. The tree lights flickered and then stayed on, sprinkling an array of colours about the darkened room. Exhaling loudly she straightened up. The only decorations hanging from the branches were the ones that Lisa had made each Christmas: seventeen of them. Meg balanced the one from the year Lisa had turned five in the palm of her hand: a clumsily cut pine tree covered in dried glue and silver sequins. Gently she let it fall and watched it swing on the long loop of blue wool.

Tomorrow Richard would be home for the first time in ten months: in a wheelchair. The guilt brought sour bile to her mouth as usual. She rubbed her hands over her face. 'Pull yourself together,' she muttered; this wasn't the time for self-pity. Alice had been wonderful. Meg thought back to the months that her friend had helped her: filling in forms f for the alteration, chivvying the builders to finish the conversions, taking Meg into her own home when the loneliness was too much for her.

She walked from room to room in the small bungalow, apprehension raising goose-bumps on the skin of her arms. Their lives would be completely different from now on. Each doorway had been widened. Through the frosted glass she could see the ramps at the front and back doors. She looked into the bathroom. There was a frame around the lavatory, similar to the one in Richard's hospital room, and rails by the wash-hand basin. The bath had been taken out and a specially converted shower installed. How would Richard react? Whatever he said, there had to be a small core of resentment in him. Would the reality of his disability hit him hard, when he saw the alterations to the home he'd looked after for so many years? Would he ever really forgive her? Because that's what she needed; his forgiveness.

In Lisa's room she sat at the desk, her chin rested on clenched fists. In front of her a pile of envelopes waited to be posted. Over the last few months it had become a routine; writing letters to people she thought might help her to expose the damage Stilboestrol caused, getting replies that had no answers. It filled the empty spaces in her day. It stopped her from thinking.

She'd come full circle; still writing letters, getting the same worthless answers. But this time she had Jackie, Avril and Rachel with her; together they would succeed; they had too; she was tired.

In the hotel there was a lull in the music again. Somewhere a car door was closed and the engine started. Tyres rattled gravel. Meg looked around. The hotel windows threw out welcoming sheets of light.

She shivered. 'It's cold, let's go in.' Holding out her hand.

Alice took it and, grunting slightly, eased herself off the wall. She picked up her hat. 'Mustn't forget this bloody thing,' she said, 'it has to go back to the hire shop tomorrow.'

Meg smiled, grateful for her friend's naive ability to diffuse tension. Still clasping hands they walked across the grass to the hotel.

Chapter Forty-Three

Always remember that you, your parents, and your grandparents did nothing wrong when it comes to having DES as part of your health histories.[44]

'I'll come back and visit soon,' Phillip said. 'It's been nice being useful.' The words 'for once' hovered at the end of the sentence.

Rachel hesitated. 'I'll miss you.' She raised her arms and folded them around his neck, pulling him down until the side of his face rested against hers. 'I'm sorry; I wasn't very nice to you when you first got here.'

'It doesn't matter, I understood.'

Rachel let him go and he slowly straightened as if unsure what to do next. 'Keep in touch, Dad,' she said, 'and come back soon. You'll need to see your new grandchild.'

'Perhaps the beginning of July?'

Rachel nodded. It was a start.

'Have you got Jake back?' Rachel wriggled uncomfortably on the narrow hospital bed.

'Yeah,' Jackie nodded. 'I picked him up and took him back to mine after I'd dropped your dad off at

---

[44] DES Grandchild Brochure: Current research regarding DES Granddaughters/ Sons DES Action USA.

the airport.'

'Thanks,' Rachel said. 'Dad got off okay then?'

'Right on time. How did the visit go?'

'Good, difficult at first but he came every day and we managed to talk about a lot of stuff. Got things sorted out in the end, hopefully,' Rachel said, tucking her hair behind her ears. It felt lank and greasy. 'It went better as the week went on.'

I'd forgotten what a nice guy he is.'

'I know. I've been a right cow, Jackie.'

'Not at all … you've had a rough time.'

'Even so.' Rachel reached under the covers of the bed and tugged at her nightdress which had rucked up around her hips. 'Do you think you could straighten my sheet if I lift up a bit?'

'Course,' Jackie glanced around the ward, 'but are you supposed to?'

'I'm allowed to sit up for fifteen minutes every two hours but I have to move a bit sometimes,' Rachel pushed herself onto one elbow. 'I ache like mad and if I carry on like this I'll have no muscles worth calling muscles; I'll have forgotten how to walk.' She glanced towards the long line of windows at the end of the ward. 'It looks lovely weather out there.'

'It is,' Jackie admitted, 'still a bit chilly in the evening sometimes though.' She pulled the sheet taut and tucked it in. 'Don't worry; you'll soon get your walking legs when you have Jake to walk *and* a pram to push around.' She gave Rachel's pillow a vigorous thump on both sides. 'There. Come on, patience, kiddo, I know it's hard but stick with it.' She grinned. 'And when you're really fed up just think how you could be trying to teach the differences between assonance and alliteration or the intricacies in the poetry of Sylvia Plath to such classes as 10SA.' She helped Rachel to lie back, 'that better?'

'What's going on?' the voice boomed across from the nurses' station, followed by the rapid squeaks of rubber soles on the tiled floor. 'If Mrs Conway needs assistance, that's what I'm here for. Please ring the bell next time.' The nurse pushed Jackie to one side and fussed around Rachel, tightening the top covers.

'I can't move at all now,' Rachel complained. It was like being a helpless baby herself with everybody looking down at her all the time.

'Good, keep it that way until the doctor sees you later.' The nurse looked pointedly at Jackie. 'He's the one who will decide what Mrs Conway can and can't do.' She strode away, throwing the words over her shoulder. 'I'll be round with the pain relief tablets in an hour. Doctor says you can have two then.'

'Cow,' Rachel muttered.

'My god,' Jackie said, 'you didn't tell me King Kong was on duty. She nearly knocked me over with that bosom of hers. That's one pair of tits I'll gladly avoid.'

Rachel giggled. Jackie perched on the bed. 'Has Meg been in while I was away?'

'Yes, a few times. But I've been meaning to say

something about Meg,' Rachel frowned. 'She's tried to hide it but seemed quite low. I wondered if it was Richard. You know, what she told us about the accident?'

'No, I don't think so. I think she felt better once we knew.' Jackie shook her head. Then she opened her eyes wide.' Oh hell, wasn't it Alice's daughter's wedding last weekend?'

'It was.' Rachel said, dismayed. 'Meg didn't mention it. Oh, Jackie, I've been so wrapped up with myself I forgot. She must be feeling dreadful.'

'I think she's worse than you for keeping things bottled up. Don't worry, I'll call on my way home, see if I can get her to come here with me tonight.' Jackie glanced around. 'Now, try and get some sleep before King Kong comes back with a cudgel and knocks you out.'

Chapter Forty-Four

Twenty years ago I talked to everyone about it; to get health care for DES exposed as well as compensation; but after years of being ignored or told that nothing could be done I feel ... I have ... to leave it behind and get on with my life. To keep hitting my head against a brick wall would drive me mad .... We were either told that only very few women were affected and there was no point in alarming women unnecessarily ... then all our letters were ignored. It goes on and on[45]

'So I thought I'd call over and see how you two are.' Jackie lay back on the blanket on the lawn, hands behind her head, the sun warm on her face, adding casually, 'and to ask if you'll come with me to see Rachel tonight.'

'Perhaps not tonight.' Meg didn't offer an excuse. She wasn't up to making cheerful conversation; not at the moment.

'Okay, no worries ... keeping him busy I see.' Jackie tipped her chin towards Richard who was at a table on the flags outside the back door, filling two hanging baskets with geranium and petunia plugs.' Looks as if he's doing a good job there.' She squinted

---

[45] Heather Justice – DES Daughter and member of DES Action UK see bio.

at Meg in the brightness. Rachel was right, Meg was unhappy.

'Richard loves pottering,' Meg said, adjusting the arms of the sun-lounger and tilting her hat over her eyes, wanting to protect herself from Jackie's probing 'He's always loved the garden. Of course we have to have someone in to cut the grass now and do the heavy work.'

Jackie rolled onto her stomach. Without looking up, she said, 'wasn't it Alice's daughter's wedding last week?'

Meg didn't answer. Don't think; stop all thoughts of that day, she told herself.

Jackie kept her head lowered. 'Is that what's wrong? The wedding?'

Silence.

Finally Meg spoke. 'I keep thinking ... I don't want to but the thought won't go away ... how all that's been taken away from Lisa: boyfriends, getting married, having children ... our grandchildren.'

'I know, sweetie.'

'I try so hard ...' her hands lay limp on her lap. Above her the leaves moved gently in the breeze, casting changing patterns of light and shade around her; the flickering brightness making her frown.

'You need a change.'

'Hmm, perhaps.' Meg said. 'But how?' She lifted the rim of her hat, her eyes sliding sideways towards Richard and immediately she felt guilty. 'No,' she said, firmly this time, 'I'm fine, really.' The misery would go; it always did. And it always came back.

Jackie closed the gate after her and walked thoughtfully to her car. She stood for a moment, as though searching for her keys in her pocket. Meg wouldn't let herself be persuaded but it was obvious she need a break. Glancing back at Meg's she crossed the road to Alice's house.

Chapter Forty-Five

Because of PayPal, international members can join, support our work, and receive the DES Action VOICE newsletter four times a year. This is particularly important in countries where organizations no longer exist. We don't want to take members away from active DES groups[46]

Dear Avril,

Richard, Meg's husband here. She says you're looking for a father's point of view about Stilboestrol and she's asked me to write to you about how I feel about the drug.

Well, how I feel is that everybody lives with their own ghosts. DES is ours. I didn't take the drug but I wanted a child just as much as Meg did. Stilboestrol was the choice she was given. She took it. That will always haunt me. Would I change that? Well, truth be told, no. We had eighteen wonderful years with Lisa, nothing and nobody can take those memories away. What I do have is bitter remorse that my daughter, that wonderful human being that we created, felt that in the end she couldn't trust us; that she was unable to talk to us. We, I, let her down.

---

[46] Quoting Fran Howell – Executive Director of DES Action USA

Thinking about that now still makes me cry...

'She's looking tired.' Alice appeared behind Richard. He jumped. 'Sorry,' she said, 'I startled you.'

'I was just writing this letter to post to the woman in Yorkshire,' he said, automatically and self-consciously turning the sheet of paper over. 'Meg asked me to write how I feel about the drug.'

'Hmm,' Alice grimaced, then tried to lighten the moment 'not for public consumption then? Too many swear words?' She spoke quietly, her hand on his shoulder; her usual gesture of concern. To his expression of enquiry she repeated her words, 'I said she looks tired.'

They turned to where Meg was lying on the sun-lounger

'She is, and a bit down as well.' He looked up at Alice with a strained smile 'Has she said anything to you?'

'Not really.' Alice was proud she'd never betrayed one confidence her friend had entrusted to her but now she was worried; it almost felt like Meg was slipping back into the dark depression that had haunted her in the months after Lisa's death. She'd been trying to get Richard on his own for days. 'I don't think Wendy's wedding help... not that she said anything bad about it,' she added hastily, feeling his muscles tighten under her palm. 'It must have been difficult for both of you, I know. But I think Meg needs a break; she's ploughed all her energies into forming this group with Jackie and Rachel.'

'I know, it's helped her … it's helped both of us but it's taken a lot out of her as well.' Richard watched Meg as she tilted her head to look up at the sky through the leaves. With a twist of nerves in his stomach he wondered what she was thinking. 'But what can I do, Alice?'

'Well, I've had a thought.' Alice folded her arms under her huge breasts and hoisted them up. 'Jackie's just been to see me; she says she's going to Yorkshire, something to do with that play. How about suggesting Meg goes with her so she can see for herself what's happening. Might buck her up; change of scenery, who knows.' Her face softened as she looked at Richard. 'Might do you both good to know what's happening properly.'

Richard shook his head. 'She won't go; she wouldn't go and leave me here on my own, whatever I said to try to persuade her.'

'But you wouldn't mind?'

'Good grief no. I think it would do her the world of good.'

'Well then, how about I move in here to give you a hand while she's away.'

'You'd do that?'

I certainly would.' She jerked her head backwards in the direction of the avenue. 'I'm rattling around that house on my tod, now Wendy's gone.'

'She won't go along with it.'

'She will, by the time I've finished with her; you

leave it to me, Richard.'

He held up his hand and she gave him a high-five.

'Thanks, Alice,' he said in a low voice. Then he gave her a huge grin. 'But no bed- baths, mind.'

She gave him such a push that the wheelchair rocked.

'Bloody old spoilsport,' she said.

'Are you sure it's alright for me to go?' Meg looked up from her lists headed, 'Things to do' and 'Things that don't need doing'. The excitement in her was balanced with apprehension; each time she asked the question she expected him to sound doubtful. Yet she had to ask; she needed to know he would be alright, she told herself

'For the hundredth time, woman, I'm sure. 'Besides it gives me and my lover some time alone; Alice can't wait to get her hands on me.'

Meg jumped up from the armchair to give him a playful punch. 'You'll be sorry; you'd be worn out, begging me to come back.' She chuckled, wrapping her arms around him. 'I love you, Mr Matthews.' She nuzzled his neck.

'And I love you. But it's no good, you can't have your wicked way with me again this year; you've had your quota.' Richard turned his head to kiss her. 'Much as I'm sorry to turn you down, of course.' His mouth smiled; there was remorse in his eyes.

Meg picked up on it at once. 'We were good though, weren't we?'

'Red-hot lovers,' he said; the fleeting moment of regret gone. 'Though I don't like to boast … yes, I was.'

'Show-off.' Meg returned his kiss, looking beyond him to the letter. 'Do you want me to read it or not? I don't mind if you don't.'

'I'd like you to.' Richard nodded towards it. 'Not sure if I've said too much.' It felt as though there was too much revealed between the words and he regretted writing some of it.

'Let me look.'

Meg sat at the side of him on the floor, took her glasses from the top of her head and began to read.

When she reached the lines: … *felt that in the end she couldn't trust us; that she was unable to talk to us. We, I, let her down Thinking about that now still makes me cry…* she bit her lip and screwed her eyes tight. Oh Richard, she thought, and me, and me. Placing her hand on his knee she kept her head down and carried on reading.

… O*ther parents living with what that drug has done to their children have the chance to help and support them. We didn't get that opportunity.*

I know, too, that the GPs prescribed it in good faith; they believed they were helping. It seems ironic to me that the only people who should feel guilty about Stilboestrol are the ones who produced it – the pharmaceutical companies, and they obviously don't. They are the ones who made money out of it, the ones who persuaded all of us, for so long, that the drug was the answer to our prayers; that it would make sure that our wives carried our babies to full term.

But, ultimately, there has to be a way to find peace. To tell ourselves we weren't to blame for believing what we were told. To stop beating ourselves up about it.

What would I want out of the Government's recognition of the harm caused? Well, not financial gain, for a start. Perhaps if Lisa had lived then we would have fought for that, to enable her to have some quality of life. Now I think all we would want is acknowledgment from someone that this happened.

Governments down the years recognised the damage caused by Thalidomide (they had no choice; the disabilities were plain to see).

Does the fact that Stilboestrol has caused damage that is only apparent years, sometimes decades, later, and even then damage that can't be seen, make the pharmaceutical companies less culpable? I think not.

If your play helps bring attention to Stilboestrol then you will have succeeded in what we, Meg and I, strived to do for years.

I wish you all the luck in the world with it.

All the best

Richard

Meg rested her head on his knee. There was no need to speak; he'd said it all.

Chapter Forty-Six - June

"There is no evidence that DES granddaughters are at higher risk of developing cervical cancer than the general population. But, once again, we run into the

old problem of no research being done, so there is no evidence either way. "Absence of evidence isn't evidence of absence." …"Given the long-term gynaecological health of DES granddaughters is not known, the most sensible and safest option is for them to be screened annually."[47]

To: Jacgay@ yahoo.com
From: Avrilbreen@sheepfold.freeserve.co.uk
Subject: Ref Play

Hi Jackie,
Attached last draft of play for you to show to the others before you come up here. Ask them to let me know if there's anything they don't like/ want taking out/ adding. Please pass on my thanks to Richard through Meg; I've used the whole of it for the father character.

---

[47] Dr Ross Pagano, Director of the DES Clinic at the Royal Women's Hospital: quoted in DESPATCH: Newsletter 56 of DES Action Australia

See you next week
Avril
x

It took a moment before Avril's eyes adjusted to the gloom of the theatre. The open doors behind her threw a square of pale light across the rows of seats. Dust motes floated around, tiny grey particles against the pale blue walls.

Georgina was a flash of purple and green in the middle of the front row. Hurrying down the slope of the aisle Avril breathed in the familiar musty smells of the theatre: the paint from the sets, the staleness of curtains and costumes.

'Sorry, emails to sort out; I've sent the last draft of the script to Jackie for her to show to the others and I've printed out two for us.' Avril's voice and the slapping sound of her flip-flops echoed slightly in the emptiness of the auditorium.

Georgina was wearing a long cotton dress with a deep vee neckline that emphasised her large breasts. Her thick black hair was tied back with a matching scarf.

'You look good,' Avril said, aware of the scruffy skirt and blouse she'd thrown on. 'Gorgeous outfit.'

'Thanks,' Georgina acknowledged the compliment absentmindedly. 'I've been thinking,' she said, flapping papers at Avril. 'I've been looking through all the letters that you passed on; all those written by Meg?' She didn't wait for an answer. 'They gave me an idea. The technician says we can get them up on a screen on the backdrop.' In her enthusiasm she stood up, scattering the letters. 'It could be a way of conveying the years of struggling for recognition ... setting the atmosphere, the mood of the script.' She bent down to pick up the papers. 'What do you think?'

'How?' Avril asked.

'I don't know,' Georgina straightened up. But he seems to think it possible to get them to slowly scroll down.'

'But the three doors open in the back drop that the minor characters appear from. Won't that affect the scrolling?'

'Not according to the technician; he says he'll time it so there are pauses between each showing ... we just have to get the timing right.'' She tidied the letters into a neat pile on the edge of the stage.

'If it can be done it sounds a fantastic idea,' Avril said, 'it will reinforce the play, emphasise the message. Fantastic, Georgina, well done.'

'Think you've spent too much time talking to Jackie,' Georgina grinned.

'Huh?'

'Fantastic? One of Jackie's favourite words?'

'Oh Lord, did I say it again?' Avril slapped her forehead in mock exasperation. 'It's got so bad even Mr Macaw's picked it up. It's driving me crazy.'

'Could be worse: could be "wicked" or "awesome"' Georgina took on a casual tone. 'You're quite friendly with Jackie, aren't you? What do you know about her?'

'You fishing, Georgina Lees?'

'Who? Me? Now why would I?'

Avril turned serious. 'If you're asking does she have a partner the answer is no, not now.' She grimaced. 'But she did have and it ended badly.'

'Are you telling me she wouldn't be interested?'

'No. How could I? I don't know her that well, Georgina. I'm just saying she's had a bad experience these last few months.'

The caretaker appeared at the side of the stage. 'Sorry, I'm off home; I've got to lock up.' '

'Okay, Tom,' Avril said. She waited in the aisle while Georgina pushed all the papers and her copy of the script into her bag. 'Fancy a coffee in The Mews? There's a couple of things we still need to discuss. And we can also discuss your fascination with the gorgeous Jackie as well, if you like?'

Georgina gave her a gentle push. 'Give over.' She grinned. 'She is rather a dish though, isn't she?'

'How should I know?' Avril laughed, 'you're the expert in that field.'

Outside they weaved their way through the bustle of shoppers, delivery vans and slow moving traffic on the High Street.

'I have a really good feeling about this play, Georgina,' Avril said. 'I think this is only the start of things.'

Chapter Forty-Seven

For us DES Daughters, and perhaps for our children, keeping current with research and legal processes being either taken, or considered on our behalf, is crucial ...[48]

'Rache?' Stephen spoke softly.'

She'd had this dream so many times in the past six months: she could almost smell his Hugo aftershave, sense his breath against her cheek as he said her name. Reluctant to wake she moaned, wrapped her arms around the hard dome of her stomach and burrowed her face deeper into the pillow, hiding from the dazzling line of sunshine that stretched across her bed through the half-closed curtains.

'Rache?'

'No,' she mumbled. His hand was fleetingly on her bare shoulder, his thumb fitting in a familiar gesture into the hollow above her collarbone and stroking her skin. Warm. Gentle. She wanted to hold onto the feeling. But the touch vanished.

'Rachel.'

She was awake. She lay still, held her breath and listened. The ward was quiet. A baby snuffled, whimpered. Another gave a tiny squealing cry. Uncomfortable, Rachel stretched her legs, slippery

---

[48] Article written by DES Action USA member Joanna Katzen – *VOICE*. Spring 2012

with sweat. Her nightdress was sticking to her buttocks. Cautiously, eyelids still closed, she rolled over onto her back. A rustling sound, so close to her ear she took a sharp intake of breath, squinted upwards.

Stephen.

He took his hand off her pillow. Ill at ease, his gaze didn't meet hers, giving her chance to study him, to get a measure of her feelings. She'd always admired his discipline, his self-control. However restrictive, it had given their lives, in the early days of their trying for a baby anyway, boundaries; an ability to concentrate on the now and not on the might have been.

But lately she'd realised that long ago the constraints had tipped over into the parts of their lives that should have been spontaneous; the laughter, the impulsive 'drop everything and go out for dinner, a day's walking in the Brecon Beacons, a holiday.'

Sex.

Rachel's mouth tightened. Of course, unknown to her, he'd been going elsewhere for that; and all the time she'd thought he was being caring, considerate, putting her needs before his. Except for the optimum days, the days most likely for her to conceive, he'd hardly been near her for the last two years. But, as she'd told him a thousand times, it wasn't the conceiving that she had trouble with, it was the holding on to that tiny morsel of life she couldn't manage.

Until this time. She rested her hand on the sheet over her stomach. As though in reply there was a ripple, a shifting of a small limb under her fingers and she held back the small secret smile, not even willing to share with Stephen the thrill it gave her to feel their ... her, baby move inside her, as though to reassure all was well.

She watched her husband under lowered lids. His strong even features seemed more carved out somehow and his skin had a strange pallid sheen. He'd lost weight. Used to seeing him immaculate in suit, shirt and tie she took in the crumpled jeans and polo shirt. There was a stain on the collar; tomato sauce, the housewife in Rachel decided before she reminded herself it was not her problem anymore. He was unshaven, there were a few silvery whiskers along his jaw line, picked out by the sunlight, and his hair needed a cut. It took her seconds to take all that in before he fixed his eyes fully on hers.

'Rachel,' he said again. There was a time when she'd melt under the gaze of those deep brown eyes; when the warmth in them made her feel she was surrounded, protected by his love; best of all where the times when one look was all the encouragement she needed to wrap her arms around him and kiss him. Or make love with him. But that seemed a long time ago; in the last few months they were together, before he'd walked out on her, she couldn't recollect a time when he'd actually looked at her, when his eyes didn't slide past her as though she was invisible. Now, when he was facing her, she saw only pleading in them, a wordless beseeching.

'What are you doing here?' Her hands were trembling; she shoved them under the bedclothes.

'I told them I was your husband.' His voice was dry, as though he had a sore throat but there was an intimation of defiance that was inconsistent with his expression. 'Which I am. Still.'

Not for long if I can help it. The thought didn't spring to mind but came gradually from nowhere. Did she really believe that? She felt so lethargic she was amazed that she had enough energy to rear up from her pillow and hiss at him, 'how the hell did you explain where you'd been for the last two months?'

Stephen didn't reply but his face flushed and he rubbed at his ear between his thumb and fingers, a habit when he was uneasy or in a difficult situation.

Rachel fell back and turned her face away from him. She knew she looked a mess and was angry that she cared. 'Go away.'

'We need to talk.' One of the babies began to wail. Stephen looked around the ward.

'Like hell we do.' Rachel wriggled so she was further down in the bed; it smelled musty, too slept-in.

She heard him take a long breath, knew he was waiting for her to emerge. Now he was here, now he'd decided to put on an appearance, he wouldn't go in a hurry. She imagined he'd have that barely concealed impatient expression on his face; the one that pulled his cheeks inwards as though he was sucking hard on the insides. Why didn't he just sod off? A shiver of agitation ran through her. The light from the sun glowed orange under the sheet and she could see the line of sweat in the crease of her elbow. It was stifling but she refused to emerge until she heard him move away from her bed. Peering from under the corner of the sheet she watched him pulling at the stack of chairs by the door. Two came away and he struggled to separate them.

The baby belonging to the woman in the next bed joined in with the first, a thin irritable cry. Rachel's face burned with mortification and fury. Damn, she thought again, why was he here? What the hell did he want? She tugged the sheet back over her head, much like she had as a child when refusing to face up to something that she'd done wrong or that had upset her. But there was no running away from this: hell she wasn't even allowed to sit up, never mind run.

More of the babies started to cry. Stephen looked around the ward, his face flushed. 'Chairs stuck,' he said to no one in particular, 'sorry.' He carried one back to Rachel's bed.

The minutes ticked by. Rachel's skin became increasingly prickly but she stayed stubbornly still. The baby didn't. But this time she didn't thrill at the feeling of it turning, pushing a tiny hand or foot against her. Now she wondered if it was feeling as upset as she was? She was getting pins and needles in the arm she was lying on. He wasn't going to leave.

She threw back the covers taking in a long grateful breath and under his gaze struggled ungainly onto her back and attempted to cross her arms over her swollen breasts. Failing, she concentrated on folding the sheet into a tidy line. 'What do you want?'

'I called your Dad when he got back to his place. He didn't half tear a strip of me; said I hadn't been straight with him. Said he'd knock my block off next time he sees me.'

Good for you, Dad. 'Why call *my* father?' She glared at him. 'He's nothing to do with you, just like this baby's nothing to do with you.' She held up her hand as he protested. 'And how did you find out I was pregnant and in here anyway.'

He shrugged; didn't answer.

'You've given up all right to know anything about me … us.' She cradled her stomach. 'You gave up that right two years ago. That's how long you've been having the affair, isn't it?'

His face took on a mottled redness.

'So?' she asked, satisfied to see the jibe hit home.

'We need to talk, Rache,' he repeated.

She winced inwardly against the familiar shortening of her name, fought against the wistful memory of the countless times it had been uttered in careless affection. He'd lost the right to use it. In fact he'd lost all say in anything she did in her life.

'I made a mistake,' he said, leaning closer to her elbows on his knees

'One that lasted two years?' Rachel pulled the sheet under her chin, wished she could at least look more dignified and not like a ... beached whale, she thought, unable to come up with a lesser worn cliché.

'Please, Rache.'

'Rachel!' she hissed, adamant he knew she didn't accept the shortening of her name. 'You've got a bloody nerve; you wait six months and now you want to talk? Well I don't want to talk to you. Not ever again.'

His face crumpled, he covered it with both hands and she heard a stifled choking gasp.

She couldn't help herself. She touched his shoulder. 'Don't.' Despite herself, compassion filtered through her anger.

'I've been stupid. 'I'm sorry.'

Rachel watched him, stroked her stomach. Waited. He'd made a mistake: impossible though it had seemed a few seconds ago the thought began to form; could she forgive him?

'Charlotte made a fool of me.'

The sound of the girl's name came as a shock. I don't want to know, I don't want to know. She drew back her hand and turned her face away.

'She's told me the baby isn't mine.' He wiped his

face across his shirtsleeve. 'There was another bloke.'

Rachel felt a flash of anger. And he thought, even she had thought, idiot that she was, that she might feel sorry for him? 'Welcome to my world,' she said.

'I thought I had a son, Rach.'

The instant hatred left her breathless. 'Sod off, Stephen.'

'What?' Snot and tears ran down his face. Her stared: uncomprehending

'You heard.'

'We need to talk.'

Rachel turned away, slid under the covers.

'It's my child too,' he said, 'I have as much right to see it. I'll fight you for access and I'll win.'

'When Hell freezes over.'

Chapter Forty-Eight - July

Dodds was always against the casual overuse of prescribing oestrogen that occurred in the 1940s, and was particularly horrified when he heard it was being used to 'prevent miscarriage'. The newly established (US) National Cancer Institute shared his concern, based on many animal studies published from 1940 onwards. But to no avail, the pharmaceutical industry's push for profits overrode the misgivings and warnings by the scientists and cancer researchers.[49]

'It's a shame your mum couldn't come with us.' Meg stared out through the side window of the Peugeot, deliberately making her voice casual. She'd pretended she hadn't seen the older version of Jackie standing at the door of that house

'Wouldn't, Meg ... not couldn't.' Jackie gripped the steering wheel and looked fixedly ahead. She knew as soon as she stepped through the door and saw her mother, still in her dressing gown, sitting at the kitchen table, a plate of congealed kipper bones in front of her, that there'd be trouble. 'I rang her last night; she said she'd come with us.'

---

[49] The Greatest Experiment Ever Performed on Women: Exploding the Estrogen Myth (2003) by Barbara Seaman 1935—2008 – extract in DESPATCH: Newsletter 57 of DES Action Australia

The scene had played over and over in her head for the last half an hour as they crossed the Pennines. Despite the hostility she'd felt an unusual pang of sadness and guilt towards her mother.

'There was no shifting her.' Jackie's face burned. 'You heard her, Meg, don't tell me you didn't. It was bloody embarrassing.'

'Don't worry about it.' Meg said. 'I can understand how she feels.'

'Can you?' Jackie blinked quickly to stop the tears blurring her vision as she indicated and moved into the inside lane of the motorway in readiness for the exit that led to Lydfield. 'Can you? Because I can't; I never have.'

'It's a mum thing,' Meg said.

Jackie glanced quickly at her before looking forward again. She nodded slowly. 'Thanks Meg.'

So,' Meg said in a casual voice. 'What was it she said?'

'You mean when she shoved me out of the door?'

'Mmm.' Meg gave a small chuckle.

'Something like "go and see your bloody clever friends with their stupid bloody play."?'

'That's it. So that's what we'll do … yes?'

'Yes.' Jackie grinned and said again, 'thanks Meg.'

Meg didn't know if she'd helped by making light of the whole thing. What she'd really wanted to do back there, was to get out of the car and hold Mary Duffy in her arms and tell her she knew how she felt.

And, as they drove into the village, neither of

them could forget the woman's parting shot; "Don't blame me when nobody believes you about the drug. Because they won't, you know. Nobody will be interested … ever. They weren't before and they won't be now."

Chapter Forty-Nine

Never mistake a woman's silence for her ignorance, her calmness for her acceptance, and her kindness for her weakness ...[50]

The theatre smelt stale, almost chilly after the walk from the car park in the sunshine. Two men were picking up sweet wrappings and other rubbish between the rows of seats, a woman was pushing a vacuum cleaner along the aisles, lips pursed against the rising dust from the carpet.

'Are you sure they don't mind?' Meg glanced anxiously around. She felt distinctly out of her depth; it was a long time since she'd been anywhere on her own and despite Richard's encouragement, she still thought it wrong that she'd left him at home.

'Don't be daft; you've more right than any of us to be here, to see just how it's panning out.' Jackie glanced around the rows. Several people were sitting in various seats on their own, reading scripts. She grasped Meg's elbow. 'Let's go further down; get a better view. You've rung Richard; you know he and Alice are managing fine; in fact he'll be loving all the fuss. Now relax.' Once settled she scrabbled inside her bag and produced two pre-packed

---

[50] Anon

sandwiches. 'Keep us going for a while. Cheese and pickle or ham salad?'

'Ham please,' Meg whispered. 'Which one is Avril?'

'The one with reddish hair in the blue top, and the one in front of the group of women by the curtains at the corner of the stage, with the kaftan and her hair tied back with the purple scarf, is Georgina. Fantastic director ... so Avril says,' Jackie added hastily when Meg grinned at her. She took a bite of her sandwich and settled back in the seat to enjoy watching Georgina as she moved quickly around the stage, studying a sheaf of papers and talking at the same time.

Avril looked out into the theatre and saw Jackie and Meg. She lifted a hand in acknowledgement.

Georgina followed the action. 'Hi, you're here at last.' She directed a wide smile at Jackie.

'Georgina.' Warmth rose from Jackie's neck to her face; it was like being a teenager all over again, she thought, glad that the bright lights onstage would probably, hopefully, mean Georgina couldn't see her blushing. She coughed self-consciously. 'Avril, this is Meg. Georgina, Meg.'

'Meg! Brilliant to meet you at last,' Avril waved again. 'Five minutes and we're stopping for a break; I'll be with you then?'

'That's fine,' Meg called. The underlying excitement surrounding everyone on the stage was infectious; she was fascinated.

'Great to see you both; chat in a bit,' Georgina said. 'There's a pile of scripts over on that seat if you want to have a read.' She pointed to the front row and glanced down at the paper in her hand. 'So,' she said to Avril, 'the narrator here, sitting downstage right, throughout the whole thing as an observer.' She dragged a chair from the wings of the stage. 'There's a lot of action in the first half, makes sense if she stays on stage; it'd lose momentum if she keeps going on and off. And three chairs downstage centre.' Georgina spaced them out in a line. 'For the three main characters; the mother in the middle.'

'That's you, Meg.' Jackie nudged her.

Meg nodded; it was a strange feeling, knowing that an actor would be using her own words; that, after all the years, her voice would be heard.

'MP upstage right?' Georgina glanced at Avril.

'Yes.' Avril raised her voice and included Jackie and Meg in her next words. 'I thought it should be a woman? You've been dealing with a woman in the Department of Health, haven't you?'

'For all the good it's done us,' Jackie said, irked just by the thought of the last letter she'd received. 'But the MP is a man.'

'Well, I thought portraying the MP as a woman would highlight the lack of understanding for the DES daughters,' Georgina said, 'so it doesn't look like a gender issue. But we don't want her completely indifferent so she'll show her reactions through body language. I'd like her as a permanent fixture in the shadows upstage, near the backdrop? At her desk.' She pulled a table at an angle to the backdrop. 'She stays there, sometimes writing, sometimes listening to what the three women are saying but she never speaks until almost at the end ... she has a long speech then.' She flipped the sheets of script over. 'The one that starts "There is no redress against any particular pharmaceutical company ..."?'

'That's right,' Avril nodded.

. The rest of the cast have their parts and they'll do some doubling up of the minor characters.' Georgina read from another list. 'A rep from the pharmaceutical company: a scientist from the time DES was discovered; two doctors; one old school, one contemporary ... think that's it.'

'No,' Avril said, scribbling on her copy of the script, 'there's still the father and DES son I've got a couple of ideas about their parts.'

'Oh, sorry, yes. Getting a bit confused.' Georgina looked out towards Jackie and laughed, 'need a shot of caffeine, I think.'

'Just quickly then,' Avril said. 'I think, because their speeches are longer than the other minor characters and they say themselves who they are, the men should appear next to the narrator right of stage without being introduced by the narrator.'

'Yes, I like that.' Georgina checked her watch. 'Right,' she said, 'break for now; we'll have the next read through at four o'clock, ok? So,' she said, 'downstairs in the café for a coffee?'

'And cake?' Avril grinned. 'I'm starving.' She left the stage and hurried up the aisle to give Meg a hug. 'I'm so glad you could come. How's Richard?'

'He's fine, thanks.' Meg gathered together her bag and coat.

'His letter was so moving.' Avril swept her away, throwing a backward glance towards Georgina. 'See you in the café.' She linked arms with Meg. 'And Rachel? How's she coping, being in bed all the time, she can't have all that long to go now, surely...'

Her voice trailed away as they left the theatre.

Georgina waited until there was no one else around before she went to where Jackie was sitting. 'Hi,' she said, holding out her hand.

Jackie stood and grasped it before pulling Georgina to her and giving her a hug. 'Hi.' She couldn't think of anything else to say. She felt her face hot again. The pulse in her neck throbbed.

'Coffee?'

'Yes.'

'I've suggested to Avril we apply to enter the play at one or two festivals afterwards,' Georgina said. 'What do you all think?'

'Great idea.'

'Not fantastic?'

'Well, if you insist ...'

Chapter Fifty -August

One of the problems is that unlike Thalidomide, where you see the problem the minute the baby was born, women who took DES had healthy babies. Problems were hidden until the teens and twenties, by which point we were forgotten about. When I asked my mum what she had taken, she didn't even remember the name of the stuff. It is a complete and utter minefield.[51]

'She's beautiful.' Stephen breathed the words, 'so tiny.' His face contorted.

'She was nearly six weeks early. We're ... I'm lucky she was allowed out of the incubator so soon.'

'How long was she in there?'

'Three weeks.' Rachel could see he was trying not to break down. His child was almost a month old and this was the first time he'd seen her. Rachel closed her eyes. How different it all could have been. She'd tried hard to hold onto the anger but it had disappeared as soon as she held her baby.

'What are you going to call her?' Stephen wiped the back of his hand across his face.

Rachel wasn't used to this humility in her

---

[51] Heather Justice – DES Daughter and member of DES Action UK. The first recorded "DES daughter" in Britain. See bio.

husband. 'Megan,' she said.

'Just Megan?' No middle name?'

Rachel knew where this was going; in the past Stephen had always insisted that a girl would have his mother's name and a boy, his father's. Rachel had never argued but she'd secretly sworn no child of hers was going to be lumbered with being called Aggie or Wilfred: over her dead body. 'No, no middle name,' she said. The baby whimpered and Rachel reached into the little plastic cot and lifted her close, breathing in the moist, soapy smell of her. 'Do you want to hold her?' she whispered.

'Can I?' He nodded. 'Please.'

She leaned towards him and they moved in synchronization, carefully holding their child, trying to avoid touching one another.

'Watch her head,' Rachel warned, 'support her head.'

Neither of them spoke as he cradled Megan.

Rachel saw the movement in his throat s he swallowed hard, his hands large and clumsy around the tiny form. Once or twice he glanced up at Rachel but she refused to meet his eyes. The baby squirmed, drawing up her legs and kicking out, her mouth puckered. She started to cry.

'Here, you'd better have her back.'

Again the cautious exchange until Megan was back with her mother.

Stephen sat back, a line of perspiration on his forehead. 'That was one of the most terrifying experiences of my life,' he said, smiling. 'She wriggles like a tadpole.'

Rachel ignored the offered familiarity.

There was a discomfited silence.

'You can have the house,' Stephen suddenly said, slapping his hands on his knees, 'and I'll pay for the upkeep.'

'Thank you,' Rachel deliberately kept the relief out of her voice; after all, it was what she and the baby deserved.

She could tell it wasn't the reaction he'd expected. When he next spoke his voice was subdued. 'I can afford it, in any case.' It was a statement, not a boast.

Rachel swayed back and forth, holding the baby against her shoulder until she quietened. 'Where will you live?' As soon as she'd spoken Rachel regretted it; she didn't want to show any interest.

'Don't worry about me,' he said.

'I'm not.' The retort was sharp. 'It's just in case we ... Megan needs you in the future.'

'I'm in the middle of moving; I'll let you know.'

'Fine.' The whimpers started again and grew until they were cries. 'She's hungry: you'll have to go.' She refused to share the intimate moment with him.

'Oh, yeah, course.' He stood, awkward in the room of couples huddled over the latest addition to their families. 'When will you be out?'

'About a week.' Rachel spoke over Megan's growing wails, suppressing her impatience. She waited for him to leave.

'Can I come to see you?'

'No,' Rachel said, 'but you can come to see Megan, once we're home.' She didn't even look up. 'I won't stop you being her father, Stephen, she deserves to know you: she deserves your love.' She bent over the baby, cupping her head in her palm as she began to unbutton the front of her nightdress. 'But you and I are finished.' She glanced up at him for a second; dismissing him. 'There's nothing left between us.'

It wasn't until night, when the ward was dimly lit and only the hushed voices of the nurses, the snores from the women and snuffling baby noises disturbed the quiet, did Rachel think about what she'd said. A sense of liberation flooded through her: she'd meant what she said. For her there was nothing between them, not love, Stephen had destroyed that, not hatred; especially not hatred, she realised with relief. Perhaps, one day, friendship. Who knew? It would make things easier.

Chapter Fifty-One

DES undermines the bonds of experience between a mother and daughter and adversely affects the development of each ... the mother who is (the daughter's) natural ally and is needed for support, is also the source of her pain. [viii52]

Richard was watching *News at One* in the living room and Meg was turning out a sponge cake when Alice appeared at the open back door.

'I've just put my washing out and I thought I'd come over. I came round the back of the house because I could see Richard watching telly and I didn't want to disturb him.' She hauled herself up the steps, holding on to the rail of the ramp for the wheelchair. 'It's blowing well; clothes should dry in no time.' She sniffed, appreciating. 'That's a bloody wonderful smell, love, I forgot it was Friday.' The grin was guileless.

'It's still hot; you'd get raging indigestion if you ate any of it. But you can have a scone; they've been out a while.'

'Never get indigestion, me; stomach like cast iron my mother always used to say,' Alice settled herself

---

[52] Roberta J Apfel, MD.,M.P.H. Susan M Fisher, M.D. To Do No Harm: DES and the Dilemmas of Modern Medicine Chapter 5 p71

on the kitchen chair, knees wide apart, one arm folded on the table, the other hand propped under her chin. 'But one of your scones will go down a treat.'

Meg buttered two scones and passed them to her. 'Your hair looks nice,' she said.

'Oh? Thanks,' Alice patted the tight curls. 'I have to be honest, love, I didn't really forget it was Friday,' she said.

'Didn't you?' Meg managed to look surprised.

'No. I was coming round sometime today anyway.' She took a bite. 'Mmm, lovely.' Watching Meg turn off the oven and nodding when she waved the kettle at her, Alice said, 'how did yesterday go?'

'Much the same as every year; always regrets, always wondering whether we could have done anything different: whether we let her down in some way.' Meg spooned coffee into two mugs and poured hot water into them, adding milk. She thought for a moment. 'No, actually, Alice, that's wrong; it wasn't quite the same this time. We still grieved; I think we always will. But it *was* different in a way.' She stirred the coffee; dissolving the last granules floating around on the surface with the back of the teaspoon. She wondered if she should feel guilty for thinking that but decided not and said, 'I think Lisa would be pleased that we've achieved so much over the last year, you know, especially with the play.' She smiled. 'Yes, to be honest I feel better than I have for a long time. Richard too, I think.'

Handing the drink to Alice and sitting down, she said, 'and it was so good to see your Wendy with the baby. It cheered us up no end and James really suits him, he's such a handsome little chap.' When she'd held him she'd waited for the old familiar grief to return. But it hadn't. All she'd felt was wonder and joy to be cuddling a child.

Alice put her large soft hand over Meg's. 'I'm glad you feel okay about it, I was a bit worried.' She leant forward; the usual smell of TCP mixed with the smell of her newly permed hair today. 'Wendy says she asked you?'

'To be godparents? Yes, she did. I said I thought we were too old but she insisted.'

'It's what she wants,' Alice squeezed Meg's fingers. 'She said it would have been Lisa ... if she'd been ...' She stopped, made slight popping noises with her lips for a moment and then rushed on, 'you're the closest people to Lisa; Wendy's thrilled you've said yes.'

Meg nodded, not trusting herself to speak. With an exclamation she jumped up. 'I forgot to make Richard a coffee.'

Alice waited until Meg came back into the kitchen before saying, 'how're the holiday plans?' She adjusted a bra strap and hoisted up her bosom with her arms. 'All set?'

'Great. I've always wanted to see the Monet Gardens. Only two weeks now.' Meg lowered her voice. 'You know it's our first time abroad since the accident. I was worried sick that Richard wouldn't cope but he's determined and the travel people have been brilliant with all the organizing.'

Alice laced her hands across the expanse of her stomach. 'And you sure you'll be back for the twenty ninth?'

'The Christening? Of course. You'll have to let us know what Wendy would like us to get for James's present: give us a few ideas. It's so exciting, Alice.' On impulse Meg reached across and hugged her. 'You deserve this. You're the best friend I've ever had. I don't know where we'd be without you.'

'Give over woman, you're squashing my perm.' Still, Alice held her close as she said, 'it's always worked both ways, you know. More so now I'm on my own across the road; with Wendy gone.'

'How're things going with the group by the way?' Alice said, letting Meg go.

She obviously wanted to change the subject; her face was rosy with embarrassment. She busied herself buttering another scone.

'Well, Rachel's out of it for now with the baby. With everything that's happened and then the caesarean, we wouldn't ask her to do anything; especially as she's on her own until her father comes back over.' A blast of air swung the back door to and fro and Meg hurried to close it. 'Weather's changing: better keep an eye on it in case it rains. I can see us having to run to get your washing in.'

'I can't,' Alice gave a screech of laughter, 'my

running days are long over.' She licked the butter of her fingers. 'Don't think they ever started actually.' She flapped her hand. 'So what else is happening?'

Meg smiled. 'Well, Richard and I are still waiting for a reply from Stewart Jones and Jackie's still bombarding that Baroness from the House of Lords with emails to see if there's anything she can do. But the play's our main hope,' Meg reminded her. 'Avril's arranged the performance for the first Saturday in November. It'll be exactly a year since my interview at Radio Carvoen.' She paused, for a moment lost in thought. 'Such a long way in twelve months. She glanced at Alice 'You will come to that with us, won't you?'

'Try and stop me,' Alice said. 'That's if they can fit me into a seat on the aeroplane.' She pulled a face in a mock dismay.

'Don't be daft.'

'Are Jackie and Rachel flying too?'

'No, driving up there with Rachel's cousin who's going to look after the baby.' Meg stood by the window. There was a low bank of steely grey cloud moving swiftly across the sky.

'What about Jackie's mother? Will she go?'

'No.'

'That's a shame ... they still don't get on?'

'No. and you're right, it is a shame ... there should always be a special bond between mothers and daughters.'

Silent Trauma

November 2002

'We must continue to bear witness...[53]

To:georginalees@btinternet.com
_info@theconways. egmath222@aol.com
From: Avrilbreen@sheepfold.freeserve.co.uk

Subject: Hi all,

Well it's time. Let's hope we get the message across to the audience without being too heavy. This play has to be a vehicle that bears witness; that acts as a voice for the thousands of people whose lives have been destroyed by DES. If we've made it do all that, then we've succeeded.
Meg: Just to prepare you; I've inserted another line right at the beginning of the play. As the curtain rises the Narrator will be centre stage. Her first words will be - "This play is in recognition of the bravery and perseverance of Meg Matthews, and in remembrance of her daughter, Lisa." I hope that's okay?
Fingers crossed girls. See you next week.
Love Avril

---

[53] DES Voices: From Anger to Action: © Pat Cody. Ch.17

The Play

"A medical myth is shattered" [ix54]

'Oh my god!'

'What? What is it?' Jackie turns in her seat to stare at Avril.

'There, there at the front, in the middle.' Avril does her best to give a gracious nod and a smile to two people sitting in the front row even though she is shaking with nerves. 'It's Patty,' she says, 'the woman I told you about; the critic from the Manchester Chronicle.' Slinking down in her seat she speaks with half-closed lips. 'She said she'd come, she's always so enthusiastic about the plays here, her cousin helps with the props....'

'Where?' Jackie cranes her neck to see, crunching one of the Polo mints she's been chomping since she arrived at the theatre.

'No, sit back.' Avril digs her in the ribs with her elbow.

'Ouch.' Jackie rubs her side but doesn't stop staring. 'The one who looks like Janet Street-Porter?'

---

[54] Report on DES Action International Colloquium 2001: From a talk given by John McLachlan, noted by Marian Vickers DES Action Australia.

she says in a stage whisper. 'What about her?'

'She's brought Peter Shaw, the producer from the Royal Venue Theatre in Manchester.' Avril pulls her crocheted shawl across her chest and folds her arms as though chilled. 'He must be interested in the play. What if he doesn't like it?'

Georgina leans across Jackie. 'Calm down, woman. It's a bloody brilliant play and you know it.'

'Stop worrying. He'll think it's as good as we do.' Rachel puts on her best encouraging smile, hoping she sounds less nervous than she feels. She gives Avril's arm a quick squeeze before checking her watch

'That's the tenth time since we arrived here,' Jackie murmured, 'Megan's safe with your cousin; she should be with the load of instructions you've left.'

'I know, but it's the first time I've left her,' Rachel hissed. Between the worry of that and the play she thinks she could easily throw up. She bends forward and looks both ways along the row towards the others. 'He'll think it's as good as we do, won't he?'

Everyone nods vigorously and Richard stuck his thumbs up as Meg manoeuvres his wheelchair in line with the row and puts the brakes on.

'He'd be bloody mad not to like it.' Jackie passes the mints down the line.

Alice squirms in her seat, a look of concentration on her face as she tries to squash her ample buttocks into the space. 'Made for midges, these things.'

'Don't think that's what you mean, Alice,' Meg says with a grin, 'just put the armrest up, give yourself a bit more room. I can manage with less.'

'Ere, you casting aspersions on my size?' In mock offence Alice sniffs haughtily and then nudges Meg as she sat next to her. 'Bloody exciting though eh? All this, Meg? Bloody exciting.'

'Let's hope it achieves something.' Meg passes Jackie's mints back.

A bell sounds.

'It's no good.' Avril untangles the curls in her hair and leaves it sticking out at all angles before standing up. 'I'll have to go for a pee.'

'Don't be long,' Georgina warns, 'you've only got five minutes.'

Avril shuffles past Rachel and runs up the aisle. At the theatre door she almost collides with a woman. 'Sorry.' She pauses; there's something familiar about the woman's face. Then she shakes her head; no.

Mary Duffy doesn't notice the expression of curiosity. She studies the ticket for her seat number and presses past the knees of the people on the back row, mumbling apologies. It's cost a fortune in the taxi but she's been saving up for two months and, though terrified by what she might see and hear, is glad she's made the effort. She cranes her neck, spotting her daughter almost immediately; her head is turned towards the woman next to her and she's laughing. It was a long time since Mary's seen her laugh like that.

'It's a good crowd,' Rachel says, glancing around the small theatre. The others turn to look. Most of the dark blue seat seats, rising in tiers, are filled by fidgety groups of middle-aged women, chatting and laughing, passing sweets along the curved rows, arranging coats over knees, clutching handbags. Here and there clusters of younger women talk in loud animated voices. There are a few couples. 'A good crowd,' she repeats as Avril returned.

'It's nearly full.' Avril raises her voice over the shrill sound of the second bell. Then, 'oh my god, here goes.' Someone closes the doors at the back of the theatre.

As though by a signal, the murmuring and restlessness dies down. There are a few muted coughs, a last rustle of sweet papers. The stage curtain ripples, accidentally pulled aside, and fleetingly reveals a bright flash of light.

Then a locked moment of absolute stillness.

Meg grabs hold of Richard's hand, Rachel checks her mobile one last time before turning it off, Georgina moves closer to Jackie, Avril holds her breath.

The lights dim. The curtain rises.

'We need never be ashamed of our tears...'[55]

---

[55] Charles Dickens: *Great Expectations*

Silent Trauma

ABOUT THE AUTHOR

Judith Barrow grew up in a small village in Saddleworth, at the foot of the Pennines in North-West England. In 1978 she moved with her husband, David, and their three children to Pembrokeshire, West Wales, where she is a creative writing tutor. .

Her short stories have been published in several of **Honno** anthologies.

Silent Trauma was first published as an eBook and is her second novel.

Her first novel, **Pattern of Shadows** was published by Honno. The sequel, **Changing Patterns** follows in May 2013.

those found in contaminated wildlife and laboratory animals, suggesting that humans may be at the same risk to the same environmental hazards as wildlife: Taken from *Our Stolen Future* © 1997 Theo Colborn, Dianne Dumanoski, & John Peterson Myers*: Appendix: The Wingspread Consensus Statement* p/p 252/254. Permission received from Abacus: A Division of Little, Brown &Co UK)

iii The rights of victims of environmental disasters worldwide were formally recognised by the United Nations Permanent Court of Arbitration at The Hague in November 2001. It was the first time a court gave legitimacy to environmental disputes between individuals and organisations. Although DES was not an environmental disaster *per se* I thought it appropriate to include this to show the kind of scatter – gun approach an amateur group might carry out, bearing in mind this story is actually basically fictional. (Judith Barrow).

.

iv *The DES Legacy Children of Women Given the Hormone DES Decades Ago Now Cope With Their Own - and Even Their Children's - Health Problems* by Leef Smith *Washington Post* September 23, 2003.

v In *The Bitter Taste of a Miracle Drug*, a documentary film about DES made by French film maker Stephane Mercurio and her mother, Catherine Sinet, a group of young, healthy –seeming women sit in a comfortable living room showing each other x-rays. Quoted in *DES Voices From Anger to Action.* ©Pat Cody 2008 Introduction p5.

[vi] Still trying for a public enquiry 2012.

[vii] Dick Clapp, DSc, MPH is an epidemiologist who has forty years of experience in public health practice, research and teaching. He is Professor Emeritus at Boston University School of Public Health and Adjunct Professor at the U. of Mass.- Lowell School of Health and Environment. He is a former co-Chair of Greater Boston Physicians for Social Responsibility and served as Director of the Massachusetts Cancer Registry from 1980-1989.

[viii] Roberta J Apfel, MD.,M.P.H. Susan M Fisher, M.D. *To Do No Harm: DES and the Dilemmas of Modern Medicine* Chapter 7 p.109 1st edition (September 10, 1984 Reproduced with the permission of the Senior Rights Assistant, Yale University Press, 47 Bedford Square, London,WC1B 3DP 06/04/2010

[ix] Until the Des experience it was believed that any harmful effect of in utero – drug exposure would show up at birth. The place of DES in modern medical history was discussed by clinicians involved with discovering the on-going health effects of DES exposure. Unfortunately … the DES lesson has not been learnt in terms of drug safety and public health

issues: paraphrasing a quote from The drug safety monitoring and reporting systems (like the Therapeutic Goods Administration here in Australia) with their voluntary "adverse drug reactions" reporting system were established in the wake of thalidomide and follow that paradigm – totally inadequate when it comes to endocrine disruptors. So with DES, a medical myth was shattered over 40 years ago, but the health authorities haven't caught up with the news! (paraphrasing a quote from Marian Vickers DES Action Australia)

Biographies:

Pat Cody, DES Mother and co-founder of DES

Action USA. She worked as Program Director from 1978 - 2004. Her years there saw passage of Congressional funding for DES research, creation of our quarterly newsletter DES Action VOICE, and assistance in setting up DES groups in the Netherlands, Australia, Canada, France, England and Ireland. But Pat was so much more. She wasn't the loudest voice in the room but she usually was the wisest. Pat knew how to get things done and you could never say "no" to Pat. She kept DES Action USA on a steady course and her spirit guides DES Action USA still. Much of what we are today and have accomplished through the years is because Pat's guiding hand kept us moving in the right direction. If she taught us anything, it's that the DES issue is one that requires the energy and expertise of many voices and many disciplines.

Fran Howell – Executive Director DES Action USA Fran thanks her late Mom for giving her a membership in DES Action USA and keeping it current for many years. When Fran had trouble starting her family she began seriously paying attention to DES issues. After numerous infertility treatments failed, Fran eventually became the adoptive mom to her wonderful, now young-adult daughter, Shelby. Fran joined the DES Action USA Board, and when the opportunity arose she assisted with media relations - working with newspaper, TV and magazine reporters to successfully place dozens of media stories about DES. That parlayed into the job of DES Action USA Executive Director in January 2005. A highlight is meeting and working with an incredibly talented group of individuals from all around the country.

Joyce Bichler - Joyce was the first DES Daughter to sue a drug company, and win, for the vaginal cancer she suffered. Her book, DES Daughter, published in 1981, told the harrowing and touching story of her fight for recognition of drug company involvement in her disease. Joyce became an active and indispensable member of DES Action USA, and co-founded the DES Cancer Network in 1982. She has appeared in numerous radio and TV interviews to promote DES awareness, and one, in San Francisco, was even conducted during an earthquake!

Jill Vanselous Murphy – President, DES Action USA Jill, a native of New Jersey, has lived her entire life knowing about her DES exposure. She is the sixth of nine pregnancies and the only survivor, no thanks to DES, which her mother took for seven of her pregnancies. At the age of 12 she started a vigilant journey of regular screenings which she has maintained over the years. Three ectopic pregnancies and the dreaded t-shaped uterus lead to yet another journey called adoption. Jill has spent more than 20 years in the non-profit community specifically in membership/fundraising, communications and marketing and now puts those skills to work aiding DES Action USA in its mission.

Marian Vickers is a DES daughter and founding member of DES Action Australia. Established in 1979, DES Action Australia is unfunded and relies on the voluntary efforts of its members. Marian's work for DES Action Australia is voluntary and is carried out around her paid employment and family commitments, usually late at night or at weekends. As she has two daughters, who are DES granddaughters, her involvement with the DES story is on-going.

Heather Justice – DES Daughter and member of DES Action UK. The first recorded "DES daughter" in Britain, Heather Justice, 59, from Jarrow, was 25 when she found out she had vaginal cancer and would have to undergo a hysterectomy and partial vaginectomy. Although she found records showing her mother had been given DES in the 1950's, she was unable to bring a case to court (in the UK because she could not identify which manufacturer had produced the drug. However, a US lawyer did help her get some compensation there. Also, she says, it is impossible for anyone to find the manufacturer of the drug in this country, not just me, as it was never patented. It was the surgeon who performed my hysterectomy who asked my mother if she knew what she had taken. He knew it must have been DES because of the rare type of cancer I had. He was also the one who found her medical records with the generic name of the drug.(written after this interview) After years of fighting the legal system, she says she feels disillusioned.

Jane Kevan - (a trustee and member of DES Action UK) Jane grew up knowing her mother had taken a drug called stilboestrol. She had her first smear test aged 14, following her Dad, a pharmacist, reading that DES was to be contraindicated for use in pregnancy because of the potential side-effects to the developing child. In 1989 her Dad told her about a programme that was going to be shown on Channel 4 about the drug. This led to Jane meeting Heather, then Michelle and others, and joining DES Action UK. She became one of the trustees in 1991 and remained so until the UK group was formally wound up in 2012. In 1993 the group's work resulted in a peak of media exposure. Also in this year Jane carried out research, contacting all health authorities in England, Scotland and Wales about DES. It was found that a minimum of 14, and possibly 19, cases of vaginal CCAC had been diagnosed at these hospitals. Jane's involvement in the group became personal in the late 1990's when she had a series of miscarriages, partly due to an incompetent cervix which is a sign of DES exposure. Happily, after a cervical suture and daily injections of heparin, Jane and her husband Rob became parents to Sarah in 2000.

Aim of DES Action UK: To provide support and information to all those exposed to DES, and to the health profession. DES Action UK started as a result of the 4 What it's Worth Channel 4 programme Unto the Second Generation - DES Children shown in November 1989.

Due to lack of funding DES Action UK has been forced to disband.

Scientific studies continue adding to a growing list of

serious medical problems caused by exposure before birth to the anti-miscarriage drug, DES. An increased risk for infertility, vaginal/cervical cancer and breast cancer are but the start.

Doctors prescribing DES told mothers it was safe and these women had no reason to doubt.

Later they learned the horrible truth that DES harmed their children.

© **Judith Barrow 2013**

Made in the USA
Charleston, SC
10 February 2013